I0667628

THAT STICK

CHARLOTTE M. YONGE

1st WORLD
LIBRARY
Literary Society

That Stick

Charlotte M. Yonge

© 1st World Library, 2007
PO Box 2211
Fairfield, IA 52556
www.1stworldlibrary.com
First Edition

LCCN: 2007927768

Softcover ISBN: 978-1-4218-4514-2
Hardcover ISBN: 978-1-4218-4430-5
eBook ISBN: 978-1-4218-4598-2

Purchase *"That Stick"*
as a traditional bound book at:
www.1stWorldLibrary.com/purchase.asp?ISBN=978-1-4218-4514-2

1st World Library is a literary, educational organization
dedicated to:

- Creating a free internet library of downloadable ebooks

  - Hosting writing competitions and offering book
  publishing scholarships.

Interested in more 1st World Library books?
contact: literacy@1stworldlibrary.com
Check us out at: www.1stworldlibrary.com

1st World Library Literary Society

Giving Back to the World

"If you want to work on the core problem, it's early school literacy."

- James Barksdale, former CEO of Netscape

"No skill is more crucial to the future of a child, or to a democratic and prosperous society, than literacy."

- Los Angeles Times

"Literacy... means far more than learning how to read and write... The aim is to transmit... knowledge and promote social participation."

- UNESCO

"Literacy is not a luxury, it is a right and a responsibility. If our world is to meet the challenges of the twenty-first century we must harness the energy and creativity of all our citizens."

- President Bill Clinton

"Parents should be encouraged to read to their children, and teachers should be equipped with all available techniques for teaching literacy, so the varying needs and capacities of individual kids can be taken into account."

- Hugh Mackay

CONTENTS

CHAPTER I

HONOURS

'Oh, there's that stick. What can he want?' sighed one of a pair of dignified elderly ladies, in black silk, to the other, as in a quiet country-town street they saw themselves about to be accosted by a man of about forty, with the air of a managing clerk, who came up breathlessly, with a flush on his usually pale cheeks.

'Miss Lang; I beg pardon! May I be allowed a few words with Miss Marshall? I know it is unusual, but I have something unusual to tell her.'

'Nothing distressing, I hope, Mr. Morton,' said one of the ladies, startled.

'Oh no, quite the reverse,' he said, with a nervous laugh; 'in fact, I have unexpectedly come into a property!'

'Indeed!' with great astonishment, 'I congratulate you,' as the colour mounted in his face, pleasant, honest, but with the subdued expression left by long years of patience in a subordinate position.

'May I ask—' began the other sister.

'I hardly understand it yet,' was the answer; 'but I must go to town by the 5.10 train, and I should like her to hear it from myself.'

'Oh, certainly; it does you honour, Mr. Morton.'

They were entering the sweep of one of those large substantial houses on the outskirts of country towns that have a tendency to become boarding-schools, and such had that of the Misses Lang been long before the days of the High School.

'Fortunately it is recreation-time,' said Miss Lang, as she conducted Mr. Morton to the drawing-room, hung round with coloured drawings, in good taste, if stiff, and chiefly devoted to interviews with parents.

'Poor little Miss Marshall!' murmured one sister, when they had shut him in.

'What a loss she will be!'

'She deserves any good fortune.'

'She does. Is it not twenty years?'

'Twenty-two next August, sister.'

Yes, it was twenty-two years since Mary Marshall had been passed from the Clergy Orphan Asylum to be English governess at Miss Lang's excellent school at Hurminster. In that town resided, with her two sons, Mrs. Morton, the widow of a horse-dealing farmer in the late Mr. Marshall's parish. On discovering the identity of the English governess with the little girl who had admired the foals, lambs, and chickens in past times, Mrs. Morton gave invitations to tea. She was ladylike, the sons unexceptionable, and no objection could reasonably be made by the Misses Lang, though the acquaintance was regretted by them.

Mr. Morton, the father, had died in debt and distress, and the eldest son had been thankful for a clerkship in the office of Mr. Burford, a solicitor in considerable practice, and man of business to several of the county magnates. Frank Morton was not remarkable for talent or enterprise, but he was plodding and trustworthy, methodical and accurate, and he had continued in the same position, except that time had made him senior instead of junior clerk. Partly from natural disposition, partly from weight of responsibility, he had always been a grave, steady youth, one of those whom their contemporaries rank as sticks and muffs, because not exalted by youthful spirits or love of daring. His mother and brother had always been his primary thought; and his recreations were of the sober-sided sort—the chess club, the institute, the choral society. He was a useful, though not a distinguished, member of the choir of St. Basil's Church, and a punctual and diligent Sunday-school teacher of the least interesting boys. To most of the world of Hurminster he was almost invisible, to the rest utterly insignificant. Even his mother was far less occupied with him than with his brother Charles, who was much handsomer, more amusing and spirited, as well as far less contented or easy to be reckoned upon. But there was one person to whom he was everything, namely, little brown-eyed, soft-voiced Mary Marshall.

She felt herself the happiest of creatures when, after two years of occasional evening teas and walks to Evensong at St. Basil's, it was settled that she should become his wife as soon as his salary should be increased, and Charlie be in condition to assist in supporting his mother. Ever since, Mary had rested on that hope, and the privileges it gave.

She had loyally informed the Misses Lang, who were scarcely propitious, but could not interfere, as long as their pupils (or they believed so) surmised nothing. So the Sunday evening intercourse became more frequent, and in the holidays, when the homeless governess had always remained to superintend cleaning and repairs, there were many pleasant hours spent with kind old Mrs. Morton, who, if she had ever wished that Frank had waited longer and chosen some one with means, never betrayed it to the girl whom she soon loved as a daughter.

Two years had at first been thought of as the period of patience. Charles had a situation as clerk in a shipping office at Westhaven, a small seaport about twenty miles off, and his mother was designing to go to keep house for him, when he announced that his banns had been asked with the daughter of the captain and part-owner of a small trading vessel of the port.

The Hurminster couple must defer their plans till further promotion; and so far from helping his mother, Charles ere long was applying to her, when in need, for family expenses.

Then came a terrible catastrophe. Charlie had been ill, and in his convalescence was taken on a voyage by his father-in-law. There was a collision in the Channel, and the *Emma Jane* and all on board were lost. The insurance did not cover the pecuniary loss; debts came to light, and nothing was left for the widow and her three children except a seaside lodging-house in which her father had invested his savings.

The children's education and great part of their maintenance must fall on their uncle; and again his marriage must wait till this burthen was lessened. Old Mrs. Morton died; and meetings thus became more difficult and

Charlotte M. Yonge

infrequent. Frank had hoped to retain the little house where he had lived so long; but his sister-in-law's demands were heavy, and he found himself obliged to sell his superfluous furniture, and commit himself to the rough attendance of the housekeeper at the office, where two rooms were granted to him.

Thus had year after year gone by, unmarked except by the growth of the young people at Westhaven and the demand of their mother on the savings that were to have been a nest-egg, while gray threads began to appear in Mary's hair, and Frank's lighter locks to leave his temples bare.

So things stood when, on this strange afternoon, Miss Marshall was summoned mysteriously from watching the due performance of an imposition, and was told, outside the door, that Mr. Morton wanted to speak to her.

It was startling news, for though the Misses Lang were kindly women, and had never thrown obstacles in the way of her engagement, they had merely permitted it, and almost ignored it, except when old Mrs. Morton was dying, and they had freely facilitated her attendance. 'Surely something as dreadful as the running down of the *Emma Jane* must have happened!' thought Mary as she sped to the drawing-room. She was a little brown mouse of a woman, with soft dark eyes, smooth hair, and a clear olive complexion, on which thirty-eight years of life and eighteen of waiting had not left much outward trace; for the mistresses were good women, who had never oppressed their underling, and though she had not met with much outward sympathy or companionship, the one well of hope and joy might at times suffer drought, but had never run dry, any more than the better fountain within and beyond.

In she came, with eyes alarmed but ready to console. 'Oh,

Frank, what is it? What can I do for you?'

'It is no bad news,' was his greeting, as he put his arm round her trembling little figure and kissed her brow. 'Only too good.'

'Oh, is Mrs. Charles going to be married?' the only hopeful contingency she could think of.

'No,' he said; 'but, Mary, an extraordinary incident has taken place. I have inherited a property.'

'A property? You are well off! Oh, thank God!' and she clasped her hands, then held his. 'At last! But what? How? Did you know?'

'I knew of the connection, but that the family had never taken notice of my father. As to the rest I was entirely unprepared. My great-grandfather was a younger son of the first Lord Northmoor, but for some misconduct was cast off and proscribed. As you know, my grandfather and father devoted themselves to horses on the old farm, and made no pretensions to gentility. The elder branch of the family was once numerous, but it must have since dwindled till the old lord was left with only a little grandson, who died of diphtheria a short time before his grandfather.'

'Poor old man!' began Mary. 'Then—oh! do you mean that he died too?'

'Yes; he was ill before, and this was a fatal blow. It appears that he was aware that I was next in the succession, and after the boy's death had desired the solicitor to write to me as heir-at-law.'

'Heir-at-law! Frank, do you mean that you are—' she said,

Charlotte M. Yonge

turning pale.

'Baron Northmoor,' he answered, 'and you, my patient Mary, will be the baroness as soon as may be.'

'Oh, Frank!'—and there was a rush of tears—'dear Frank, your hard work and cares are all over!'

'I am not sure of that,' he said gravely; 'but, at least, this long waiting is over, and I can give you everything.'

'But, oh!' she cried, sobbing uncontrollably, with her face hidden in her handkerchief.

'Mary, Mary! what does this mean? Don't you understand? There's nothing to hinder it now.'

She made a gesture as if to put him back from her, and struggled for utterance.

'It is very dear, very good; but—but it can't be now. You must not drag yourself down with me.'

'That is just nonsense, Mary. You are far fitter for this than I am. You are the one joy in it to me.'

'You think so now,' she said, striving to hold herself back; 'but you won't by and by.'

'Do you think me a mere boy to change so easily?' said the new lord earnestly. 'I look on this as a heavy burthen and very serious responsibility: but it is to you whom I look to sweeten it, help me through with it, and guard me from its temptations.'

'If I could.'

'Come, Mary, I am forced to go to London immediately, and then on to the funeral. I shall miss the train if I remain another minute. Don't send me away with a sore heart. Tell me that your affection has not been worn out by these weary years.'

'You cannot think so, Frank,' she sobbed. 'You know it has only grown. I only want to do what is best for you.'

'Not another word,' he said, with a fresh kiss. 'That is all I want for the present.'

He was gone, while Mary crept up to her little attic, there to weep out her agitated, uncertain feelings.

'Oh, he is so good! He deserves to be great. That I should be his first thought! Dear dear fellow! But I ought to give him up. I ought not to be a drag on him. It would not be fair on him. I can love him and watch him all the same; but oh, how dreary it will be to have no Sunday afternoons! Is this selfish? Is this worldly? Oh, help me to do right, and hold to what is best for him!'

And whenever poor Mary had any time to herself out of sight of curious eyes, she spent it in concocting a letter that went near to the breaking of her constant heart.

Charlotte M. Yonge

CHAPTER II

HONOURS REFLECTED

On the beach at Westhaven, beyond the town and harbour, stood a row of houses, each with a garden of tamarisk, thrift, and salt-loving flowers, frequented by lodgers in search of cheap sea breezes, and sometimes by families of yachting personages who liked to have their headquarters on shore.

Two girls were making their way to one of these. One was so tall though very slight, that in spite of the dark hair streaming in the wind, she looked more than her fifteen years, and her brilliant pink-and-white complexioned face confirmed the impression. Her sister, keeping as much as she could under her lee, was about twelve years old, much more childish as well as softer, smaller, with lighter colouring and blue eyes. Going round the end of the house, they entered by the back door, and turning into a little parlour, they threw off their hats and gloves. The younger one began to lay the table for dinner, while the elder, throwing herself down panting, called out—

'Ma, here's a letter from uncle. I'll open it. I hope he's not crusty about that horrid low millinery business.'

'Yes, do,' called back a voice across the tiled passage. 'I've had no time. This girl has put me about so with Mrs. Leeson's luncheon that I've not had a moment. Of all the sluts I've ever been plagued with, she's the very worst, and so I tell her till I'm ready to drop. What is it then, Ida?' as an inarticulate noise was heard.

'Ma! ma! uncle is a lord!' came back in a gasp.

'What?'

'Uncle's a lord! Oh!'

'Your uncle! That stick of a man! Don't be putting your jokes on me, when I'm worried to death!' exclaimed Mrs. Morton, in fretful tones.

'No joke. It's true—Lord Northmoor.' And this brought Mrs. Morton out of the kitchen in her apron and bib, with a knife in one hand and a bunch of parsley in the other. She was a handsome woman, in the same style as Ida, but her complexion had grown harder than accorded with the slightly sentimental air she assumed when she had time to pity herself.

'It is! it is!' persisted Ida, reading scraps from the letter; "'Title and estates devolve on me—family bereave-ments—elder line extinct.'"

'Give me the letter. Oh, you gave me such a turn!' said Mrs. Morton, sinking into a chair.

'What's the row?' said another voice, as a sturdy bright-eyed boy, between the ages of his sisters, came bouncing in. 'I say, I want my grub—and be quick!'

'Oh, Herbert, my dear boy,' and his mother hugged him, 'your uncle is a lord, and you'll be one one of these days.'

'I say, don't lug a man's head off. Who has been making a fool of you?'

'Uncle Frank is Lord Northmoor,' said Ida impressively.

'I say, that's a good one!' and Herbert threw himself into a chair in fits of laughter.

'It is quite true, Herbert,' said his mother. 'Here is the letter.'

A bell rang sharply.

'Bless me! I shall not hear much more of that bell, I hope. Run up, Conny, and say Mrs. Leeson's lunch will be up in a moment, but we were hindered by unexpected news,' said Mrs. Morton, bustling into the kitchen. 'Oh dear! one doesn't know where one is.'

'Let her ring,' said Ida. 'Send her off, bag and baggage! We've done with lodgings and milliners and telegraphs, and all that's low. We shall all be lords and ladies, and ever so rich.'

'Hold hard!' said Herbert, who had got possession of the letter. 'He doesn't say so.'

'He'll be nasty and mean, I daresay,' said Ida. 'What does he say? I hadn't time to see.'

Herbert read from the neat, formal, distinct writing: "I do not yet know what is in my power, nor what means I may be able to command; but I hope to make your position more comfortable and to give my nephew and nieces a really superior education. You had better, however, not take any steps till you hear from me again." There, Ida, lots of schooling, that's all.'

'Nonsense, Bertie; he must—if he is a lord, what are we?'

Hunger postponed this great question for a little while; but dinner had been delayed till the afternoon school hour had passed, and indeed the young people agreed that they were far above going to their present teachers any more.

'We must acquire a few accomplishments,' said Ida. 'Uncle never would afford me lessons on the piano—such a shame; but he can't refuse me now. Dancing lessons, too, we will have; and then, oh, Conny! we will go to Court, and how they will admire us!'

At which Herbert burst out laughing loudly, and his mother rebuked him. 'You will be a nobleman, Herbert, and your sisters a nobleman's sisters. Why should they not go to Court like the best of them?'

'That's all my eye!' said Herbert. 'The governor has got a young woman of his own, hasn't he?'

'That dowdy old teacher!' said Ida. 'Of course he won't marry her now.'

'She will be artful enough to try to hold him to it, you may depend on it,' said Mrs. Morton; 'but I shall take care he knows what a shame and disgrace it would be. Oh no; he will not dare.'

'She is awfully old,' said Ida.

'Not near so old as Miss Pottle, who was married yesterday,' said Constance, who, at the time of her father's death, and at other times when the presence of a young child was felt to be inconvenient at home, had stayed with her grandmother at Hurminster, and had grown fond of Miss Marshall.

Charlotte M. Yonge

'Don't talk about what you know nothing about, Constance,' broke in her mother. 'Your uncle, Lord Northmoor, ain't going to lower and demean himself by dragging a mere school teacher up into the peerage, to cut out poor Herbert and all his family. There's that bell again! I shall go and let Mrs. Leeson know how we are situated, and that I shall give her notice one of these days. Clear the table, girls; we don't know who may be dropping in.'

This done, chiefly by Constance, the sisters put on their hats, and sallied forth with their astounding news to such of their friends as were within reach, and by the time they had finished their expedition they were convinced of their own nobility, and prepared to be called Lady Ida and Lady Constance Northmoor on the spot.

When they came in they found the parlour being prepared for company, and were sent to procure sausages and muffins for tea. Mrs. Morton had, on reflection, decided that it was inexpedient to answer her brother-in-law till she had ascertained, as she said, her just rights, and she had invited to tea Mr. and Mrs. Rollstone and, to Constance's delight, his little daughter Rose, their neighbours a few doors off; but as Rose was attending classes, it had been useless to go to her before.

Mr. Rollstone was a great authority, for he had spent the best part of his life in what he termed the first families of the highest circles. He had been hall boy to a duke, footman to a viscountess, valet to an earl, butler to a right honourable baronet, M.P., and when he had retired on the death of the baronet and marriage with the housekeeper he had brought away a red volume, by name *Burke's Peerage*, by which, as well as by his previous knowledge, he was enabled to serve as an oracle respecting all owners of yachts worthy of consideration. If their names were not recorded in that book, he scorned them as 'parvenoos,' however perfect their vessels might be in the eyes of mariners. The edition was indeed a quarter of a century old, but he had kept it up to date, by marking in neatly all the births, deaths, and marriages from the *Gazette*—his daily study. His daughter, a nice, modest-looking girl of fourteen, Constance's chief friend, came too.

His wife was detained by her lodgers, but when he rolled in, with the book under his arm, there was a certain resemblance between himself and it, for both were broad and slightly dilapidated—the one from gout, the other from wear, and the red cover had faded into a nondescript whity-brown, or browny-white, not unlike the complexion of a close-shaven face. He was carefully arrayed in evening costume, and was very choice in his language, being, in fact, much grander than all his aristocratic masters rolled into one; so that though Mrs. Morton tried to recollect that she was a great lady and he had been a servant, force of habit made her feel his condescension when he held out his puffy white hand; and, with a gracious bend of his yellow-gray head, said, 'Allow me to offer my congratulations, Mrs. Morton. I little suspected my proximity to a lady so nearly allied to the aristocracy.'

'I am sure you are very kind, Mr. Rollstone. I had no notion—Ida can tell you I was quite overcome—though when I came to think of it, my poor, dear Morton always did say he had high connections, but I always thought it was one of his jokes.'

'Then as I understand, Mrs. Morton, the lamented deceased was junior to the present Lord Northmoor?'

'Yes, poor dear! Oh, if he had but lived and been eldest, he would have become his honours ever so much better!'

'And oh, Mr. Rollstone, what are we?' put in Ida breathlessly, while Rose squeezed Constance's hand in schoolgirl fashion.

'Indeed, Miss Ida, I fear I cannot flatter you with any change in your designation. If your respected parent had survived he might have become the Honourable Charles, but only by special grant from Her Majesty. It was so in the case of the Honourable Frances Fordingham, when her brother inherited the title.'

'Then at least I am an Honourable!' exclaimed Mrs. Morton.

'I am afraid not, Mrs. Morton. I know of no precedent for such honours being bestowed on a relict; but as I understand that Lord Northmoor is no longer in his first youth, your son might succeed to the title, and, in that case, his sisters might be'—he paused for a word— 'ennobled.'

'Then does not it really make any difference to us?' exclaimed Mrs. Morton.

'That would rest in the bosom of his lordship,' said Mr. Rollstone solemnly.

'I declare it is an awful shame,' burst out Ida, while Constance cooed 'Dear uncle!'

'Hush, hush, Ida!' said her mother. 'Your uncle has always treated us handsomely, and we have every reason to expect that he will continue to do so.'

'He ought to have us to live with him in his house in London, and take us to Court,' said Ida. 'Oh, Mr. Rollstone, is he not bound to do that?'

And Constance breathed, 'How delicious!'

Mr. Rollstone perhaps had his doubts of the figures Mrs. and Miss Morton would cut in society, but he contented himself with saying, 'It may be well to moderate your expectations, Miss Ida, and to remember that Lord Northmoor is not compulsorily bound to consult any interests but his own.'

'If he does not, it is perfectly abominable,' cried Mrs. Morton, 'towards his poor, only brother's children, with Herbert his next heir-apparent.'

'Heir-presumptuous,' solemnly corrected Mr. Rollstone, at which Ida looked at Constance, but Constance respected Rosie's feelings, and would not return her sister's glance, only blushed, and sniggered.

'Heir-apparent is only the eldest son, who cannot be displaced by any contingency.'

'And there's a horrid, little, artful school teacher, who drew him in years ago—before I was married even,' said Mrs. Morton. 'No doubt she will try to keep him now. Most likely she always knew what was going to happen. Cannot he be set free from the entanglement?'

'Oh!' gasped Constance.

'That is serious,' observed Mr. Rollstone gravely. 'It would be an unfortunate commencement to have an action for breach of promise of marriage.'

'She would never dare,' said Mrs. Morton. 'She is as poor as a rat, and could not do it!'

'Well, Mrs. Morton,' said Mr. Rollstone, 'if I may be

Charlotte M. Yonge

allowed to tender my poor advice, it would be that you should be very cautious and careful not to give any offence to his lordship, or to utter what might be reported to him in a sinister manner.'

'Oh, I know every one has enemies!' said Mrs. Morton, tossing her head.

After this disappointment there was rather less interest displayed when Mr. Rollstone proceeded to track out and explain the whole Northmoor pedigree, from the great lawyer, Sir Michael Morton, who had gained the peerage, down to the failure of the direct line, tracing the son from whom Francis and Charles Morton were descended. Certainly Miss Marshall must have been wonderfully foresighted if she had engaged herself with a view to the succession, for at the time it began, the last Lord Northmoor had two sons and a brother living! There was also a daughter, the Honourable Bertha Augusta.

'Is she married?' demanded Mrs. Morton.

'It is not marked here, and if it had been mentioned in the papers, I should not have failed to record it.'

'And how old is she?'

'The author of this peerage would never be guilty of the solecism of recording a lady's age,' said Mr. Rollstone gravely; 'but as the Honourable Arthur was born in 1848, and the Honourable Michael in 1850, we may infer that the young lady is no longer in her first youth.'

'And not married? Nearly Fr—Lord Northmoor's age. She must be an old cat who will set her mind on marrying him,' sighed Mrs. Morton, 'and will make him cut all his own relations.'

'Then Mary Marshall might be the better lookout,' said Ida.

'She could never be unkind,' breathed little Constance.

'There is no knowing,' said Mr. Rollstone oracularly; 'but the result of my observations has been that the true high-bred aristocracy are usually far more affable and condescending than those elevated from a lower rank.'

'Oh, I do hope for Miss Marshall,' said Constance in a whisper to Rose.

'Nasty old thing—a horrid old governess,' returned Ida; and they tittered, scarcely pausing to hear Mr. Rollstone's announcement of the discovery that he had entered the marriage in 1879 of the Honourable Arthur Michael to Lady Adela Emily, only daughter of the Earl of Arlington, and the death of the said Honourable Arthur by a carriage accident four years later.

Then Herbert tumbled in, bringing a scent of tea and tar, and was greeted with an imploring injunction to brush his hair and wash his hands—both which operations he declared that he had performed, spreading out his brown hands, which might be called clean, except for ingrained streaks of tar. Mr. Rollstone tried to console his mother by declaring that it was aristocratic to know how to handle the ropes; and Herbert, sitting among the girls, began, while devouring sausages, to express his intention of having a yacht, in which Rose should be taken on a voyage. No, not Ida; she would only make a fool of herself on board; and besides, she had such horrid sticking-out ears, with a pull at them, which made her scream, and her mother rebuke him; while Mr. Rollstone observed that the young gentleman had much to learn if he was to conform to aristocratic manners, and Herbert

Charlotte M. Yonge

under his breath hung aristocratic manners, and added that he was not to be bored, at any rate, till he was a lord; and then to salve any shock to his visitor, proceeded to say that his yacht should be the *Rose*, and invite her to a voyage.

'Certainly not till you can behave yourself,' replied Rose; and there was a general titter among the young people.

CHAPTER III

WHAT IS HONOUR?

'Here is a bit of news for you,' said Sir Edward Kenton, as, after a morning of work with his agent, both came in to the family luncheon. 'Mr. Burford tells me that the Northmoor title has descended on his agent, Morton.'

'That stick!' exclaimed George, the son and heir.

'Not altogether a stick, Mr. Kenton,' said the bald-headed gentlemanly agent. 'He is very worthy and industrious!'

Frederica Kenton and her brother looked at each other as if this character were not inconsistent with that of a stick.

'Poor man!' said their mother. 'Is it not a great misfortune to him?'

'I should think him sensible and methodical,' said Sir Edward. 'By the way, did you not tell me that it was his diligence that discovered the clause to which our success was owing in the Stockpen suit?'

'Yes, Sir Edward, through his indefatigable diligence in reading over every document connected with the matter. I take shame to myself,' he added, smiling, 'for it was in a letter that I had read and put aside, missing that passage.'

'Then I am under great obligations to him?' said Sir Edward.

'I could also tell of what only came to my knowledge many years later, and not through himself, of attempts made to tamper with his integrity, and gain private information from him which he had steadily baffled.'

'There must be much in him,' said Lady Kenton, 'if only he is not spoilt!'

'I am afraid he is heavily weighted,' said Mr. Burford. 'His brother's widow and children are almost entirely dependent on him, more so, in my opinion, than he should have allowed.'

'Exactly what I should expect from such a sheep,' said George Kenton.

'There is this advantage,' said the lawyer, 'it has prevented his marrying.'

'At least that fatal step has been averted,' said the lady, smiling.

'But unluckily there is an entanglement, an endless engagement to a governess at Miss Lang's.'

'Oh,' cried Freda, who once, during a long absence of the family abroad, had been disposed of at Miss Lang's, 'there was always a kind of whisper among us that Miss Marshall was engaged, though it was high treason to be supposed to know.'

'Was that the one you called Creepmouse?' asked

her brother.

'George, you should not bring up old misdeeds! She was a harmless old thing. I believe the tinies were very fond of her, but we elders had not much to do with her, only we used to think her horridly particular.'

'Does that mean conscientious?' asked her father.

'Perhaps it does; and though I was rather a goose then, I really believe she was very kind, and did not want to be tiresome.'

'A lady?' asked her mother.

'I suppose so, but she was so awfully quiet there was no knowing.'

'Poor thing!' observed Lady Kenton, in a tone of commiseration.

'I think Morton told me that she was a clergy-orphan,' said Mr. Burford, 'and considered her as rather above him, for his father was a ruined farmer and horse-breeder, and I only took him into my office out of respect for his mother, though I never had a better bargain in my life. Of course, however, this unlucky engagement cannot stand.'

'Indeed!' said the Baronet drily. 'Would you have him begin his career with an act of baseness?'

'No—no, Sir Edward, I did not mean—' said Mr. Burford, rather abashed; 'but the lady might be worked on to resign her pretensions, since persistence might not be for the happiness of either party; and he really ought to marry a lady of fortune, say his cousin, Miss Morton, for I under-stand that the Northmoor property was never

Charlotte M. Yonge

considerable. The late Mr. Morton was very extravagant, and there are heavy burthens on the estate, by the settlement on his widow, Lady Adela, and on the late Lord's daughter. Miss Lang tells me likewise that Miss Marshall is full of doubts and scruples, and is almost persuaded that it is incumbent on her to drop the engagement at any cost to herself. She is very conscientious!'

'Poor thing!' sighed more than one voice.

'It is a serious question,' continued the solicitor, 'and I own that I think it would be better for both if she were induced to release him.'

'Has she no relations of her own?'

'None that I ever heard of. She has always spent her holidays at Miss Lang's.'

'Well, Mr. Burford,' exclaimed Freda, 'I think you are frightfully cruel to my poor little Creep-mouse.'

'Nay, Freda,' said her mother; 'all that Mr. Burford is considering is whether it would be for the happiness or welfare of either to be raised to a position for which she is not prepared.'

'I thought you were on her side, mother.'

'There are no sides, Freda,' said her father reprovingly. 'The whole must rest with the persons chiefly concerned, and no one ought to interfere or influence them in either direction.' Having thus rebuked Mr. Burford quite as much as his daughter, he added, 'Where is Lord Northmoor now?'

'He wrote to me from Northmoor after the funeral, Sir

Edward, saying that he would return on Saturday. Of course, though three months' notice would be due, I should not expect it, as I told him at first; but he assures me that he will not leave me till my arrangements for supplying his place are complete, and he will assist me as usual.'

'It is very proper of him,' said Sir Edward.

'It will be awkward in some ways,' said Mr. Burford. 'Yet I do not know what I could otherwise have done, he had become so necessary to me.'

'Stick or no stick,' was the family comment of the Kentons, 'there must be something in the man, if only his head is not turned.'

'Which,' observed Sir Edward, 'is not possible to a stick with a real head, but only too easy to a sham one.'

Charlotte M. Yonge

CHAPTER IV

HONOURS WANING

'And who is the man?' So asked a lady in deep mourning of another still more becraped, as they sat together in the darkened room of a Northmoor house on the day before the funeral.

The speaker had her bonnet by her side, and showed a kindly, clever, middle-aged face. She was Mrs. Bury, a widow, niece of the late Lord; the other was his daughter, Bertha Morton, a few years younger. She was not tearful, but had dark rings round her eyes, and looked haggard and worn.

'The man? I never heard of him till this terrible loss of poor little Mikey.'

'Then did he put in a claim?'

'Oh no, but Hailes knew about him, and so, indeed, did my father. It seems that three generations ago there was a son who followed the instincts of our race further than usual, and married a jockey's daughter, or something of that sort. He was set up in a horse-breeding farm and cut the connection; but it seems that there was always a sort of communication of family events, so that Hailes knew exactly where to look for an heir.'

'Not a jockey!'

'Oh no, nothing so diverting. That would be fun!' Bertha said, with a laugh that had no merriment in it. 'He is a clerk—an attorney's clerk! What do you think of that, Lettice?'

'Better than the jockey.'

'Oh, very respectable, they say'—with a sound of disgust.

'Is he young?'

'No; caught early, something might be done with him, but there's not that hope. He is not much less than forty. Fancy a creature that has pettifogged, as an underling too, all his life.'

'Married?'

'Thank goodness, no, and all the mammas in London and in the country will be running after him. Not that he will be any great catch, for of course he has nothing—and the poor place will be brought to a low ebb.'

'And what do you mean to do, Birdie?'

'Get out of sight of it all as fast as possible! Forget that horses ever existed except as means of locomotion,' and Bertha got up and walked towards the window as if restless with pain, then came back.

'I shall get rid of all I can—and come to live as near as I can to Whitechapel, and slum! I'm free now.' Then looking at her cousin's sorrowful, wistful face, 'Work,

Charlotte M. Yonge

work, work, that's all that's good for me. Soberly, Lettice, this is my plan,' she added, sitting down again. 'I know how it all is left. This new man is to have enough to go on upon, so as not to be too beggarly and bring the title into contempt. He is only coming for to-morrow, having to wind up his business; but I shall stay on till he comes back, and settle what to do with the things here. Adela and I have our choice of them, and don't want to leave the place too bare. Then I shall sell the London house, and all the rest of the encumbrances, and set up for myself.'

'Not with Adela?'

'Oh no; Adela means to stick by the old place, and I couldn't do that for a constancy—oh no,' with a shudder.

'Does she?' in some wonder.

'Her own people don't want her. The Arlingtons are with her now, but I fancy she would rather be sitting with us— or alone best of all, poor dear. You see, she is a mixture of the angel that is too much for some people. How she got it I don't know, not among us, I should think, though she came to us straight out of the schoolroom, or I fancy she would never have come at all. But oh, Lettice, if you could have seen her how patient she has been throughout with my father, reading him all about every race, just because she thought it was less gall and wormwood to her than to me, and going out to the stables to satisfy him about his dear Night Hawk, and all the rest of it. When she was away for that fortnight over poor little Michael, I found to the full what she had been, and then after that, back she comes again, as white as a sheet, but all she ever was to my father, and more wonderful than all, setting herself to reconcile him to the notion of this new heir of his—and I do believe, if my father had not so suddenly grown worse, she would have made us have him up to be introduced—all out of rectitude and duty, you know, for Adela is the shyest of mortals, and recoils by nature from the underbred far more than we do. In fact, I rather like it. It gives me a sensation. I had ten times rather this man were a common sailor, or a tinker, than just a stupid stick of a clerk!'

'Then Adela means to stay at the Dower House?'

'Yes, she has rooted herself there by all her love to her poor people, and I fancy, too, that she does not want to bring Amice up among all the Arlington children, who are not after her pattern, so she intends to bear the brunt of it, and not leave Northmoor, unless the new-comers turn out unbearable.'

'She goes away with her brother now.'

'Oh yes, she must, and Lord Arlington is fond of her in a way! Can't you stay on with me, Lettice?'

'I wish I could, my dear Birdie, but I am anxious about Mary; I don't think I must stay later than Sunday.'

'Yes; you are too devoted a mother for me to absorb. Never mind, you will be in London, and I shall soon be within reach of you. You are a comfortable person, Lettice.'

Charlotte M. Yonge

CHAPTER V

THE PEER

Poor Miss Lang! After all her care that her young pupils' heads should not be turned by folly about marriage and noblemen, the very event she had always viewed as most absurdly improbable had really occurred, and it was impossible to keep it a secret; though Miss Marshall did her very best to appear as usual, heard lessons with her accustomed diligence, conducted the daily exercises, watched over the instructions by masters, and presided over the needlework. But she grew whiter, more pinched, and her little face more mouse-like every day, and the elder girls whispered fancies about her. 'She had no doubt heard that Lord Northmoor had broken it off!'—'A little poky attorney's clerk, of course he would.'—'Poor dear thing, she will go into a consumption! Didn't you hear her cough last night?'—'And then we'll all throw wreaths into her grave!'—'Oh, that was only Elsie Harris!'—'Nonsense, Mabel, I'm sure it was her, poor thing. Prenez garde, la vieille Dragonne vient.'

That Lord Northmoor was to come back by the mail train was known, and Miss Lang had sent a polite note to invite him to afternoon tea on the Sunday. The church to which he had been for many years devoted was a district one, and Miss Lang's establishment had their places in the old parish church, so there was not much chance of meeting in the morning, though one pupil observed to another that 'she should think him a beast if they did not meet him on the way to church.'

It is to be feared that she had to form this opinion, but on the other hand, by the early dinner-time, tidings pervaded the school that Lord Northmoor had been at St. Basil's, and sung in his surplice just as if nothing had happened! The more sensational party of girls further averred that he had been base enough to walk thither with Miss Burford, and that Miss Marshall had been crying all church time. Whether this was true or not, it was certain that she ate scarcely any dinner, and that Miss Lang insisted on administering a glass of wine.

Moreover, when dinner was finally over, she quietly crept up to her own room, and resumed her church-going bonnet—a little black net, with a long-enduring bunch of violets. Then she knelt down and entreated, 'Oh, show me Thy will, and give me strength and judgment to do that which may be best for him, and may neither of us be beguiled by the world or by ambition.'

Then she peeped out to make sure that the coast was clear—not that she was not quite free to go where she pleased, but she dreaded eyes and titters—out at the door, to the corner of the lane where for many a Sunday afternoon there had been a quiet tryste and walk. Her heart beat so as almost to choke her, and she hardly durst raise her eyes to see if the accustomed figure awaited her. Was it the accustomed figure? Her eyes dazzled so under her little holland parasol that she could hardly see, and though there was a movement towards her, she felt unable to look up till she heard the words, 'Mary, at last!' and felt the clasp of the hand.

Charlotte M. Yonge

'Oh, Frank—I mean—'

'You mean Frank, your own Frank; nothing else to you.'

'Ought you?' And as she murmured she looked up. It was the same, but still a certain change was there, almost indescribable, but still to be felt, as if a line of toil and weariness had passed from the cheek. The quiet gray eyes were brighter and more eager, the bearing as if ten years had been taken from the forty, and though Mary did not perceive the details, the dress showing that his mourning had not come from the country town tailor and outfitter, even the soft hat a very different article from that which was wont to replace the well-cherished tall one of Sunday mornings.

'I had not much time,' he said, 'but I thought this would be of the most use,' and he began clasping on her arm a gold bracelet with a tiny watch on it. 'I thought you would like best to keep our old ring.'

'If—if I ought to keep it at all,' she faltered.

'Now, Mary, I will not have an afternoon spoilt by any folly of that sort,' he said.

'Is it folly? Nay, listen. Should you not get on far far better without such a poor little stupid thing as I am?'

'I always thought I was the stupid one.'

'You—but you are a man.'

'So much the worse!'

'Yes; but, Frank, don't you see what I mean? This thing has come to you, and you can't help it, and you are descended from these people really; but it would be choice for me, and I could not bear to feel that you were ashamed of me.'

'Never!' he exclaimed. 'Look here, Mary. What should I do without you to come back to and be at rest with? All the time I was talking to those ladies and going through those fine rooms, I was thinking of the one comfort I should have when I have you all to myself. See,' he added, going over the arguments that he had no doubt prepared, 'it is not as if you were like poor Emma. You are a lady all over, and have always lived with ladies; and yet you are not too grand for me. Think what you would leave me to—to be wretched by myself, or else—I could never be at home with those high-bred folk. I felt it every moment, though Miss Morton was very kind, and even wanted me to call her Birdie. I *did* feel thankful I could tell her I was engaged.'

'You did!'

'Yes; and she was very kind, and said she was glad of it, and hoped soon to know you.'

'Oh, Frank dear, I am sure no one ever was more really noble-hearted than you,' she almost sobbed; 'you know how I shall always feel it; but yet, but yet I can't help thinking you ought to leave it a little more unsettled till you have looked about a little and seen whether I should be a very great disadvantage to you.'

'Seen whether I could find such a dear, unselfish little woman, eh? No, no, Mary, put all that out of your head. We have not loved one another for twenty years for a trumpery title to come between us now! And you need not fear being too well off for the position. The agent, Hailes, has been continually apologising to me for the smallness

Charlotte M. Yonge

of the means. He says either we must have no house in London, or else let Northmoor. He cannot tell me yet exactly what income we shall have, but the farms don't let well, and there is not much ready money.'

'Every one says you ought to marry a lady of fortune.'

'My dear Mary, to what would you condemn me? What sort of lady of fortune do you think would take an old stick like me for the sake of being my Lady? I really shall begin to believe you are tired of it.'

'Stick! oh no, no. Staff, if'—and the manner in which she began to cling was answer full and complete; indeed, as she saw that her resistance had begun to hurt him as much as herself, she felt herself free to throw herself into the interests, and ask, 'Is Northmoor a very nice place?'

'Not so pretty as Cotes Kenton outside. A great white house, with a portico for carriages to drive under, and not kept up very well, patches of plaster coming off; but there is a beautiful view over the woods, with a purple moor beyond.'

'And inside?'

'Well, rather dreary, waiting for you to make it homelike. They have not lived there much for some time past. Lady Adela has lived in the Dower House, and will continue there.'

'Did you see much of them?'

'Not Lady Adela. Poor lady, she had her own relations with her. She had not by any means recovered the loss of her little boy, and I can quite understand that it must have been too trying for her to see me in his place. I understand from Hailes—'

'Your Mr. Burford,' said Mary, smiling.

'That she is a very refined, rather exclusive and domestic lady, devoted to her little girl, and extremely kind to the poor. Indeed, so is Miss Morton, but she prefers the London poor, and is altogether rather flighty, and what Hailes calls an unconventional young lady. There was a very nice lady with her, Mrs. Bury, the daughter of a brother of the late Lord, a widow, and very kind and friendly. Both were very good-natured, Miss Morton always acted hostess, and talked continually.'

'About her father?'

'Oh no, I do not think he had been a very affectionate father, and their habits and tastes had been very different. Lady Adela seems to have latterly been more to him. Miss Morton was chiefly concerned to advise me about politics and social questions, and how to deal with the estate and the tenants.'

He seemed somewhat to shudder at the recollection, and Mary certainly conceived a dread of the ladies of Northmoor. It was further elicited that he meant to help Mr. Burford through all the work and arrangements consequent on his own succession, indeed, to remain at his post either till a successor was found, or the junior sufficiently indoctrinated to take the place. Of course, as he said, six months' notice was due, but Mr. Burford has waived this. During this time he meant to go to see 'poor Emma' at Westhaven, but it was not an expedition he seemed much to relish, and he wished to defer it till he could definitely tell what it would be in his power to do for her and her children, for whose education he was really anxious, rejoicing that they were still young enough

Charlotte M. Yonge

to be moulded.

Then came the tea at Miss Lang's—a stately meal, when the two ladies were grand; Lord Northmoor became shy and frozen, monosyllabic, and only spasmodically able to utter; and Mary felt it in all her nerves and subsided into her smallest self, under the sense that nobody ever would do him justice.

CHAPTER VI

THE WEIGHT OF HONOURS

The next was a fortnight of strange and new experiences.
Lord Northmoor spent most of his days over the papers in
the office, so much his usual self, that Mr. Burford generally forgot, and called to him as 'Morton' so naturally that
after the first the other clerks left off sniggering.

There Sir Edward called on him, and in an interview in
his sitting-room at the office asked him to a quiet dinner,
together with the solicitor; but this was hardly a success,
for Mr. Burford, being at home with the family, did all the
talking, and Frank could not but feel in the presence of his
master, and had not a word to say for himself, especially
as George and Freda looked critical, and as if 'That stick'
was in their minds, if not on their lips. The only time
when he approached a thaw was when in the hot summer
evening Lady Kenton made him her companion in a
twilight stroll on the terraces, when he looked at the roses
with delight, and volunteered a question about the best
sorts, saying that the garden at Northmoor had been much
neglected, and he wanted to have it in good order, 'that
is'—blushing and correcting himself—'if we can live
there.'

Lady Kenton noted the 'we' and was sorry to be here

Charlotte M. Yonge

interrupted. 'We shall do nothing with him till we get him alone,' she said. 'We must have him apart from Mr. Burford.'

Before this, however, they had to meet him at a very splendid party, given with all the resources of the Burford family at their villa, when the county folks, who had no small curiosity to see the new peer, were invited in full force, and the poor peer felt capable of fewer words than ever to throw at them.

Lady Kenton ventured on asking Mrs. Burford to introduce her to Miss Marshall, taking such presence for granted.

'Oh, Lady Kenton, really now I did not think that foolish affair should be encouraged. It is such an unfortunate thing for him; and as Miss Lang and I agreed, it would be so much better for both of them if it were given up.'

'Is there anything against her?'

'Oh no, not at all; only that, poor thing, she is quite unfitted for the position, and between ourselves, in the condition of the property, it is really incumbent on his Lordship to marry a lady of fortune. At his age he cannot afford romance,' she added with a laugh, being in fact rather inferior to her husband in tone, or perhaps in manners. Indeed, she was of all others the person who most shrivelled up the man whom she had always treated like a poor dependent, till her politeness became still more embarrassing. Among all the party, Sir Edward and Lady Kenton were those with whom he was most nearly at ease, for they had nothing to revoke in their manners towards him, and could, without any change, treat him as an equal whom they respected; nor did they try to force him forward into general conversation—as did his host—with the best intentions.

Lady Kenton, under cover of Miss Burford's piano, asked him whether she might call on Miss Marshall, and saw him flush with gratitude and pleasure, as he answered, 'It will be very kind in you.'

Lady Kenton knew enough of the ways of the school to understand when to make her visit, so as to have a previous conversation with Miss Lang, whom of course she already knew. That lady received her in one of the drawing-rooms, the folding doors into the other were shut.

'I have told Miss Marshall,' said Miss Lang, 'that the room is always at her service to receive Lord Northmoor, though, in fact, he never comes till after business hours.'

'He is behaving very well.'

'Very honourably indeed; but poor Miss Marshall is in a very distressing position.'

'Indeed! Is she not very happy in his constancy?'

'She is in great doubt and difficulty,' said Miss Lang, 'and we really hardly know how to advise her. She seems sure of his affection, but she shrinks from entering on a position for which she is so unfit.'

'Is she really unfit?'

Miss Lang hesitated. 'She is a complete lady, and as good and conscientious a creature as ever existed; but you see, Lady Kenton, her whole life has been spent here, ever since she was sixteen, she has known nothing beyond the schoolroom, and how she is ever to fulfil the duties of a peeress, and the head of a large establishment, I really cannot see. It might be just misery to her, and to him, too.'

'Has she good sense?'

'Yes, very fair sense. We can trust to her judgment implicitly in dealing with the girls, and she teaches well, but she is not at all clever, and could never shine.'

'Perhaps a person who wanted to shine might be embarrassing,' said Lady Kenton, rather amused.

'Well, it might be so. The poor man is certainly no star himself, but surely he needs some one who would draw him out, and push him forward, make a way in society, in fact.'

'That might not be for his domestic happiness.'

'Perhaps not, but your Ladyship has not seen what a poor little insignificant creature she is—though, indeed, we are both very fond of her, and should be very much relieved not to think we ought to strengthen her scruples. For, indeed,' and tears actually came into the good lady's eyes, 'I am sure that though she would release him for his good, that it would break her heart. Shall I call her? Ah!' as a voice began to become very audible on the other side of the doors, 'she has a visitor.'

'Not Lord Northmoor. It is a woman's voice, and a loud one.'

Presently, indeed, there was a tone that made Lady Kenton say, 'People do scent things very fast. It must be some one wanting to apply for patronage.'

'I am a little afraid it is that sister-in-law of his,' said Miss Lang, lowering her voice. 'I saw her once at the choral festival—and—and I wasn't delighted.'

'Perhaps I had better come another day,' said Lady Kenton. 'We seem to be almost listening.'

Even as the lady was taking her leave, the words were plainly heard—

'Artful, mean-spirited, time-serving viper as you are, bent on dragging him down to destruction!'

Charlotte M. Yonge

CHAPTER VII

MORTONS AND MANNERS

'Shillyshally,' quoth Mrs. Charles Morton over her brother-in-law's letter. 'Does he think a mother is to be put off like that?'

So she arrayed herself in panoply of glittering jet and nodding plumes, and set forth by train to Hurminster to assert her rights, and those of her children, armed with a black sunshade, and three pocket-handkerchiefs. She did not usually wear mourning, but this was an assertion of her nobility.

In his sitting-room, wearing his old office coat, pale, wearied, and worried, the Frank Morton, 'who could be turned round the finger of any one who knew how,' appeared at her summons.

She met him with an effusive kiss of congratulation. 'Dearest Frank! No, I must not say Frank! I could hardly believe my eyes when I read the news.'

'Nor I,' said he.

'Nor the dear children. Oh, if your dear brother were only here! We are longing to hear all about it,' she said, as she settled herself in the arm-chair, a relic of his mother.

He repeated what he had told Mary about the family, the Park, and the London house.

'I suppose there is a fine establishment of servants and carriages?'

'The servants are to be paid off. As to the carriages and the rest of the personal property, they go to Miss Morton; but the executors are arranging about my paying for such furniture as I shall want.'

'And jewels?'

'There are some heirlooms, but I have not seen them. How are the children?'

'Very well; very much delighted. Dear Herbert is the noblest boy. He was ready to begin on his navigation studies this next term, but of course there is no occasion for that now.'

'It is a pity, with his taste for the sea, that he is too old to be a naval cadet.'

'The army is a gentleman's profession, if he must have one.'

'I must consider what is best for him.'

'Yes, my Lord,' impressively. 'I am hoping to know what you mean to do for your dear brother's dear orphans,' and her handkerchief went up to her eyes.

'I hope at any rate to give Herbert the education of a gentleman, and to send his sisters to good schools. How

Charlotte M. Yonge

are they getting on?'

'Dear Ida, she is that clever and superior that a master in music and French is all she would want. Besides, you know, she is that delicate. Connie is the bookish one; she is so eager about the examination that she will go on at her school; though I would have taken her away from such a low place at once.'

'It is a good school, and will have given her a good foundation. I must see what may be best for them.'

'And, of course, you will put us in a situation becoming the family of your dear brother,' she added, with another application of the handkerchief.

'I mean to do what I can, you may be sure, but at present it is impossible to name any amount. I neither know what income is coming to me, nor what will be my expenses. I meant to come and see you as soon as there was anything explicit to tell you; but of course this first year there will be much less in hand than later.'

'Well,' she said, pouting, 'I can put up with something less in the meantime, for of course your poor dear brother's widow and children are your first consideration, and even a nobleman as a bachelor cannot have so many expenses.'

'I shall not long continue a bachelor,' was the answer, given with a sort of shy resolution.

'Now, Lord Northmoor! You don't mean to say that you intend to go on with that ridiculous affair; when, if you marry at all, it ought to be one who will bring something handsome into the family.'

'Once for all, Emma, I will hear no more on that subject.

A twenty years' engagement is not lightly to be broken.'

'A wretched little teacher,' she began, but she was cut short.

'Remember, I will hear no more of this, and' (nothing but despair of other means could have inspired him) 'it is for your own interest to abstain from insulting my future wife and myself by such remonstrances.'

Even then she muttered, 'Very hard! Not even good-looking.'

'That is as one may think,' said he, mentally contrasting the flaunting, hardened complexion before him with the sweet countenance he had never perceived to be pinched or faded; and as he heard something between a scornful sniff and a sob, he added, 'I am wanted in the office, so, if you have no more to say of any consequence, I must leave you, and Hannah shall give you some tea.'

'Oh, oh, that you should leave your poor brother's widow in this way!' and she melted into tears and sobs.

'I can't help it, Emma,' he said, distressed and perplexed. 'They want me about some business of Mr. Claughton's, and I can't keep them waiting. These are office hours, you know. Have some tea, and I will come to you again.'

But Mrs. Emma swallowed her sobs as soon as he was gone, and instead of waiting for the tea, set forth for Miss Lang's. On asking for Miss Marshall she was shown into the drawing-room, where, after she had waited a few minutes, nursing her wrath to keep it warm, the small figure appeared, whom she had no hesitation in accosting thus—

Charlotte M. Yonge

'Now, Miss Marshall, do I understand that you are resolved to attempt thrusting yourself on his Lordship, Lord Northmoor's family?'

Mary, entirely taken by surprise, could only falter, 'I can only do whatever he wishes.'

'That is just a mere pretence. I wonder you are not ashamed to play on his honourable feelings, when you know everything is changed, and that it is absolutely ridiculous and derogatory for a peer of the realm to stoop to a mere drudge of a teacher.'

'It is,' owned Mary; but she went back to her formulary, 'it must be as he wishes.'

'If he is infatuated enough to pretend to wish it, I tell you it is your simple duty to refuse him.'

Whatever might be Mary's own views of her duty, to have it inculcated in such a manner stirred her whole soul into opposition, which was shown, not in words, but in a tiny curve of the lips, such as infuriated her visitor, so that vulgarity and violence were under no restraint, and whether all self-command was lost in passion, or whether there was an idea that bullying might gain the day, Mrs. Morton's voice rose into a shrill scream as she denounced the nasty, mean-spirited viper, worming herself—

The folding doors suddenly opened and in a dignified tone Miss Lang announced, 'Lady Kenton wishes to be introduced to you, Miss Marshall.'

Mary made her little formal bend as well as her trembling limbs would allow her. Her cheeks were hot, her eyes swam, her hand shook as Lady Kenton took it kindly, while Mrs. Morton, too strong in her own convictions to perceive how the land lay, exclaimed, 'Your Ladyship is come for the same purpose as me, to let Miss Marshall know how detrimental and improper it is in her to persist in holding my brother, Lord Northmoor, to the unfortunate engagement she inveigled him into.'

To utter this with moderate coolness cost such an effort that she thought Mr. Rollstone could not have done it better, and was astonished when Lady Kenton replied, 'Indeed, I came to have the pleasure of congratulating Miss Marshall on, if it be not impertinent to say so, a beautiful and rare perseverance and constancy being rewarded.'

'As if she had not known what she was about,' muttered Mrs. Morton, not even yet quite confounded, but as she saw the lady lay another hand over that of still trembling Mary, she added, 'Well, if that is the case, my lady, and she is to be encouraged in her obstinacy, I have no more to say, except that it is a cruel shame on his poor dear brother's children, that—that he has made so much of, and have the best right—' and she began to sob again.

'Come,' said Miss Lang, as if talking to a naughty girl, 'if you are overcome like that, you had better come away.'

Wherewith authoritative habits made it possible to her to get Mrs. Morton out of the room; while Mary, well used to self-restraint, was struggling with choking tears, but when warm-hearted Lady Kenton drew her close and kissed her, they began to flow uncontrollably, so that she could only gasp, 'Oh, I beg your pardon, my lady!'

'Never mind,' was the answer; 'I don't wonder! There's no word for that language but brutal.'

'Oh, don't,' was Mary's cry. 'She is *his*, Lord Northmoor's

Charlotte M. Yonge

sister-in-law, and he has done everything for her ever since his brother's death.'

'That is no reason she should speak to you in that way. I must ask you to excuse me, but we could not help hearing, she was so loud, and then I felt impelled to break in.'

'It was very very kind! But oh, I wish I knew whether she is not in the right after all!'

'I am sure Lord Northmoor is deeply attached—quite in earnest,' said Lady Kenton, feeling rather as if she was taking a liberty.

'Yes, I know it would grieve him most dreadfully, if it came to an end now, dear fellow. I know it would break my heart, too, but never mind that, I would go away, out of his reach, and he might get over it. Would it not be better than his being always ashamed of an inferior, incompetent creature, always dragging after him?'

'I do not think you can be either, after what my daughter and Miss Lang have told me.'

'You see, it is not even as if I had been a governess in a private family, I have always been here. I know nothing about servants, or great houses, or society, not so much as our least little girl, who has a home.'

'May I tell you what I think, my dear,' said Lady Kenton, greatly touched. 'You have nothing to unlearn, and there is nothing needful to the position but what any person of moderate ability and good sense can acquire, and I am quite sure that Lord Northmoor would be far less happy without you, even in the long-run, besides the distress you would cause him now. It is not a brilliant, showy person that he needs, but one to understand and make him a real home.'

'That is what he is always telling me,' said Mary, somewhat cheered.

'Yes, and he could not help showing where his heart is,' said the lady. 'Now the holidays are near, are they not?'

'The 11th of July.'

'Then, if you have no other plans, will you come and stay with me? We are very quiet people, but you would have an opportunity of understanding something of the kind of life.'

'Oh, how very kind of you! Nobody has been so good to me.'

'I think I can help you in some of the difficulties if you will let me,' said Lady Kenton, quite convinced herself, and leaving a much happier woman than she had found.

Charlotte M. Yonge

CHAPTER VIII

SECOND THOUGHTS

Though Miss Lang was shocked and indignant at Mrs. Morton's violence, she was a wise woman, and felt that it would be better tact not to let such a person depart without an attempt at pacification; so she did her best at dignified soothing, and listened to a good deal of grumbling and lamentation.

She contrived, however, to give the impression that as things stood, Mrs. Morton would be far wiser to make no more resistance, but to consult family peace by accepting Miss Marshall, who, she assured the visitor, was a very kind and excellent person, not likely to influence Lord Northmoor against his own family, except on great provocation.

Mrs. Morton actually yielded so far as to declare she had only spoken for her dear brother-in-law's own good, and that since he was so infatuated, she supposed, for her dear children's sake, she must endure it. Having no desire to encounter him again, she went off by the next train, leaving a message that she had had tea at Miss Lang's. She related at home to her expectant daughter that Lord Northmoor had grown 'that high and stuck-up, there was no speaking to him, and that there Miss Marshall was an artful puss, as knew how to play her cards and get *in* with the quality.'

'I wish you had taken me, ma,' said Ida, 'I should have known what to say to them.'

'I can't tell, child, you might only have made it worse. I see how it is now, and we must be mum, or it may be the worse for us. He says he will do what he can for us, but I know what that means. She will hold the purse-strings, and make him meaner than he is already. He will never know how to spend his fortune now he has got it! If your poor, dear pa had only been alive now, he would never have let you be wronged.'

'But you gave it to them?' cried Ida.

'That I did! Only that lady, Lady Kenton, came in all stuck-up and haughty, and cut me short, interfering as she had no business to, or I would have brought Miss Mary to her marrow-bones. She hadn't a word to say for herself, but now she has got those fine folks on her side, the thing will go on as sure as fate. However, I've done my dooty, that's one comfort; and now, I suppose I shall have to patch it up as best I can.'

'I wouldn't!' said Ida hotly.

'Ah, Ida, my dear, you don't know what a mother won't do for her children.'

A sigh that was often reiterated as Mrs. Morton composed a letter to her brother-in-law, with some hints from Ida on the spelling, and some from Mr. Rollstone on the address. The upshot was that her dear brother and his *fiancee* were to believe her actuated by the purest sense of the duty and anxiety she owed to them and her dear children, the

Charlotte M. Yonge

orphans of his dear deceased brother. Now that she had once expressed herself, she trusted to her dear Frank's affectionate nature to bury all in oblivion, and to believe that she should be ready to welcome her new sister-in-law with the warmest affection. Therewith followed a request for five pounds, to pay for her mourning and darling Ida's, which they had felt due to him!

Lord Northmoor did not quite see how it was due to him, nor did he intend to give whatever his dear sister-in-law might demand, but she had made him so angry that he felt that he must prove his forgiveness to himself. Mary had not thought it needful to describe the force of the attack upon herself, or perhaps his pardon might not have gone so far. He sent the note, and added that as he was wanted at Northmoor for a day or two, he would take his nephew Herbert with him.

This was something like, as Mrs. Morton said, a kind of tangible acknowledgment of their relationship and of Herbert as his heir, and it was a magnificent thing to tell all her acquaintances that her son was gone to the family seat with his uncle, Lord Northmoor. She would fain have obtained for him some instructions in the manners of the upper ten thousand from Mr. Rollstone, but Herbert entirely repudiated listening to that old fogey, observing that after all it was only old Frank, and he wasn't going to bother himself for the like of him.

The uncle was fond of his brother's boy, and had devised this plan partly for the sake of the pleasure it would give, and partly because it was impossible to form any judgment of his character while with the mother. He was a fine, well-grown, manly boy, and when seen among his companions, had an indefinable air of good blood about him. He had hitherto been at a good day-school which prepared boys for the merchant service, and his tastes were so much in the direction of the sea, that it was much to be regretted that at fourteen and a half it was useless to think of preparation for a naval cadetship. He was sent up by train to join his uncle at Hurminster, and the first question after the greeting was, 'I say, uncle, shan't you have a yacht?'

'I could not afford it, if I wished it,' was the answer, while *Punch* was handed over to him, and Lord Northmoor applied himself to a long blue letter.

'Landlubber!' sighed Herbert to himself, with true marine contempt for a man who had sat on an office-stool all his life. 'He doesn't look a bit more of a swell than he used to. It is well there's some one with some pluck in the family.'

Charlotte M. Yonge

CHAPTER IX

THE HEIR-PRESUMPTUOUS

Herbert began to be impressed when, on the train arriving at a little country station, a servant in mourning, with finger to his hat, inquired after his Lordship's luggage, and another was seen presiding over a coroneted brougham.

'I say,' he breathed forth, when they were shut in, 'is this yours?'

'It is Miss Morton's, I believe, at present. I am to arrange whether to keep it or not.'

They were driving over an open heath in its summer carpet-like state of purple heather, dwarf gorse, and bracken. Lord Northmoor looked out, with thoughtfulness in his face. By and by there was a gate, a lodge, a curtse-ying woman, and as they passed it, he said, 'Now, this is Northmoor.'

'Yours, uncle?'

'Yes.'

'My—!' was all Herbert could utter. It semed to his

town-bred eyes a huge space before they reached, through some rather scanty plantations, another lodge, and a park, not very extensive, but with a few fine trees, and they thundered up beneath the pillars to what was, to his idea, a palace—with servants standing about in a great hall.

His uncle would have turned one way, but a servant said, 'Miss Morton is in the morning-room, my Lord,' and ushered them into a room where a lady in black came forward.

'You did not expect to find me here still,' she said cordially; 'but Adela is gone to her brother's, and I thought I had better stay for the division of—of the things.'

'Oh, certainly—I am—glad,' he stammered, with a blush as one not quite sure of the correctness of the proceeding. 'I wouldn't have intruded—'

'Bosh! I'm the intruder. Letitia Bury is gone—alas—but,' said she, laughing, 'Hailes is here—staying,' she added to relieve him and to lessen the confusion that amused her, 'and I see you have a companion. Your nephew—?'

'Yes, Herbert, my late brother's son. I would not have brought him if I had known.'

'A cousin,' she said, smiling, and shaking hands with him. 'Boys are my delight. This is quite a new experience.'

Herbert looked up surprised, not much liking to become an experience. He had had less intercourse with ladies than many boys of humbler pretensions, for his mother had always scouted the idea of sending her children to a Sunday-school, and she was neither like his mother's friends nor his preconceived notions. 'There! for want of an introduction, I must introduce myself. Your cousin

Charlotte M. Yonge

Bertha, or Birdie, whichever you like best.'

Frank was by no means prepared to say even Bertha, and was in agonies lest Herbert should presume on the liberty given him; but if the boy had been in the palace of Truth, he would have said, 'You old girl, you are awfully old to call yourself Birdie!' For Birdie had been a pet name of Rose Rollstone; and Bertha Morton, though slim and curly-headed, had a worn look about her eyes, and a countenance such as to show her five-and-thirty years, and to the eyes of fourteen was almost antediluvian; indeed, older observers might detect a worn, haggard, strained look. He was somewhat disgusted, too, at the thin rolls of bread-and-butter on the low table, whence she proceeded to hand teacups, as he thought of the substantial meals at home. When they had been conducted to their rooms, and his uncle followed to his, he broke out with his perpetual, 'I say, uncle, is this all the grub great swells have? I'm awfully peckish!'

'That's early tea, my boy,' was the answer, with a smile. 'There's dinner to come, and I hope you will behave yourself well, and not use such expressions.'

'Dinner! that's not such a bad hearing, but I suppose one must eat it like a judge?'

'Certainly; I am afraid I am not a very good model, but don't you do anything you don't see me do. And, Herbert, don't take wine every time the servants offer it.'

At which Herbert made a face.

'Have you got any evening shoes? No! If I had only known that the lady was here! It can't be helped to-day, only wash your face and hands well; there's some hot water.'

'Why, they ain't dirty,' said the boy, surveying them as one to whom the remains of a journey were mere trifles, then, with a sigh, 'It's no end of a place, but you swells have a lot of bores, and no mistake!'

Upstairs Herbert roamed about studying with great curiosity the appliances of the first bedchamber he had ever beheld beyond the degree of his mother's 'first floor,' but downstairs, he was in the mood of the savage, too proud to show wonder or admiration or the sense of awe with which he was inspired by being waited on by the very marrow of Mr. Rollstone, always such grand company at home. This daunted him far more than the presence of the lady, and though his was a spirit not easily daunted, he almost blushed when that personage peremptorily resisted his endeavour to present the wrong glass for champagne, which fortunately he disliked too much at the first taste to make another attempt. Lord Northmoor, for the first time at the foot of his own table, was on thorns all the time, lest he should see his nephew commit some indiscretion, and left most of the conversation to Miss Morton and Mr. Hailes, the solicitor, a fine-looking old gentleman, who was almost fatherly to her, very civil to him, but who cast somewhat critical eyes on the cub who might have to be licked into a shape befitting the heir.

They tried to keep their host in the conversation, but without much success, though he listened as it drifted into immediate interests and affairs of the neighbourhood, and made response, as best he could, to the explanations which, like well-bred people, they from time to time directed to him. He thus learnt that Lady Adela with her little Amice had been carried off 'by main force,' Bertha said, 'by her brother. But she will come back again,' she added. 'She is devoted to the place and her graves—and the poor people.'

'I do not know what they would do without her,' said Mr. Hailes.

'No. She is lady-of-all-work and Pro-parsoness—with all her might'; then seeing, or thinking she saw, a puzzled look, she added, 'I don't know if you discovered, Northmoor, that our Vicar, Mr. Woodman, has no wife, and Adela has supplied the lack to the parish, having a soul for country poor, whereas they are too tame for me. I care about my neighbours, of course, after a sort, but the jolly city sparrows of the slums for me! I long to be away.'

What to say to this Lord Northmoor knew as little as did his nephew, and with some difficulty he managed to utter, 'Are not they very uncivilised?'

'That's the beauty of it,' said Bertha; 'I've spotted my own special preserve of match-girls, newsboys, etc., and Mr. Hailes is going to help me to get a scrumptious little house, whence I can get to it by underground rail. Oh, you may shake your head, Mr. Hailes, but if you will not help me, I shall set my unassisted genius to work, and you'll only suffer agonies in thinking of the muddle I may be making.'

'What does Lady Adela say?' asked Mr. Hailes.

'She thinks me old enough to take care of myself, whatever you do, Mr. Hailes; besides, she knows I can come up to breathe! I long for it!'

The dinner ended by Bertha rising, and proposing to Herbert to come with her. It was not too dark, she said, to look out into the Park and see the rabbits scudding about.

'Ah!' said Mr. Hailes, shaking his head as they went, 'the

rabbits ought not to be so near, but there has been sad neglect since poor Mr. Morton's death.'

It was much easier to get on in a *tete-a-tete*, and before long Mr. Hailes had heard some of the perplexities about Herbert, the foremost of which was how to make him presentable for ladies' society in the evening. If Miss Morton's presence had been anticipated, either his uncle would not have brought him, or would have fitted him out beforehand, for though he looked fit for the fields and woods in male company, evening costume had not yet dawned on his imagination. Mr. Hailes recommended sending him in the morning to the town at Colbeam, under charge of the butler, Prowse—who would rather enjoy the commission, and was quite capable of keeping up any needed authority. For the future training, the more important matter on which he was next consulted, Mr. Hailes mentioned the name of a private tutor, who was likely to be able to deal with the boy better under present circumstances than a public school could do—since at Herbert's age, his ignorance of the classics on the one hand, and of gentlemanly habits on the other, would tell too much against him.

'But,' said Mr. Hailes, 'Miss Morton will be a very good adviser to you on that head.'

'She is very good-natured to him,' said Frank.

'No one living has a better heart than Miss Morton,' said Mr. Hailes heartily; 'a little eccentric, owing to—to circumstances. She has had her troubles, poor dear; but she has as good a heart as ever was, as you will find, my Lord, in all arrangements with her.'

Nevertheless, Lord Northmoor's feelings towards her might be startled the next morning, when he descended to

Charlotte M. Yonge

the dining-room. A screen cut off the door, and as he was coming round it, followed by his nephew, Bertha's clear voice was heard saying, 'Yes, he is inoffensive, but he is a stick. There's no denying it, Mr. Hailes, he is a dreadful stick.'

Frank was too far advanced to retire, before the meaning dawned on him, partly through a little explosion of Herbert behind him, and partly from the guilty consternation and colour with which the other two turned round from the erection of plants among which they were standing.

Yet it was the shy man who spoke first in the predicament, like a timid creature driven to bay.

'Yes, Miss Morton, I know it is too true; no one is more sensible of it than myself. I can only hope to do my best, such as it is.'

'Oh, Northmoor, it was very horrid and unguarded in me, and I can only be sorry and beg your pardon,' and while she laughed and held out her hand, there was a dew in her eyes.

'Truths do not need pardon,' he said, as he gave a cousinly grasp, 'and I think you will try kindly to excuse my deficiencies and disadvantages.'

There was a certain dignity in his tone, and Bertha said heartily—

'Thank you. It is all right in essentials, and chatter is of very little consequence. Now come and have some breakfast.'

They got on together far better after that, and began to

feel like relations, before Herbert was sent off with Mr. Prowse to Colbeam. Indeed, throughout the transactions that followed, Bertha showed herself far less devoted to her own interests than to what might be called the honour of the family. Her father's will had been made in haste, after the death of his little grandson, and was as concise as possible, her influence having told upon it. Knowing that the new heir would have nothing to begin with, and aware that if he inherited merely the title, house, and land, he would be in great straits, the old Lord had bequeathed to him nearly what would have been left to the grandson, a fair proportion of the money in the funds and bank, and all the furniture and appurtenances of Northmoor House, excepting such articles as Bertha and Lady Adela might select, each up to a certain value.

Lady Adela's had been few, and already chosen, and Bertha's were manifestly only matters of personal belonging, and not up altogether to the amount named; so as to avoid stripping the place, which, at the best, was only splendid in utterly unaccustomed eyes. Horses and carriages had to be bought of her, and it was she who told him what was absolutely necessary, and fixed the price as low as she could, so as not to make them a gift. And he was not so ignorant in this matter as she had expected— for the old habits of his boyhood served him, he could ride well, and his scruples at Miss Morton's estimate proved that he knew a horse when he saw it—as she said. She would, perhaps, have liked him better if he had been a dissipated horsey man like his father. He would have given her sensations—and on his side, considering the reputation of the family, he was surprised at her eager, almost passionate desire to be rid of the valuable horses and equipages as soon as possible.

When, in the afternoon, she went out of doors to refresh herself with a solitary ramble in the Park after her morning of business, she heard an altercation, and presently encountered a keeper, dragging after him a trespasser, in whom, to her amazement, she recognised Herbert Morton, at the same moment as he exclaimed: 'Cousin Bertha! Miss—Look at this impudent fellow, though I told him I was Lord Northmoor's own nephew.'

'And I told him, ma'am,' said the keeper, touching his hat, 'that if he was ten nephews I wouldn't have him throwing stones at my pheasants, nor his Lordship wouldn't neither, and then he sauced me, and I said I would see what his Lordship said to that.'

'You must excuse him this time, Best,' said Miss Morton; 'he is a town-bred boy, and knows no better, and you had better not worry his Lordship about it.'

'Very well, Miss Morton, if it is your pleasure, but them pheasants are my province, and I must do my dooty.'

'Of course, quite right, Best,' she answered; 'but my cousin here did not understand, and you must make allowance for him.'

Best touched his hat again, and went off with an undercurrent of growl.

'Oh, Herbert, this is a pity!' Miss Morton exclaimed.

'Cheeky chap!' said Herbert sulkily. 'What business had he to meddle with me? A great big wild bird gets up with no end of a row, and I did nothing but shy a stone, and out comes this fellow at me in a regular wax, and didn't care half a farthing when I told him who I was. I fancy he did not believe me.'

'I don't wonder,' said Bertha; 'you have yet to learn that in the eyes of any gentleman, nothing is much more sacred than a pheasant.'

'I never meant to hurt the thing, only one just chucks a stone,' muttered Herbert, abashed, but still defensive and offended. 'I thought my uncle would teach the rascal how to speak to me.'

'I'll tell you what, Herbert, if you take that line with good old servants, who are only doing their duty, you won't have a happy time of it here. I suppose you wish to take your place as a gentleman. Well, the greatest sign of a gentleman is to be courteous and well-behaved to all about him.'

'He wasn't courteous or well-behaved to me.'

'No, because you did not show yourself such a gentleman as he has been used to. If you acted like a tramp or a poacher, no wonder he thought you one'; then, after a pause, 'You will find that much of your pleasure in sport depends on the keepers, and that it would be a great disadvantage to be on bad terms with them, so I strongly advise you, on every account, to treat them with civility, and put out of your head that there is any dignity in being rude.'

Herbert liked Miss Morton, and had been impressed as well as kindly treated by her, and though he sulked now, there was an after-effect.

CHAPTER X

COMING HONOURS

With great trepidation did Mary Marshall set forth on her visit to Coles Kenton. She had made up her mind—and a determined mind it could be on occasion—that on it should turn her final acceptance of her twenty years' lover.

Utterly inexperienced as she was, even in domestic, not to say high life, she had perhaps an exaggerated idea, alike of its requirements and of her own deficiencies; and she was resolved to use her own judgment, according to her personal experience, whether she should be hindrance or help to him whom she loved too truly and unselfishly to allow herself to be made the former.

She was glad that for the first few days she should not see him, and should thus be less distracted and biased, but it was with a sinking heart that she heard that Lady Kenton had called to take her up in the carriage. Grateful as she was for the kindness, which saved her the dreariness of a solitary arrival, she was a strange mixture of resolution and self-distrust, of moral courage and timidity, as had been shown by her withstanding all Miss Lang's endeavours to make her improve her dress beyond what was absolutely necessary for the visit, lest it should be presuming on the future.

Lady Kenton had a manner such as to smooth away shyness, and, with tact that perceived with what kind of nature she had to deal, managed to make the tea-table serve only as a renewal of acquaintance with Frederica, and an introduction to Sir Edward, after which Mary was taken to the schoolroom and made known to the governess, a kindly, sensible woman, who, according to previous arrangement, made the visitor free of her domains as a refuge.

The prettiness and luxury of the guest-chamber was quite a shock, and Mary would rather have faced a dozen naughty girls than have taken Sir Edward's arm to go in to dinner. However, her hostess had decided on a quiet course of treatment such as not to frighten this pupil, and it had been agreed only to take enough notice of her to prevent her from feeling herself neglected, until she should begin to be more at ease. Nor was it long before a certain sparkle in the brown eyes showed that she was amused by, and appreciative of, the family talk.

It was true, as Lady Kenton had told her, that she had nothing to unlearn, all she wanted was confidence, experience, and ease, and in so humble, gentle, and refined a nature as hers, the acquisition of these could not lead to the disclosure of anything undesirable. So, after the first day of novelty, when she had learnt the hours, could distinguish between the young people, knew her way about the house so as to be secure of not opening the wrong doors, and when she had learnt where and when she would be welcome and even helpful, she began to enjoy herself and the life, the beauty, and the leisure.

She made friends heartily with the governess, fraternised with Freda, taught the younger girls new games, could hold a sort of conversation with Sir Edward, became less afraid of George, and daily had more of filial devotion to Lady Kenton. The books on the tables were a real delight and pleasure to her, when she found that it was not ill-mannered to sit down and read in the forenoon, and the discussion of them was a great help in what Freda called teaching her to talk. Visitors were very gradually brought upon her, a gentleman or two at first, who knew nothing about her, perhaps thought her the governess and merely bowed to her. There was only one real *contretemps*, when some guests, who lived rather beyond the neighbourhood, arrived for afternoon tea, and, moreover, full of curiosity about Lord Northmoor. Was it true that he was an attorney's clerk, and was not he going to marry a very inferior person?

'Certainly not,' said Lady Kenton. 'He is engaged to my friend, Miss Marshall.'

The said Miss Marshall was handing the sugar, while Freda was pouring out the tea. She had been named on the ladies' entrance, and the colour rose to her eyes but she said nothing, while there was a confusion of, 'I beg pardon. I understand.'

'Report makes a good many mistakes,' said Lady Kenton coolly. 'Mary, my dear, you have given me no sugar.'

It was the first time of calling her by her Christian name, and done for the sake of making the equal intimacy apparent. In fact, Mary was behaving herself better than the visitors, as Lady Kenton absolutely told her when a sort of titter was heard in the hall, where they were expressing to Freda their horror at the scrape, and extorting that Miss Marshall was really a governess.

'But quite a lady,' said Freda stoutly, 'and we are all as

fond of her as possible.'

It showed how much progress she had made that even this shock did not set her to express any more faint-hearted doubts, and, when Lord Northmoor arrived the next day, the involuntary radiance on both their faces was token enough that they were all the world to each other. Mary allowed herself to venture on getting Lady Kenton's counsel on the duties of household headship that would fall on her; and instead of being terrified at the great garden-party and dinner-party to be held at Coles Kenton, eagerly availed herself of instruction in the details of their management. She had accepted her fate, and when the two were seen moving about among the people of the party they neither of them looked incongruous with the county aristocracy. Quiet, retiring, and insignificant they might be, but there was nothing to remark by the most curious eyes of those who knew they were to see the new peer and his destined bride; in fact, as George and Freda privately remarked, they were just the people that nobody ever would see at all, unless they were set up upon a pedestal.

Mary still feebly suggested, when the marriage was spoken of, that it might be wiser for Frank to wait a year, get over his first expenses and feel his way; but he would not hear of her going back to her work, and pleaded his solitude so piteously that she could not but consent to let it take place as soon as possible. They would fain have kept it as private as possible, but their good friends were of opinion that it was necessary to give them a start with some *eclat*, and insisted that it should take place with all due honours at Coles Kenton, where Mary was treated like a favoured niece, and assisted with counsel on her *trousseau*. The savings she had made during the long years of her engagement were enough to fit her out sufficiently to feel that she was bringing her own wardrobe, and Lady Kenton actually went to London with her to superintend the outlay.

'Whom would they like to have asked to the wedding?' the lady inquired, herself naming the Langs and Burfords. 'Of course,' she added, smiling, 'Freda and Alice will be only too happy to be bridesmaids. Have you any one whom you would wish to ask? Your old scholars perhaps.'

'I think,' said Mary, hesitating, 'that one reason why we think we ought to decline your kindness was—about *his* relations.'

Lady Kenton had given full license to the propriety of calling *him* Frank with intimate friends, but Mary always had a shyness about it.

'Indeed, I should make no question about asking them, if I had not doubted whether, after what passed—'

'That is all forgotten,' said Mary gently. 'I have had quite a nice letter since, and—'

'Of course they must be asked,' said Lady Kenton; 'I should have proposed it before, but for that scene.'

'That is nothing,' said Mary; 'the doubt is whether, considering the style of people, it would not be better for us to manage it otherwise, and not let you be troubled.'

'Oh, that's nothing! On such an occasion there's no fear of their not behaving like the rest of the world. There are girls, I think; they should be bridesmaids.'

This very real kindness overcame all scruples, and indeed a great deal might be forgiven to Miss Marshall in consideration of the glory of telling all Westhaven of the invitation to be present 'at my brother Lord Northmoor's wedding, at Sir Edward Kenton's, Baronet.' He gave the dresses, not only the bridesmaids' white and cerise (Freda's choice), but the chocolate moire which for a minute Mrs. Morton fancied 'the little spiteful cat' had chosen on purpose to suppress her, till assured by all qualified beholders, especially Mrs. Rollstone and a dressmaker friend, that in nothing else would she have looked so entirely quite the lady.

And Lady Kenton's augury was fulfilled. The whole family were subdued enough by their surroundings to comport themselves quite well enough to pass muster.

Charlotte M. Yonge

CHAPTER XI

POSSESSION

So Francis Morton, Baron Northmoor of Northmoor, and Mary Marshall, daughter of the late Reverend John Marshall, were man and wife at last. Their honeymoon was ideally happy. It fulfilled a dream of their life, when Frank used, in the holidays spent by Mary with his mother, to read aloud the Waverley novels, and they had calculated, almost as an impossible castle in the air, the possibility of visiting the localities. And now they went, as assuredly they had never thought of going, and not much impeded by the greatness that had been thrust on them. The good-natured Kentons had dispensed his Lordship from the encumbrance of a valet, and though my Lady could not well be allowed to go maidless, Lady Kenton had found a sensible, friendly person for her, of whom she soon ceased to be afraid, and thus felt the advantage of being able to attend to her husband instead of her luggage.

Tourists might look and laugh at their simple delight as at that of a pair of unsophisticated cockneys. This did not trouble them, as they trod what was to them classic ground, tried in vain the impossible feat of 'seeing Melrose aright,' but revelled in what they did see, stood with bated breath at Dryburgh by the Minstrel's tomb, and tracked his magic spells from the Tweed even to Staffa, feeling the full delight for the first time of mountain, sea, and loch. Their enjoyment was perhaps even greater than that of boy and girl, for it was the reaction of chastened lives and hearts 'at leisure from themselves,' nor were spirit and vigour too much spent for enterprise.

They tasted to the full every innocent charm that came in their way, and, above all, the bliss of being together in the perfect sympathy that had been the growth of so many years. Their maid, Harte, might well confide to her congeners that though my lord and my lady were the oldest couple she had known, they were the most attached, in a quiet way.

They were loth to end this state of felicity before taking their new cares upon them, and were glad that the arrangements of the executors made it desirable that they should not take possession till October, when they left behind them the gorgeous autumn beauty of the western coast and journeyed southwards.

The bells were rung, the gates thrown wide open, and lights flashed in the windows as Lord and Lady Northmoor drove up to their home, but it was in the dark, and there was no demonstrative welcome, the indoor servants were all new, the cook-housekeeper hired by Lady Kenton's assistance, and the rest of the maids chosen by her, the butler and his subordinate acquired in like manner.

It was a little dreary. The rooms looked large and empty. Miss Morton's belongings had been just what gave a homelike air to the place, and when these were gone, even the big fires could not greatly cheer the huge spaces. However, these two months had accustomed the new arrivals to their titles, and likewise to being waited upon, and they were less at a loss than they would have been previously, though to Mary especially it was hard to realise that it was her own house, and that she need ask no one's leave. Also that it was not a duty to sit with a fire. She could not well have done so, considering how many were doing their best to enliven the house, and finally she spent the evening in the library, not a very inviting room in itself, but which the late lord had inhabited, and where the present one had already held business interviews. It was, of course, lined with the standard books of the last generation, and Mary, who had heard of many, but never had access to them, flitted over them while her husband opened the letters he had found awaiting him. To her, what some one has called the 'tea, tobacco, and snuff' of an old library where the books are chiefly viewed as appropriate furniture, were all delightful discoveries. Even to 'Hume's *History of England*—nine volumes! I did not know it was so long! Our first class had the Student's *Hume*. Is there much difference?'

'Rather to the Student's advantage, I believe. Half these letters, at least, are mere solicitations for custom! And advertisements!'

'How the books stick together! I wonder when they were opened last!'

'Never, I suspect,' said he. 'I do not imagine the Mortons were much disposed to read.'

'Well, they have left us a delightful store! What's this? Smollett's *Don Quixote*. I always wanted to know about that. Is it not something about giants and windmills? Have you read it?'

'I once read an odd volume. He was half mad, and too good for this world, and thought he was living in a romance. I will read you some bits. You would not like it all.'

'Oh, I do hope you will have time to read to me! Gibbon's *Decline and Fall of the Roman Empire*. All these volumes! They are quite damp. You have read it?'

'Yes, and I wish I could remember all those Emperors. I must put aside this letter for Hailes—it is a man applying for a house.'

'How strange it sounds! Look, here is such an immense *Shakespeare*! Oh! full of engravings,' as she fell upon Boydell's *Shakespeare*—another name reverenced, though she only knew a few selected plays, prepared for elocution exercises.

Her husband, having had access to the Institute Library, and spent many evenings over books, was better read than she, whose knowledge went no farther than that of the highest class, but who knew all very accurately that she did know, and was intelligent enough to find in those shelves a delightful promise of pasture. He was by this time sighing over requests for subscriptions.

'Such numbers! Such good purposes! But how can I give?'

'Cannot you give at least a guinea?' asked Mary, after hearing some.

'I do not know whether in this position a small sum in the list is not more disadvantageous than nothing at all. Besides, I know nothing of the real merits. I must ask Hailes. Ah! and here is Emma, I thought that she would be a little impatient. She says she shall let her house for the winter, and thinks of going to London or to Brighton, where she may have masters for the girls.'

Charlotte M. Yonge

'Oh, I thought you meant them to go to a good school?'

'So I do, if I can get Emma's consent; but I doubt her choosing to part with Ida. She wants to come here.'

'I suppose we ought to have her?'

'Yes, but not immediately. I do not mean to neglect her—at least, I do hope to do all that is right; but I think you ought to have a fair start here before she comes, so that we will invite her for Christmas, and then we can arrange about Ida and Constance.'

'Dear little Connie, I hope she is as nice a little girl as she used to be!'

'With good training, I think, she will be; and the tutor gives me good accounts of Herbert in this letter.'

'Shall we have him here on Sunday week?'

'Yes, I am very anxious to see him. I hope his master gives him more religious instruction than he has ever had, poor boy!'

Though not brilliant or playful, Lord and Lady Northmoor had, it may be perceived, no lack of good sense in their strange new surroundings. It was hard not to feel like guests on sufferance, and next morning, a Sunday, was wet. However, under their waterproofs and umbrellas trudging along, they felt once more, as Mary said, like themselves, as if they had escaped from their keepers. Nobody on the way had the least idea who the two cloaked figures were, and when they crept into the seat nearest the door they were summarily ejected by a fat, red-faced man, who growled audibly, 'You've no business in my pew!'

However, with the words, 'Beg your pardon,' they stepped out with a little amusement in their eyes, when a spruce young woman sprang up from the opposite pew, with a scandalised whisper—

'Mr. Ruddiman, it's his Lordship! Allow me, my Lord— your own seat—'

And she marshalled them up to the choir followed closely by Mr. Ruddiman, ruddier than ever, and butcher all over, in a perfect agony of apology, which Lord Northmoor in vain endeavoured to suppress or silence, till, when the guide had pointed to a handsome heavy carved seat with elaborate cushions, he gave a final gasp of, 'You'll not remember it in the custom, my Lord,' and departed, leaving his Lordship almost equally scarlet with annoyance at the place and time of the demonstration, though, happily, the clergyman had not yet appeared, in his long and much-tumbled surplice.

It was a case of a partial restoration of a church in the dawn of such doings, when the horsebox was removed, but the great family could not be routed out of the chancel, so there were the seats, where the choir ought to have sat, beneath a very ugly east window, bedecked with the Morton arms. In the other division of the seat was a pale lady in black, with a little girl, Lady Adela Morton, no doubt, and opposite were the servants, and the school children sat crowded on the steps. It was not such a service as had been the custom of the Hurminster churches; and the singing, such as it was, depended on the thin shrill voices of the children, assisted by Lady Adela and the mistress; the sermon was dull and long, and altogether there was something disheartening about the whole.

Lady Adela had a gentle, sweet countenance and a simple

devout manner; but it was disappointing that she did not attempt to address the newcomers, though they passed her just outside the churchyard, talking to an old man. Lady Kenton would surely have welcomed them.

CHAPTER XII

THE BURTHEN OF HONOURS

A fearful affair to the new possessors of Northmoor was the matter of morning calls. The first that befell them, as in duty bound, was that from the Vicar. They were peaceably writing their letters in the library, and hoping soon to go out to explore the Park, when Mr. Woodman was announced, and was found a lonely black speck in the big dreary drawing-room, a very state room, indeed, which nobody had ever willingly inhabited. The Vicar was accustomed to be overridden; he was an elderly widower, left solitary in his old age, and of depressed spirits and manner. However, Frank had been used to intercourse with clergy, though his relations with them seemed reversed, and instead of being patronised, he had to take the initiative; or rather, they touched each other's cold, shy, limp hands, and sat upright in their chairs, and observed upon the appropriate topic of early frosts, which really seemed to be affecting themselves.

There was a little thaw when Lord Northmoor asked about the population, larger, alas, than the congregation might have seemed to show, and Mary asked if there were much poverty, and was answered that there was much suffering in the winter, there was not much done for the poor except by Lady Adela.

Charlotte M. Yonge

'You must tell us how we can assist in any way.'

The poor man began to brighten. 'It will be a great comfort to have some interest in the welfare of the parish taken here, my Lord. The influence hitherto has not been fortunate. Miss Morton, indeed—latterly—but, poor thing, if I may be allowed to say so, she is flighty—and uncertain—no wonder—'

At that moment Lady Adela was ushered in, and the Vicar looked as if caught in talking treason, while a fresh nip of frost descended on the party.

Not that the lady was by any means on stiff terms with the Vicar, whom, indeed, she daily consulted on parochial subjects, and she had the gracious, hereditary courtesy of high breeding; but she always averred that this same drawing-room chilled her, and she was fully persuaded that any advance towards familiarity would lead to something obnoxious on the part of the newcomers, so that the proper relations between herself and them could only be preserved by a judicious entrenchment of courtesy. Still, it was more the manner of the Vicar than of herself that gave the impression of her being a formidable autocrat. After the frost had been again languidly discussed, Mr. Woodman faltered out, 'His Lordship was asking—was so good as to ask—how to assist in the parish.'

Lady Adela knew how scarce money must be, so she hesitated to mention subscriptions, and only said, 'Thank you—very kind.'

'Is there any one I could read to?' ventured Mary.

'Have you been used to the kind of thing?' asked Lady Adela, not unkindly, but in a doubting tone.

'No, I never could before; but I do wish to try to do something.'

The earnest humility of the tone was touching, the Vicar and the autocrat looked at one another, and the former suggested, 'Old Swan!'

'Yes,' said Lady Adela, 'old Swan lives out at Linghill, which is not above half a mile from this house, but too far off for me to visit constantly. I shall be very much obliged if you can undertake the cottages there.'

'Thank you,' said Mary, as heartily as if she were receiving a commission from the Bishop of the diocese.

'Did not Miss Morton mention something about a boys' class?' said Frank. 'I have been accustomed to a Sunday school.'

Mr. Woodman betrayed as much surprise as if he had said he was accustomed to a coal mine; and Lady Adela observed graciously, 'Most of them have gone into service this Michaelmas; but no doubt it will be a relief to Mr. Woodman if you find time to undertake them.'

This was the gist of the first two morning calls, and there were many more such periods of penance, for the bride and bridegroom were not modern enough in their notions to sit up to await their visitors, and thankful they were to those who would be at the expense of finding conversation, though this was not always the case; for much of the neighbourhood was of a description to be awed by the mere fact of a great house, and to take the shyness of titled people for pride. Those with whom they prospered best were a good-natured, merry old dowager duchess, with whom they felt themselves in the altitude to which they were accustomed at Hurminster; a loud-voiced, eager

Charlotte M. Yonge

old squire, who was bent on being Lord Northmoor's guide and prompter in county business; also an eager, gushing lady, the echoes of whose communications made Frank remark, after her departure, 'We must beware of encouraging gossip about the former family.'

'Oh, I wish I had the power of setting people down when they say what is undesirable, like Miss Lang, or Lady Adela!' sighed Mary.

'Try to think of them like your school girls,' he said.

The returning of the calls was like continually pulling the string of a shower-bath, and glad were the sighs when people proved to be not at home; but on the whole, being entertained was not half so formidable as entertaining, and a bride was not expected to do more than sit in her white silk, beside the host.

But the return parties were an incubus on their minds. Only they were not to be till after Christmas.

CHAPTER XIII

THE DOWER HOUSE

Over the hearth of the drawing-room of the Dower House, in the sociable twilight that had descended on the afternoon tea-table, sat three ladies—for Lady Adela and Miss Morton had just welcomed Mrs. Bury, who, though she had her headquarters in London, generally spent her time in visits to her married daughters or expeditions abroad.

Amice had just exhibited her doll, Elmira's last acquisition, a little chest of drawers, made of matchboxes and buttons, that Constance Morton had taught her to make, and then she had gone off to put the said Elmira and her companions to bed, after giving it as her grave opinion that Lady Northmoor was a great acquisition.

'Do you think so?' said Mrs. Bury, after the laugh at the sedate expression.

'She is very kind to Amice, and I do not think she will do her any harm,' said Lady Adela.

'Governessing was her *metier*,' added Bertha, 'so it is not likely.'

'And how does it turn out?'

Charlotte M. Yonge

'Oh, it might be a good deal worse. I see no reason for not living on here.'

'And you, Birdie?'

'No, I *couldn't*! I've been burning to get away these seven years, and as Northmoor actually seems capable of taking my boys, my last tie is gone. I'm only afraid he'll bore them with too much Sabbatarianism and temperance. He is just the cut of the model Sabbath-school teacher, only he vexes Addie's soul by dashes of the Ritualist.'

'Well,' said Mrs. Bury, 'the excellent Mr. Woodman is capable of improvement.'

'But how?' said Lady Adela. 'Narrow ritualism without knowledge or principle is a thing to be deprecated.'

'Is it without knowledge or principle?'

'How should an attorney's clerk get either?'

'But I understand you that they are worthy people, and not obnoxious.'

'Worthy!' exclaimed Bertha. 'Yes, worthy to their stiff backbones, worthy to the point of utter dulness; they haven't got enough vulgarity even to drop their h's or be any way entertaining. I should like them ever so much better if they ate with their knives and drank out of their saucers, but she can't even mispronounce a French word worse than most English people.'

'No pretension even?'

'Oh no; if there were, one could get some fun out of it. I have heard of bearing honours meekly, but they don't even do that, they just let them hang on them, like the stick and stock they are. If I were Addie, it would be the deadly liveliness that would drive me away.'

'Nay,' said Adela; 'one grows to be content with mere negations, if they are nothing worse. I *could* be driven away, or at least find it an effort to remain, if Lady Northmoor were like her sister-in-law.'

'Ah, now, that's just what would make it tolerable to me. I could get a rise or two out of that Mrs. Morton. I did get her to be confidential and to tell me how much better the honours would have sat upon her dear husband. I believe she thinks that if he were alive he would have shared them like the Spartan kings. She wishes that "her brother, Lord Northmoor" (you should hear the tone), "were more worldly, and she begs me to impress on him the duty of doing everything for her dear Herbert, who, in the nature of things, must be the heir to the peerage."'

'I am sure I hope not,' said Lady Adela. 'He is an insufferable boy. The people about the place can't endure him. He is quite insolent.'

'The animal, man, when in certain stages of development, has a peculiar tendency to be unpleasant,' observed Bertha philosophically. 'To my mind, Master Herbert is the most promising of the specimens.'

'Birdie! He is much worse than his uncle.'

'Promising, I said, not performing. Whatever promise there may have been in Northmoor must have been nipped upon the top of a high stool, but if he has sense enough to put that boy into good hands he may come to something. I like him enough myself to feel half inclined to do what I can towards licking him into shape, for the

Charlotte M. Yonge

honour of the family! It is that girl Ida that riles me most.'

'Yes,' said Lady Adela, 'she behaved fairly well in company, but I saw her tittering and whispering with Emily Trotman in a tone that I thought very bad for Emily.'

'She's spoilt; her mother worships her,' said Bertha. 'I had a pleasing confidence or two about how she is already admired, or, as Mrs. Morton calls it, how the gentlemen are after her; but now she shall not put up with anything but a *real* gentleman, and of course her uncle will do something handsome for her.'

'Poor man! I wish him joy. Has he more belongings?'

'Providentially, no. We have the honour of standing nearest to him, and she seems to have none at all, unless they should be attracted by the scent.'

'That is not likely,' said Lady Adela; 'she was a clergy orphan, and never heard of any relations.'

'Then you really know no harm of them, in these four or five months?' said Mrs. Bury.

'No; except having these relations,' said Adela.

'Except being just sensible enough not to afford even the pleasure of laughing at them,' said Bertha. 'Nay, just worthy enough'—she said it spitefully—'not even to give the relief of a good grumble.'

'Well, I think you may be thankful!'

'Exactly what one doesn't want to be!' said Bertha. 'I like sensations. Now Letitia is going to come down with a prediction that they are to become the blessings of our lives, so I am off!'

And as the door closed on her, Lady Adela sighed, and Mrs. Bury said—

'Poor Birdie; is she always in that tone?'

'Yes,' said Lady Adela; 'there seems to be always a bitter spot in her heart. I am glad she should try to work it out.'

'I suppose living here with her father tended to brooding. Yet she has always done a good deal.'

'Not up to her powers. Lord Northmoor never ceased to think her a mere girl, and obstructed her a good deal; besides, all his interest being in horses, she never could get rid of the subject, and wounds were continually coming back on us—on her.'

'On you as well, poor Addie.'

'He did not understand. Besides, to me these things were not the raw scene they were to her. It has been a very sad time for her. You see, there is not much natural softness in her, and she was driven into roughness and impatience when he worried her over racing details and other things. And then she was hurt at his preferring to have me with him. It has been very good and generous in her not to have been jealous of me.'

'I think she was glad he could find comfort in you. And you have never heard of Captain Alder?'

'Never! In justice, and for the sake of dear Arthur's wishes, I should be glad to explain; but I wonder whether, as she is now, it would be well that they should meet.'

Charlotte M. Yonge

'If it is so ordained, I suppose they will. What's that?'

It was Lord and Lady Northmoor, formally announced, and as formally introduced, to Mrs. Bury.

They had come, the lady said, when they were seated, with a message from 'Old Swan,' to ask for a bit of my lady's plaster for his back to ease his rheumatism at night. His daughter was only just come in from work, so they had ventured to bring the message.

'Is any one coming for it?'

'I said we would bring it back,' replied Mary, 'if you would kindly let us have it.'

'Why, it is a mile out of your way!'

'It is moonlight, and we do so enjoy a walk together,' she answered.

'Well, Adela,' said Mrs. Bury, when they were gone with the roll of plaster, 'I agree that they might be worse—and by a great deal!'

'Did he speak all the time?'

'Yes, once. But there are worse faults than silence; and she seems a bonny little woman. Honeymooning still— that moonlight walk too.'

'I can fancy that it is a treat to escape from Mrs. Morton. She is depths below them in refinement!'

'On the whole, I think you may be thankful, Adela.'

'I hope I am. I believe you would soon be intimate with

them; but then you always could get on with all sorts of people, and I have a shrinking from getting under the surface—if I *could*.'

And indeed, further intercourse, though not without shocks and casualties, made Mary Northmoor wish that Letitia Bury had been the permanent inhabitant; above all, when she undertook to come and give her counsel and support for that first tremendous undertaking—the dinner-party. Lady Kenton was equally helpful at their next; and Sir Edward gave much good advice to his lordship as to not letting himself be made the tool of the loud-voiced squire, who was anxious to be his guide, philosopher, and friend in county business—advice that made Frank's heart sink, for thus far he felt only capable of sitting still and listening.

Charlotte M. Yonge

CHAPTER XIV

WESTHAVEN VERSIONS OF HONOURS

'Thank you, a bit of partridge, Mr. Rollstone, if you please.'

'Excuse me, Mrs. Grover. This is a grouse from Lord Northmoor's own moors, I presume,' replied Mr. Rollstone, to the tune of a peal of laughter from Herbert and exclamation—'Not know a grouse!'—for which Ida frowned at him.

'Yes, indeed,' said his mother; 'we had so much game up at my brother's, Lord Northmoor's, that I shall quite miss it now I am come away.'

'Flimsy sort of grub!' growled an old skipper. 'Only fit for this sort of a tea—not to make a real meal on, fit for "a man"!'

The young folk laughed. Captain Purdy was only invited as a messmate of Mrs. Morton's father.

'You'll excuse this being only a tea,' went on Mrs. Morton. 'I hope to have a dinner in something more of style if ever I return here, but I could not attempt it with my present establishment after what we have got accustomed to.

Why, we never sat down to dinner without two menservants!'

'Only two?' said Mr. Rollstone. 'I have never been without three men under me; and I always had two to wait, even when the lady dined alone.'

Mrs. Grover, who had been impressed for a moment, took courage to say—

'I don't think so much of your grouse, Mrs. Morton. It's tasty and 'igh.'

'High game goes with high families,' wickedly murmured Herbert, causing much tittering at his corner of the table; and this grew almost convulsive, while another matron of the party observed—

'Mrs. Macdonald, Mr. Holt's sister in Scotland, once sent us some, and really, Mrs. Morton, if you boil them down, they are almost as good as a pat-ridge!'

'Oh, really now, Mrs. Holt! I hope you didn't tell Mrs. Macdonald so!' said Mrs. Morton. 'It is a real valuable article, such as my brother, Lord Northmoor, would only send to us, and one or two old friends that he wishes to compliment at Hurminster. But one must be used to high society to know how such things should be relished!'

'Are Lord Northmoor's moors extensive?' asked Mr. Rollstone.

'There's about four or five miles of them,' responded Herbert; 'and these grouse are awfully shy.'

'Ah, the Earl of Blackwing owns full twenty miles of heather,' said the ex-butler.

'Barren stuff!' growled the skipper; 'breeding nothing worth setting one's teeth into!'

'There are seven farms besides,' put in Mrs. Morton. 'My brother is going to have an audit-day next week.'

'You should have seen the Earl's audits,' said Mr. Rollstone. 'Five-and-twenty substantial tenant-farmers, besides artisans, and all the family plate on the sideboard!'

'Ah, you should see the Northmoor plate!' said Mrs. Morton. 'There are racing cups, four of them—not that any one could drink out of them, for they are just centre-pieces for the table. There's a man in armour galloping off headlong with a girl behind him— Who did your uncle say it was, Conny?'

'The Templar and Rowena, mamma,' said Constance.

'Yes, that was the best—all frosted. I liked that better than the one where the girl with no clothes to speak of was running like mad after a golden ball. They said that was an heirloom, worth five hundred—'

'Lord Burnside's yachting cups are valued at five thousand,' said Mr. Rollstone. 'I should know, for I had the care of them, and it was a responsibility as weighed on my mind.'

So whatever Mrs. Morton described as to the dignities and splendours of Northmoor, Mr. Rollstone continued to cap with more magnificent experiences, so that, though he never pretended to view himself in the light of a participator in the grandeur he described, he continued, quite unintentionally, so to depreciate the glories of Northmoor, that Mrs. Morton began to recollect how far above him her sphere had become, and to decide against his future admission to her parties.

The young ladies, as soon as tea was over, retired into corners in pairs, having on their side much to communicate. Rose Rollstone was at home for a holiday, after having begun to work at an establishment for art and ecclesiastical needlework, and it was no small treat to her and Constance to meet and compare their new experiences. Rose, always well brought up by her father, was in a situation carefully trained by a lady head, and watched over by those who deepened and cultivated her religious feeling; and Constance had to tell of the new facilities of education offered to them. Ida was too delicate for school, their mother said, and was only to have music lessons at Brighton, or in London whenever the present house could be parted with; but Herbert had already begun to work with a tutor for the army, and Constance was to go to the High School at Colbeam and spend her Sundays at Northmoor, where a prettily-furnished room was set apart for her. She described it with so much zest that Rose was seized with a sort of alarm. 'You will live there like all the lords and ladies that papa talks of, and grow worldly and fashionable.'

'Oh no, no,' cried Constance, and there was a girlish kissing match, but Rose seemed to think worldliness inevitable.

'The Earl my papa lived with used to bet and gamble, and come home dreadfully late at night, and so did my lady and her daughters, and their poor maid had to sit up for them till four o'clock in the morning. Then their bills! They never told his lordship, but they sold their diamonds and wore paste. His lordship did not know, but their maid did, and told papa.'

Constance opened her eyes and declared that Uncle Frank

Charlotte M. Yonge

and Aunt Mary never could do such things. Moreover, she averred that Lady Adela was always going about among the cottages, and that Miss Morton had not a bit of pride, and was going to live in London to teach the dust-pickers and match-box makers. 'Indeed, I don't think they are half as worldly in themselves,' she said, 'as Ida is growing with thinking about them.'

'Ah, don't you remember the sermon that said worldliness didn't depend on what one has, but what one is?'

'Talking of nothing better than sermons!' said Herbert, coming on them. 'Have you caught it of the governor, Con? I believe he thinks of nothing but sermons.'

And Constance exclaimed, 'I am sure he doesn't preach!'

'Oh no, nothing comes out of his mouth that he can help; trust him for that.'

'Then how do you know?'

'By the stodgy look of him. He would be the awfullest of prosers if he had the gift of the gab.'

'You are an ungrateful boy,' said Rose. 'I am sure he must be very kind to you.'

'Can't help it,' said Herbert. 'The old fellow would be well enough if he had any go in him.'

'I am sure he took you out hunting,' exclaimed Constance indignantly, 'the day they took us to the meet. And he leapt all the ditches when you—'

He broke in, 'Well, what was I to do when I've never had the chance to learn to sit a horse? You'll see next winter.'

'Did you hurt yourself?' asked Rose, rather mischievously.

To which Herbert turned a deaf ear and began to expatiate upon the game of Northmoor, till other sounds led him away to fall upon the other *tete-a-tete* between Ida and Sibyl Grover. In Ida's mind the honours of Northmoor were dearly purchased by the dulness and strictness of the life there.

'My uncle was as cross as two sticks if ever Herbert or I were too late for prayers, and he said it was nonsense of Herbert to say that kneeling at church spoilt his trousers— kneeling just like a school child! It made me so faint!'

'And it looks so!'

'I tried, because Lady Adela and Miss Bertha and all do,' said Ida, 'and they looked at me! But it made me faint, as I knew it would,' and she put her head on one side.

'Poor dear! So they were so very religious! Did that spoil it all?'

'Well, we had pretty things off the Christmas-tree, and we lived quite as ladies, and drove out in the carriage.'

'No parties nor dances? Or were they too religious?'

'Ma says it is their meanness; but my aunt, Lady Northmoor, did say perhaps it would be livelier another year, and then we should have had some dancing and deportment lessons. I up and told her I could dance fast enough now, but she said it would not be becoming or right to Lady Adela's and Miss Morton's feelings.'

'Do they live there?'

Charlotte M. Yonge

'Not in the house. Lady Adela has a cottage of her own, and Miss Morton stops with her. Lady Adela is as high and standoffish as the monument,' said Ida, pausing for a comparison.

'High and haughty,' said Sibyl, impressed. 'And the other lady?'

'Oh, she is much more good-natured. We call her Bertha; at least, she told us that we might call her anything but that horrid Cousin Bertha, as she said. But she's old, thirty-six years old, and not a bit pretty, and she says such odd things, one doesn't know what to do. She thought I made myself useful and could wash and iron,' said Ida, as if this were the greatest possible insult, in which Sibyl acquiesced.

'And she thought I should know the factory girls, just the hands,' added Ida, greatly disgusted. 'As if I should! But ma says low tastes are in the family, for she is going to live in London, and go and sit with the shop-girls in the evening. Still I like her better than Lady Adela, who keeps herself to herself. Mamma says it is pride and spite that her plain little sickly girl hasn't come to be my Lady.'

'What, doesn't she speak to them?' said Sibyl, quite excited.

'Oh yes, she calls, and shakes hands, and all that, but one never seems to get on with her. And Emily Trotman, she's the doctor's daughter, such a darling, told me *such* a history—so interesting!'

'Tell me, Ida, there's a dear.'

'She says they were all frightfully dissipated' (Ida said it quite with a relish)—'the old Lord and Mr. Morton, Lady

Adela's husband, you know, and Miss Bertha—always racing and hunting and gambling and in debt. Then there came a Captain Alder, who was ever so much in love with Miss Bertha, but most awfully in debt to her brother, and very passionate besides. So he took him out in his dog-cart with a fiery horse that was sure to run away.'

'Who did?'

'Captain Alder took Mr. Morton, though they begged and prayed him not, and the horse ran away and Mr. Morton was thrown out and killed.'

'Oh!' with extreme zest. 'On purpose?'

'Miss Bertha was sure it was, so that she might have all the fortune, and so she told him, and flung the betrothal ring in his face, and he went right off, and never has been heard of since.'

'Well, that *is* interesting. Do you think he shot himself?'

'No, he was too mean. Most likely he married a hideous millionaire: but the Mortons were always dreadful, and did all sorts of wicked things.'

'I declare it's as good as any tale—like the sweet one in the *Young Ladies' Friend* now—"The Pride of Pedro." Have you seen it?'

'No, indeed, uncle and aunt only have great old stupid books! They wanted me to read those horrid tiresome things of Scott's, and Dickens's too, who is as old as the hills! Why, they could not think of anything better to do on their wedding tour but to go to all the places in the Waverley novels.'

Charlotte M. Yonge

'Why, they are as bad as history! Jim brought one home once, and pa wanted me to read it, but I could not get on with it—all about a stupid king of France. I'm sure if I married a lord I'd make him do something nicer.'

'I mean ma to do something more jolly,' said Ida, 'when we get more money, and I am come out. I mean to go to balls and tennis parties, and I shall be sure to marry a lord at some of them.'

'And you will take me,' cried Sibyl.

'Only you must be very genteel,' said Ida. 'Try to learn style, *do*, dear. It must be learnt young, you know! Why, there's Aunt Mary, when she has got ever so beautiful a satin dress on, she does not look half so stylish as Lady Adela walking up the road in an old felt hat and a shepherd's-plaid waterproof! But they all do dress so as I should be ashamed. Only think what a scrape that got Herbert into. He was coming back one Saturday from his tutor's, and he saw walking up to the house an awfully seedy figure of fun, in an old old ulster, and such a hat as you never saw, with a knapsack on her back, and a portfolio under her arm. So of course he thought it was a tramp with something to sell, and he holloaed out, "You'd better come out of this! We want none of your sort." She just turned round and laughed, which put him in such a rage, that though she began to speak he didn't wait, but told her to have done with her sauce, or he would call the keepers. He thinks she said, "You'd better," and I believe he did move his stick a little.'

'Ida, have done with that!' cried Herbert's voice close to her. 'Hold your tongue, or I'll—' and his hand was near her hair.

'Oh, don't, don't, Herbert. Let me hear,' cried Sibyl.

'That's the way girls go on,' said Herbert fiercely, 'with their nonsense and stuff.'

'But who—?'

'If you go on, Ida—' he was clutching her braid.

Sibyl sprang to the defence, and there was a general struggle and romp interspersed with screams, which was summarily stopped by Mr. Rollstone explaining severely, 'If you think that is the deportment of the aristocracy, Miss Ida, you are much mistaken.'

'Bother the aristocracy!' broke out Herbert.

Calm was restored by a summons to a round game, but Sibyl's curiosity was of course insatiable, and as she sat next to Herbert, she employed various blandishments and sympathetic whispers, and after a great deal of fuss, and 'What will you give me if I tell?' to extract the end of the story, 'Did he call the keeper?'

'Oh yes, the old beast! His name's Best, but it ought to be Beast! He guffawed ever so much worse than she did!'

'Well, but who was it?'

And after he had tried to make her guess, and teased his fill, he owned, 'Mrs. Bury—a sort of cousin, staying with Lady Adela. She isn't half a bad old party, but she makes a guy of herself, and goes about sketching and painting like a blessed old drawing-master.'

'A lady? and not a young lady.'

'Not as old as—as Methuselah, or old Rolypoly there, but I believe she's a grandmother. If she'd been a boy, we should have been cut out of it. Oh yes, she's a lady—a born Morton; and when it was over she was very jolly about it—no harm done—bears no malice, only Ida makes such an absurd work about every little trifle.'

CHAPTER XV

THE PIED ROOK

Constance Morton was leaning on the rail that divided the gardens at Northmoor from the park, which was still rough and heathery. Of all the Morton family, perhaps she was the one who had the most profited by the three years that had passed since her uncle's accession to the title. She had been at a good boarding-house, attending the High School in Colbeam, and spending Saturday and Sunday at Northmoor. It had been a happy life, she liked her studies, made friends with her companions, and enjoyed to the very utmost all that Northmoor gave her, in country beauty and liberty, in the kindness of her uncle and aunt, and in the religious training that they were able to give her, satisfying longings of her soul, so that she loved them with all her heart, and felt Northmoor her true home. The holiday time at Westhaven was always a trial. Mrs. Morton had tried Brighton and London, but neither place agreed with Ida: and she found herself a much greater personage in her own world than elsewhere, and besides could not always find tenants for her house. So there she lived at her ease, called by many of her neighbours the Honourable Mrs. Morton, and finding listeners to her alternate accounts of the grandeur of Northmoor, and murmurs at the meanness of its master in only allowing her 300 pounds a year, besides educating her children,

Charlotte M. Yonge

and clothing two of them.

Ida considered herself to be quite sufficiently educated, and so she was for the society in which she was, or thought herself, a star, chiefly consisting of the families of the shipowners, coalowners, and the like. She was pretty, with a hectic prettiness of bright eyes and cheeks, and had a following of the young men of the place; and though she always tried to enforce that to receive attentions from a smart young mate, a clerk in an office, a doctor's assistant, or the like, was a great condescension on her part, she enjoyed them all the more. Learning new songs for their benefit, together with extensive novel reading, were her chief employments, and it was the greater pity because her health was not strong. She dreamt much in a languid way, and had imagination enough to work these tales into her visions of life. Her temper suffered, and Constance found the atmosphere less and less congenial as she grew older and more accustomed to a different life.

She was a gentle, ladylike girl, with her brown hair still on her shoulders, as on that summer Saturday she stood looking along the path, but with her ears listening for sounds from the house, and an anxious expression on her young face. Presently she started at the sound of a gun, which caused a mighty cawing among the rooks in the trees on the slopes, and a circling of the black creatures in the sky. A whistling then was heard, and her brother Herbert came in sight in a few minutes more, a fine tall youth of sixteen, with quite the air and carriage of a gentleman. He had a gun on his shoulder, and carried by the claws the body of a rook with white wings.

'Oh, Herbert,' cried Constance in dismay, 'did you shoot that by mistake?'

'No; Stanhope would not believe there was such a crittur,

and betted half a sov that it was a cram.'

'But how could you? Our uncle and aunt thought so much of that poor dear Whitewing, and Best was told to take care of it. They will be so vexed.'

'Nonsense! He'll come to more honour stuffed than ever he would flying and howling up there. When I've shown him to Stanhope, I shall make that old fellow at Colbeam come down handsomely for him. What a row those birds kick up! I'll send my other barrel among them.'

'Oh no, don't, Bertie. Uncle Frank has one of his dreadful headaches to-day.'

'Seems to me he is made of headaches.'

'Yes, Aunt Mary is very anxious. Oh, I would have done anything that you had not vexed them now and killed this poor dear pretty thing!' said Constance, stroking down the glossy feathers of the still warm victim, and laying them against her cheek, almost tearfully.

'Well, you are not going to tell them. Perhaps they won't miss it. I would not have done it if Stanhope had not been such a beast,' said Herbert.

'I shall not tell them, of course,' said Constance; 'but, if I were you, I should not be happy till they knew.'

'Oh, that's only girl's way! I can't have the old Stick upset now, for I'm in horrid want of tin.'

'Oh, Bertie, was it true then?'

'What, you don't mean that they have heard?'

'That you were out at those Colbeam races!'

'To be sure I was, with Stanhope and Hailes and a lot more. We all went except the little kids and Sisson, who is in regular training for as great a muff as the governor there. Who told him?'

'Mr. Hailes, who is very much concerned about his grandson.'

'Old sneak; I wonder how he ferreted it out. Is there no end of a jaw coming, Con?'

'I don't know. Uncle Frank seemed quite knocked down and wretched over it. He said something about feeling hopeless, and the old blood coming out to be your ruin.'

'Of course it's the old blood! How did he miss it, and turn into the intolerable old dry fogey that he is, without a notion of anything fit for a gentleman?'

'Now, Herbert—'

'Oh yes. You should just hear what the other fellows say about him. Their mothers and their sisters say there is not so stupid a place in the county, he hasn't a word to say for himself, and they would just as soon go to Portland at once as to a party here.'

'Then it is a great shame! I am sure Aunt Mary works hard to make it pleasant for them!'

'Oh yes, good soul, she does, she can't help it; but when people have stuck in the mud all their lives, they can't know any better, and it is abominably hard on a fellow who does, to be under a man who has been an office cad all his life, and doesn't know what is expected of a gentleman! Screwing us all up like beggars—'

'Herbert, for shame! for shame! As if he was obliged to do anything at all for us!'

'Oh, isn't he? A pretty row my mother would kick up about his ears if he did not, when I must come after him at this place, too!'

'I think you are very ungrateful,' said Constance, with tears, 'when they are so good to us.'

'Oh, they are as kind as they know how, but they don't know. That's the thing, or old Frank would be ashamed to give me such a dirty little allowance. He has only himself to thank if I have to come upon him for more. Found out about the Blackbird colt, has he? What a bore! And tin I must have out of him by hook or by crook if he cuts up ever so rough. I must send off this bird first by the post to confute Stanhope and make him eat dirt, and then see what's to be done.'

'Indeed, Bertie, I don't think you will see him to-night. His head is dreadful, and Aunt Mary has sent for Mr. Trotman.'

'Whew! You have not got anything worth having, I suppose, Conny?'

'Only fifteen shillings. I meant it for— But you shall have it, dear Bertie, if it will only save worrying them.'

'Fifteen bob! Fifteen farthings you might as well offer. No, no, you soft little monkey, I must see what is to be made of him or her ladyship, one or the other, to-day or to-morrow. If they know I have been at the place it is half the battle. Consequence was! Provided they don't smell

Charlotte M. Yonge

out this unlucky piebald! I wish Stanhope hadn't been such a beast!'

At that moment, too late to avoid her, Lady Northmoor, pale and anxious, came up the path and was upon them. 'Your uncle is asleep,' she began, but then, starting, 'Oh, Conny. Poor Whitewing. Did you find him?'

Constance hung her head and did not speak. Then her aunt saw how it was.

'Herbert! you must have shot him by mistake; your uncle will be so grieved.'

Herbert was not base enough to let this pass. He muttered, 'A fellow would not take my word for it, so I had to show him.'

She looked at him very sadly. 'Oh, Herbert, I did not think you would have made that a reason for vexing your uncle!'

The boy was more than half sorry under those gentle eyes. He muttered something about 'didn't think he would care.'

She shook her head, instead of saying that she knew this was not the truth; and unable to bear the sting, he flung away from her, carrying the rook with him, and kicking the pebbles, trying to be angry instead of sorry. And just then came a summons to Lady Northmoor to see the doctor.

Yet Herbert Morton was a better boy than he seemed at that moment; his errors were chiefly caused by understanding *noblesse oblige* in a different way from his uncle. Moreover, it would have been better for him if his tutor had lived beyond the neighbourhood of Northmoor, where he heard, losing nothing in the telling, the remarks of the other pupils' mothers upon his uncle and aunt; more especially as it was not generally the highest order of boy that was to be found there. If he had heard what the fathers said, he would have learnt that, though shy and devoid of small talk, and of the art of putting guests together, Lord Northmoor was trusted and esteemed. He might perhaps be too easily talked down; he could not argue, and often gave way to the noisy Squire; but he was certain in due time to see the rights of a question, and he attended thoroughly to the numerous tasks of an active and useful county man, taking all the drudgery that others shirked. While, if by severe stress he were driven to public speaking, he could acquit himself far better than any one had expected. The Bishop and the Chairman of the Quarter Sessions alike set him down on their committees, not only for his rank, but for his industry and steadiness of work. Nor had any one breathed any imputation upon the possession of what used to be known as gentility, before that good word was degraded, to mean something more like what Mrs. Morton aspired to. Lord and Lady Northmoor might not be lively, nor a great accession to society, but the anticipations of either amusement or annoyance from vulgarity or arrogance were entirely disappointed. No one could call them underbred, or anything but an ingrain gentleman and lady, while there were a few who could uphold Lady Northmoor as thoroughly kind, sweet, sensible, and helpful to her utmost in all that was good.

All this, however, was achieved not only unconsciously but with severe labour by a man whose powers could only act slowly, and who was not to the manner born. Conscientiousness is a costly thing, and Strafford's watchword is not to be adopted for nothing. The balance of duties, the perplexities of managing an impoverished and involved estate, the disappointment of being unable to

Charlotte M. Yonge

carry out the responsibilities of a landlord towards neglected cottagers, the incapacity of doing what would have been desirable for the Church, and the worry and harass that his sister-in-law did not spare, all told as his office work had never done, and in spite of quiet, happy hours with his Mary, and her devoted and efficient aid whenever it was possible, a course of disabling neuralgic headaches had set in, and a general derangement of health, which had become alarming, and called for immediate remedy.

CHAPTER XVI

WHAT IS REST?

'Rest, there is nothing for it but immediate rest and warm baths,' said Lady Northmoor to Constance, who was waiting anxiously for the doctor's verdict some hours later. 'It is only being overdone—no, my dear, there is nothing really to fear, if we can only keep business and letters out of his way for a few weeks, my dear child.'

For Constance, who had been dreadfully frightened by the sight of the physician's carriage, which seemed to her inexperienced eyes the omen of something terrible, fairly burst into tears of relief.

'Oh, I am so glad!' she said, as caresses passed—which might have been those of mother and daughter for heartfelt sympathy and affection.

'You will miss your Saturdays and Sundays, my dear,' continued the aunt, 'for we shall have to go abroad, so as to be quite out of the way of everything.'

'Never mind that, dear aunt, if only Uncle Frank is better. Will it be long?'

'I cannot tell. He says six weeks, Dr. Smith says three

Charlotte M. Yonge

months. It is to be bracing air—Switzerland, most likely.'

'Oh, how delightful! How you will enjoy it!'

'It has always been a dream, and it is strange now to feel so downhearted about it,' said her aunt, smiling.

'Uncle Frank is sure to be better there,' said Constance. 'Only think of the snowy mountains—

> Mont Blanc is the monarch of mountains;
> They crown'd him long ago
> On a throne of rocks, in a robe of clouds,
> With a diadem of snow.'

And the girl's eyes brightened with an enthusiasm that the elder woman felt for a moment, nor did either of them feel the verse hackneyed.

'Ah, I wish we could take you, my dear,' said Lady Northmoor; then, 'Do you know where Herbert is?'

'No,' said Constance. 'Oh, aunt, I am so sorry! I don't think he would have done it if the other boys had not teased him.'

'Perhaps not; but, indeed, I am grieved, not only on the poor rook's account, but that he should have the heart to vex your uncle just now. However, perhaps he did not understand how ill he has been all this week. And I am afraid that young Stanhope is not a good companion for him.'

'I do not think he is,' said Constance; 'it seems to me that Stanhope leads him into that betting, and makes him think it does not signify whether he passes or not, and so he does not take pains.'

Herbert was not to be found either then or at dinner-time. It turned out that he had taken from the stables the horse he was allowed to ride, and had gone over to display his victim to Stanhope, and then on to the bird-stuffer; had got a meal, no one wished to know how, only returning in time to stump upstairs to bed.

He thus avoided an interview with his uncle over the rook, unaware that his aunt had left him the grace of confession, being in hopes that, unless he did speak of his own accord, the vexatious knowledge might be spared to one who did not need an additional annoyance just then.

Lord Northmoor was not, however, to be spared. He was much better the next day, Sunday, a good deal exhilarated by the doctor's opinion; and, though concerned at having to break off his work, ready to enjoy what he was told was absolutely essential.

The head-keeper had no notion of sparing him. Mr. Best regarded him with a kind of patronising toleration as an unfortunate gentleman who had the ill-hap never to have acquired a taste for sport, and was unable to do justice to his preserves; but towards 'Mr. Morton' there was a very active dislike. The awkward introduction might have rankled even had Herbert been wise enough to follow Miss Morton's advice; but his nature was overbearing, and his self-opinion was fostered by his mother and Ida, while he was edged on by his fellow-pupils to consider Best a mere old woman, who could only be tolerated by the ignorance of 'a regular Stick.'

With the under-keeper Herbert fraternised enough to make him insubordinate; and the days when Lord Northmoor gave permission for shooting or for inviting his companions for a share in the sport, were days of mutual offence, when the balance of provoking sneer and

Charlotte M. Yonge

angry insult would be difficult to cast, though the keeper was the most forbearing, since he never complained of personal ill-behaviour to himself, whereas Herbert's demonstrations to his uncle of 'that old fool' were the louder and more numerous because they never produced the slightest effect.

However, Best felt aggrieved in the matter of the rook, which had been put under his special protection, and being, moreover, something of a naturalist, he had cherished the hope of a special Northmoor breed of pied rooks.

So while, on the way from church, Lady Adela was detaining Lady Northmoor with inquiries as to Dr. Smith, Best waylaid his master with, 'Your lordship gave me orders about that there rook with white wings, as was not to be mislested.'

'Has anything happened to it?' said Frank wearily.

'Well, my lord, I sees Mr. Morton going up to the rookery with his gun, and I says to him that it weren't time for shooting of the branchers, and the white rook weren't to be touched by nobody, and he swears at me for a meddling old leggings, and uses other language as I'll not repeat to your lordship, and by and by I hears his gun, and I sees him a-picking up of the rook that her ladyship set such store by, so it is due to myself, my lord, to let you know as I were not to blame.'

'Certainly not, Best,' was the reply. 'I am exceedingly displeased that my nephew has behaved so ill to you, and I shall let him know it.'

'His lordship will give it to him hot and strong, the young upstart,' muttered Best to himself with great satisfaction, as he watched the languid pace quicken to overtake the boy, who had gone on with his sister.

Perhaps the irritability of illness had some effect upon the ordinary gentleness of Lord Northmoor's temper, and besides, he was exceedingly annoyed at such ungrateful slaughter of what was known to be a favourite of his wife; so when he came upon Herbert, sauntering down to the stables, he accosted him sharply with, 'What is this I hear, Herbert? I could not have believed that you would have deliberately killed the creature that you knew to be a special delight to your aunt.'

Herbert had reached the state of mind when a third, if not a fourth, reproach on the same subject on which his conscience was already uneasy, was simply exasperating, and without the poor excuse he had offered his aunt and sister, he burst out that it was very hard that such a beastly row should be made about a fellow knocking down mere trumpery vermin.

'Speak properly, Herbert, or hold your tongue,' said his uncle. 'I am extremely displeased at finding that you do not know how to conduct yourself to my servants, and have presumed to act in this lawless, heartless manner, in defiance of what you knew to be your aunt's wishes and my orders, and that you replied to Best's remonstrance with insolence.'

'That's a good one! Insolent to an old fool of a keeper,' muttered Herbert sullenly.

'Insolence is shameful towards any man,' returned his uncle. 'And from a foolish headstrong boy to a faithful old servant it is particularly unbecoming. However, bad as this is, it is not all that I have to speak of.'

Charlotte M. Yonge

Then Herbert recollected with dismay how much his misdemeanour would tell against his pardon for the more important act of disobedience, and he took refuge in a sullen endeavour at indifference, while his uncle, thoroughly roused, spoke of the sins of disobedience and the dangers of betting. Perhaps the only part of the lecture that he really heard was, 'Remember, it was these habits in those who came before us that have been so great a hindrance in life to both you and me, and made you, my poor boy, so utterly mistaken as to what becomes your position. How much have you thrown away?'

Herbert looked up and muttered the amount—twelve pounds and some shillings.

'Very well, I will not have it owed. I shall pay it, deducting two pounds from your allowance each term till it is made up. Give me the address or addresses.'

At this Herbert writhed and remonstrated, but his uncle was inexorable.

'The fellows will be at me,' he said, as he gave Stanhope's name.

'You will see no more of Stanhope after this week. I have arranged to send you to a tutor in Hertfordshire, who I hope will make you work, and where, I trust, you will find companions who will give you a better idea of what becomes a gentleman.'

In point of fact, this had been arranged for some time past, though by the desire of Herbert's present tutor it had not been made known to the young people, so that, coming thus, there was a sound of punishment in it to Herbert.

The interview ended there. The annoyance, enhanced in his mind by having come on a Sunday, brought on another attack of headache; but late in the evening he sent for Herbert, who always had to go very early on the Monday. It was to ask him whether he would not prefer the payment being made to Stanhope and the other pupil after he had left them. Herbert's scowl passed off. It was a great relief. He said they were prepared to wait till he had his allowance, and the act of consideration softened him, as did also the manifest look of suffering and illness, as his uncle lay on the couch, hardly able to speak, and yet exerting himself thus to spare the lad.

'Thank you, sir,' actually Herbert said, and then, with a gulp, 'I am sorry about that bird—I wish I'd never told them, but it was Stanhope who drove me to it, not believing.'

'I thought it was not your better mind,' said his uncle, holding out his hand. 'I should like you to make me a promise, Herbert, not to make a bet while I am away. I should go with an easier mind.'

'I will, uncle,' said Herbert, heartily reflecting, perhaps, it must be owned, on the fewer opportunities in that line at Westhaven, except at the regatta, but really resolving, as the only salve to his conscience. And there was that in his face and the clasp of his hand that gave his uncle a sense of comfort and hope.

Charlotte M. Yonge

CHAPTER XVII

ON THE SURFACE

Lady Adela, though small and pale, was one of the healthy women who seem unable to believe in any ailments short of a raging fever; and when she heard of neuralgia, decided that it was all a matter of imagination, and a sort of excuse for breaking off the numerous occupations in which she felt his value, but only as she would have acknowledged that of a good schoolmaster. Their friendly intercourse had never ripened into intimacy, and was still punctiliously courteous; each tacitly dreaded the influence of the other on the Vicar-in-Church matters, and every visit of the Westhaven family confirmed Lady Adela's belief that it was undesirable to go below the surface.

Bertha, who came down for a day or two to assist at the breaking-up demonstration of the High School at Colbeam, was as ever much more cordial. The chief drawbacks with her were that cynical tone, which made it always doubtful whether she were making game of her hearers, and the philanthropy, not greatly tinged with religion, so as to confuse old-fashioned minds. She used to bring down strange accounts of her startling adventures in the slums, and relate them in a rattling style, interluded with slang, being evidently delighted to shock and puzzle her hearers; but still she was always good-natured in deed if not in word, and Lord Northmoor was very grateful for her offer of hospitality to Herbert, who was coming to London for his preliminary examination.

She had come up to call, determined to be of use to them, and she had experience enough of travelling to be very helpful. Finding that they shuddered at the notion of fashionable German '*baden*,' she exclaimed—

'I'll hit you off! There's that place in the Austrian Tyrol that Lettice Bury frequents—a regular primitive place with a name—Oh, what is it, Addie, like rats and mice?'

'Ratzes,' said Adela.

'Yes. The tourists have not molested it yet, and only natives bathe there, so she goes every year to renovate herself and sketch, and comes back furbished up like an old snake, with lots of drawings of impossible peaks, like Titian's backgrounds. We'll write and tell her to make ready for the head of her house!'

'Oh, but—' began Frank, looking to his wife.

'Would it not be intruding?' said Mary.

'She will be enchanted! She always likes to have anything to do for anybody, and she says the scenery is just a marvel. You care for that! You are so deliciously fresh, beauties aren't a bore to you.'

'We are glad of the excuse,' said Frank gravely.

'You look ill enough to be an excuse for anything, and Mary too! How about a maid? Is Harte going?'

'No,' said Mary; 'she says that foreign food made her so ill once before that she cannot attempt going again. I meant to do without.'

'That would never do!' cried Bertha. 'You have quite enough on your hands with Northmoor, and the luggage and the languages.'

'Is not an English maid apt to be another trouble?' said Mary. 'I do not suppose my French is good, but I have had to talk it constantly; and I know some German, if that will serve in the Tyrol.'

'I'll reconcile it to your consciences,' said Bertha triumphantly. 'It will be a real charity. There's a bonny little Swiss girl whom some reckless people brought home and then turned adrift. It will be a real kindness to help her home, and you shall pick her up when you come up to me on your way, and see my child! Oh, didn't I tell you? We had a housemaid once who was demented enough to marry a scamp of a stoker on one of the Thames steamers. He deserted her, and I found her living, or rather dying, in an awful place at Rotherhithe, surrounded by tipsy women, raging in opposite corners. I got her into a decent room, but too late to save her life—and a good thing too; so I solaced her last moments with a promise to look after her child, such a jolly little mortal, in spite of her name— Boadicea Ethelind Davidina Jones. She is two years old, and quite delicious—the darling of all the house!'

'I hope you will have no trouble with the father,' said Frank.

'I trust he has gone to his own locker, or, if not, he is only too glad to be rid of her. I can tackle him,' said Bertha confidently. 'The child is really a little duck!'

She spoke as if the little one filled an empty space in her heart; and, even though there might be trouble in store, it was impossible not to be glad of her present gladness, and her invitation was willingly accepted. Moreover, her recommendations were generally trustworthy, and Mary only hesitated because, she said—

'I thought, if I could do without a maid, we might take Constance. She is doing so very well, and likely to pass so well in her examinations, that it would be very nice to give her this pleasure.'

'Good little girl! So it would. I should like nothing better; but I am afraid that if you took her without a maid, Emma would misunderstand it, and say you wanted to save the expense.'

'Would it make much difference?'

'Not more than we could bear now that we are in for it, but I fear it would excite jealousies.'

'Is that worse than leaving the poor child to Westhaven society all the holidays?'

'Perhaps not; and Conny is old enough now to be more injured by it than when she was younger.'

'You know I have always hoped to make her like a child of our own when her school education is finished.'

Frank smiled, for he was likewise very fond of little Constance.

There was a public distribution of prizes, at which all the grandees of the neighbourhood were expected to assist, and it was some consolation to the Northmoors, for the dowager duchess being absent, that the pleasure of taking the prize from her uncle would be all the greater—if—

The whole party went—Lady Adela, Miss Morton, and all—and were installed in chairs of state on the platform, with the bright array of books before them—the head-mistress telling Lady Northmoor beforehand that her niece would have her full share of honours. No one could be a better or more diligent girl.

It quite nerved Lord Northmoor when he looked forth upon the sea of waving tresses of all shades of brown, while his wife watched in nervousness, both as to how he would acquit himself and how the exertion would affect him; and Bertha, as usual, was anxious for the credit of the name.

He did what was needed. Nobody wanted anything but the sensible commonplace, kindly spoken, about the advantages of good opportunities, the conscientiousness of doing one's best. And after all, the inferiority of mere attainments in themselves to the discipline and dutifulness of responding to training,—it was slowly but not stammeringly spoken, and Bertha did not feel critical or ashamed, but squeezed Mary's hand, and said, 'Just the right thing.'

One by one the girls were summoned for their prizes, the little ones first. Lord Northmoor had not the gift of inventing a pretty speech for each, he could do no more than smile as he presented the book, and read its name; but the smile was a very decided one when, in the class next to the highest, three out of the seven prizes were awarded to Constance Elizabeth Morton, and it might be a question which had the redder cheeks, the uncle or the niece, as he handed them to her. It was one of the few happinesses that he had derived from his brother's family!

After such achievements on Constance's part, it was impossible to withhold—as they drove back to Northmoor—the proposal to take her with them, and the effect was magical. Constance opened her eyes, bounded up, as if she were going to fly out of the carriage, and then launched herself, first on her uncle, then on her aunt, for an ecstatic kiss.

'Take care, take care, we shall have the servants thinking you a little lunatic!'

'I am almost! Oh, I am so glad! To be with you and Aunt Mary all the holidays! That would be enough! But to go and see all the places,' she added, somehow perceiving that the desire to escape from home was, at least ought not to be approved of, and yet there was some exultation, when she hazarded a supposition that there was no time to go home.

Charlotte M. Yonge

CHAPTER XVIII

DESDICHADO

Home—that is to say, Westhaven—was in some commotion when Herbert came back and grimly growled out his intelligence as to his own personal affairs. Mrs. Morton had been already apprized, in one of Lord Northmoor's well-considered letters, of his intentions of removing his nephew to a tutor more calculated to prepare for the army, and she had accepted this as promotion such as was his due. However, when the pride of her heart, the tall gentlemanly son, made his appearance in a savage mood, her feelings were all on the other side, and those of Ida exaggerated hers.

'So I'm to go to some disgusting hole where they grind the fellows no end,' was Herbert's account of the matter.

'But surely with your connection there's no need for grinding?' said his mother.

Herbert laughed, 'Much you know about it! Nobody cares a rap for connections nowadays, even if old Frank were a connection to do a man any good.'

'But you'll not go and study hard and hurt yourself, my dear,' said his mother, though Herbert's looks by no means suggested any such danger, while Ida added, 'It is not as if he had nothing else to look to, you know. He can't keep you out of the peerage.'

'Can't he then? Why, he can and will too, for thirty or forty years more at least.'

'I thought his health was failing,' said Ida, putting into words a hope her mother had a little too much sense of propriety to utter.

'Bosh, it's only neuralgia, just because he is such a stick he can't take things easy, and lark about and do every one's work—he hasn't the least notion what a gentleman ought to do.'

'It is bred in the bone,' said his mother; 'he always was a shabby poor creature! I always said he would not know how to spend his money.'

'He is a regular screw!' responded Herbert. 'What do you think now! He was in no end of a rage with me just because I went with some of the other fellows to the Colbeam races; and one can't help a bet or two, you know. So I lost twelve pound or so, and what must he do but stop it out of my allowance two pound at a time!'

There was a regular outcry at this, and Mrs. Morton declared her poor dear boy should not suffer, but she would make it up to him, and Herbert added that 'it had been unlucky, half of it was that they were riled with him, first because he had shot a ridiculous rook with white wings that my lady made no end of a fuss about.'

'Ah, then it is her spite,' said Ida. 'She's a sly cat, with all her meek ways.'

Charlotte M. Yonge

Herbert was not displeased with this evening's sympathy, as he lay outspread on the sofa, with the admiring and pitying eyes of his mother and sister upon him; but he soon began to feel—when he had had his grumble out, and could take his swing at home—that there could be too much of it.

It was all very well to ease his own mind by complaining, but when he heard of Ida announcing that he had been shamefully treated, all out of spite for killing a white rook, his sense of justice made him declare that the notion was nothing but girl's folly, such as no person with a grain of sense could believe.

The more his mother and her friends persisted in treating him as an ill-used individual, the victim of his uncle's avarice and his aunt's spite, the more his better nature revolted and acknowledged inwardly and sometimes outwardly the kindness and justice he had met with. It was really provoking that any attempt to defend them, or explain the facts, were only treated as proofs of his own generous feeling. Ida's partisanship really did him more good than half a dozen lectures would have done, and he steadily adhered to his promise not to bet, though on the regatta day Ida and her friend Sibyl derided him for not choosing to risk even a pair of gloves; and while one pitied him, the other declared that he was growing a skinflint like his uncle.

He talked and laughed noisily enough to Ida's friends, but he had seen enough at Northmoor to feel the difference, and he told his sister that there was not a lady amongst the whole kit of them, except Rose Rollstone, who was coming down for her holiday.

'Rose!' cried Ida, tossing her head. 'A servant's daughter and a hand at a shop! What will you say next, I wonder?'

'Lady is as lady acts,' said Herbert, making a new proverb, whereat his mother and sister in chorus rebuked him, and demanded to know whether Ida were not a perfect lady.

At which he laughed with a sound of scoffing, and being tired of the discussion sauntered out of the house to that inexhaustible occupation of watching the boats come in, and smoking with old acquaintances, who were still congenial to him, and declared that he had not become stuck-up, though he was turned into an awful swell! Perhaps they were less bad for him than Stanhope, for they inspired no spirit of imitation.

When he came back a later post had arrived, bringing the news of Constance's successes and of the invitation to her to share the expedition of her uncle and aunt. There was no question about letting her go, but the feeling was scarcely of congratulation.

'Well, little Conny knows how to play her cards!'

'Stuff—child wouldn't know what it meant,' said Herbert glumly.

'Well,' said his sister, 'she always was the favourite, and I call it a shame.'

'What, because you've been such a good girl, and got such honours and prizes?' demanded Herbert.

'Nonsense, Herbert,' said his mother. 'Ida's education was finished, you know.'

'Oh, she wasn't a bit older than Conny is now.'

'And I don't hold with all that study, science and logic, and what d'ye call it; that's no use to any one,' continued

his mother. 'It's not as if your sisters had to be gover-
nesses. Give me a girl who can play a tune on the piano
and make herself agreeable. Your uncle may do as he
pleases, but he'll have Constance on his hands. The men
don't fancy a girl that is always after books and lectures.'

'Not of your sort, perhaps,' said Herbert, 'but I don't care
what I bet that Conny gets a better husband than Ida.'

'It stands to reason,' Ida said, almost crying, 'when uncle
takes her about to all these fine places and sets her up to
be the favourite—just the youngest. It's not fair.'

'As if she wasn't by a long chalk the better of the two,'
said Herbert.

'Now, Bertie,' interposed his mother, 'I'll not have you
teasing and running down your sister, though I do say it is
a shame and a slight to pick out the youngest, when poor
Ida is so delicate, and both of you two have ever so much
better a right to favours.'

'That's a good one!' muttered Herbert, while Ida
exclaimed—

'Of course, you know, aunt has always been nasty to me,
ever since I said ma said I was not strong enough to be
bothered with that horrid school; and as to poor Herbert,
they have spited him because he shot that—'

'Shut up, Ida,' shouted Herbert. 'I wouldn't go with them if
they went down on their knees to me! What should I do,
loafing about among a lot of disputing frog-eaters,
without a word of a Christian language, and old Frank
with his nose in a guide-book wanting me to look at
beastly pictures and rum old cathedrals. You would be a
fish out of water, too, Ida. Now Conny will take to it like

a house afire, and what's more, she deserves it!'

'Well, ma,' put in the provoked Ida, 'I wonder you let Conny go, when it would do me so much good, and it is so unfair.'

'My dear, you don't understand a mother's feelings. I feel the slight for you, but your uncle must be allowed to have his way. He is at all the expense, and to refuse for Conny would do you no good.'

'Except that she will be more set up than ever,' murmured Ida.

'Oh, come now! I wonder which looks more like the set-up one,' said Herbert, whose wider range had resulted in making him much alive to Ida's shortcomings, and who looked on at her noisy style of flirtation with the eye of a grave censor. Whatever he might be himself, he knew what a young lady ought to be.

He triumphed a little when, during the few days spent in London, Constance wrote of a delightful evening when, while her uncle and aunt and Miss Morton had gone to an entertainment for Bertha's match-box makers, she had been permitted to have Rose Rollstone to spend the time with her, the carriage, by their kind contrivance, fetching the girl both in going and coming.

The two young things had been thoroughly happy together. Rose had gone on improving herself; her companions in the art embroidery line were girls of a good class, with a few ladies among them, and their tone was good and refined. It was the fashion among them to attend the classes, Bible and secular, put in their way, and their employers conscientiously attended to their welfare, so that Rose was by no means an unfitting companion for

Charlotte M. Yonge

the High School maiden, and they most happily compared notes over their very different lives, when they were not engaged in playing with little Cea, as the unwieldy name of Miss Morton's *protegee* had been softened. She was a very pretty little creature, with big blue eyes and hair that could be called golden, and very full of life and drollery, so that she was a treat to both; and when the housemaid, whose charge she was, insisted on her coming to bed, they begged to superintend her evening toilet, and would have played antics with her in her crib half the night if they had not been inexorably chased away.

Then they sat down on low stools in the balcony, among the flowers, in convenient proximity for the caresses they had not yet outgrown, and had what they called 'a sweet talk.'

Constance had been much impressed with the beauty of the embroidery, and thought it must be delightful to do such things.

'Yes, for the forewoman,' said Rose, 'but there's plenty of dull work; the same over and over again, and one little stitch ever so small gone amiss throws all wrong. Miss Grey told us to recollect it was just like our lives!'

'That's nice!' said Constance. 'And it is for the Church and Almighty God's service?'

'Some of it,' said Rose, 'but there's a good deal only for dresses, and furniture, and screens.'

'Don't you feel like Sunday when you are doing altar-cloths and stools?' asked Constance reverently.

'I wish I did,' said Rose; 'but I don't do much of that kind yet, and one can't keep up the being serious over it always, you know. Indeed, Miss Grey does not wish us to be dull; she reads to us when there is time, and explains the symbols that have to be done; but part of the time it is an amusing book, and she says she does not mind cheerful talk, only she trusts us not to have gossip she would not like to hear.'

'I wonder,' said Constance, 'whether I should have come with you if all this had not happened? It must be very nice.'

'But your school is nice?'

'Oh yes. I do love study, and those Saturdays and Sundays at Northmoor, they are delicious! Uncle Frank reads with me about religion, you know.'

'Like our dear Bible class?'

'Yes; I never understood or felt anything before; he puts it so as it comes home,' said Constance, striving to express herself. 'Then I have a dear little class at the Sunday school.'

'I am to have one, by and by.'

'Mine are sweet little things, and I work for them on Saturdays, while Aunt Mary reads to me. I do like teaching—and, do you know, Rose, I think I shall be a High School teacher!'

'Oh, Conny, I thought you were all so rich and grand!'

'No, we are not,' said Constance lazily; 'we have nothing but what Uncle Frank gives us, and I can't bear the way mamma and Ida are always trying to get more out of him, when I know he can't always do what he likes, and nasty

Charlotte M. Yonge

people think him shabby. I am sure I ought to work for myself.'

'But if Herbert is a lord?'

'I hope he won't be for a long long time,' cried Constance. 'Besides, I am sure he would want all his money for himself! And as to being a teacher, Aunt Mary was, and Miss Arden, who is so wise and good, is one. If I was like them I think it would be doing real work for God and good—wouldn't it, Rose? Oh dear, oh dear, there's the carriage stopping for you!'

CHAPTER XIX

THE DOLOMITES

The summer was a very hot one, and the travellers, in spite of the charm of new scenes, and the wonders of everything to their unsophisticated eyes, found it trying. Constance indeed was in a state of constant felicity and admiration, undimmed except by the flagging of her two fellow-travellers in the heated and close German railway cars. Her uncle's head suffered much, and Lady Northmoor secretly thought her maid's refusal to accompany them showed her to be a prudent woman. However, the first breath of mountain air was a grand revival to Lord Northmoor, and at Innsbruck he was quite alive, and walked about in fervent delight, not desisting till he and Constance had made out every statue on Maximilian's monument. His wife was so much tired and worn-out, that she heartily rejoiced in having provided him with such a good little companion, though she was disappointed at being obliged to fail him, and get what rest she could at the hotel. But then, as she told him, if he learnt his way about it now, he would be able to show it all to her when they had both gained strength at Ratzes.

Bertha had obtained full instructions and a welcome for them from Mrs. Bury, a kindly person, who, having married off her children while still in full health and

Charlotte M. Yonge

vigour, remained at the service of any relation who needed her, and in the meantime resorted to out-of-the-way places abroad.

The railway took them to Botzen, which was hotter still, and thence on to Castelruth, whence there was no means of reaching Ratzes but by mule or *chaise a porteux*. Both alike were terrible to poor Mary; however, she made up her mind to the latter, and all the long way was to her a dream of terror and discomfort, and of trying to admire— what she knew she ought to admire—the wonderful pinnacle-like aiguilles of the Schern cleaving the air. For some time the way lay over the great plateau of the Scisser Alp—a sea of rich grass, full of cattle, where her husband and niece kept on trying to bring their mules alongside of her to make her participate in their ecstasy, and partake of their spoils—mountain pink, celestially blue gentian, brilliant poppy, or the like. Here the principal annoyance was that their mules were so obstinately bent on not approaching her that she was in constant alarm for them, while Constance was absolutely wild with delight, and even grave Frank was exhilarated by the mountain air into boyish spirits, such as impressed her, though she resolutely prevented herself from lowering them by manifesting want of sympathy, though the aiguilles that they admired seemed to her savage, and the descent, along a perilous winding road, cut out among precipices, horrified her—on, on, through endless pine forests, where the mules insisted on keeping her in solitude, and where nothing could be seen beyond the rough jolting path. At last, when a whole day had gone by, and even Constance sat her mule in silence and looked very tired, the fir trees grew more scanty. The aiguilles seemed in all their wildness to be nodding overhead; there was a small bowling-green, a sort of chalet in two divisions, united by a gallery: but Mary saw no more, for at that moment a loose slippery stone gave way, and the bearers stumbled and fell, dragging the chair so that it tipped over.

Constance, who had ridden on in front with her uncle, first heard a cry of dismay, and as both leaped off and rushed back, they saw her aunt had fallen, and partly entangled in the chair.

'Do not touch her!' cried Frank, forgetting that he could not be understood, and raising her in his arms, as the chair was withdrawn; but she did not speak or move, and there was a distressing throng and confusion of strange voices, seeming to hem them in as Constance looked round, unable to call up a single word of German, or to understand the exclamations. Then, as she always said, it was like an angel's voice that said, 'What is it?' as through the crowd came a tall lady in a white hat and black gown, and knelt down by the prostrate figure, saying, 'I hope she is only stunned; let us carry her in. It will be better to let her come round there.'

The lady gave vigorous aid, and, giving a few orders in German, helped Lord Northmoor to carry the inanimate form into the hotel, a low building of stone, with a high-pitched shingle roof. Constance followed in a bewilderment of fright, together with Lenchen, the Swiss maid, who, as well as could be made out, was declaring that a Swiss bearer never made a false step.

Lady Northmoor was carried into a bedroom, and Constance was shut out into a room that photographed itself on her memory, even in that moment—a room like a box, with a rough table, a few folding-chairs, an easel, water-coloured drawings hung about in all directions, a big travelling-case, a few books, a writing-case, Mrs. Bury's sitting-room in fact, which, as a regular sojourner, she had been able to secure and furnish after her need.

From the window, tall, narrow, latticed, with a heavy outside shutter, she saw a village green, a little church with a sharp steeple, and pointed-roof houses covered with shingle, groups of people, a few in picturesque Tyrolese costume, but others in the ordinary badly cut edition of cosmopolitan human nature. There was a priest in a big hat and white bordered bands discussing a newspaper with a man with a big red umbrella; a party drinking coffee under a pine tree, and beyond, those strange wild pointed aiguilles pointing up purple and red against the sky.

How delightful it would all have been if this quarter of an hour could be annihilated! She could find out nothing. Lenchen and the good-natured-looking landlady came in and out and fetched things, but they never stayed long enough to give her any real information, the landlady shouting for 'Hemzel,' etc., and Lenchen calling loudly in German for the boxes, which had been slung on mules. She heard nothing definite till her uncle came out, looking pale and anxious.

'She is better now,' he said, with a gasp of relief, throwing himself into a chair, and holding out his hand to Constance, who could hardly frame her question. 'Yes, quite sensible—came round quickly. The blow on the head seems to be of no consequence; but there may be a strain, or it may be only the being worn out and overdone. They are going to undress her and put her to bed now. Mrs. Bury is kindness itself. I did not look after her enough on that dreadful road.'

'Isn't there a doctor?' Constance ventured to ask.

'No such thing within I know not how many miles of these paths! But Mrs. Bury seems to think it not likely to be needed. Over-fatigue and the shake! What was I about?

This air and all the rest were like an intoxication, making me forget my poor Mary!'

He passed his hand over his face with a gesture as if he were very much shocked and grieved at himself, and Constance suggested that it was all the mule's fault, and Aunt Mary never complained.

'The more reason she should not have been neglected,' he said; and it was well for the excluded pair that just then the boxes were reported as arrived, and he was called on for the keys, so that wild searching for things demanded occupied them.

After a considerable time, Mrs. Bury came and told Lord Northmoor that he might go and look at his wife for a few moments, but that she must be kept perfectly quiet and not talked to or agitated. Constance was not to go in at all, but was conducted off by the good lady to her own tiny room, to get herself ready for the much-needed meal that was imminent.

They met again in the outer room. There was a great Speise saal, a separate building, where the bathers dived *en masse*; but since Mrs. Bury had made the place her haunt, she had led to the erection of an additional building where there was a little accommodation for the travellers of the better class who had of late discovered the glories of the Dolomites, though the baths were scarcely ever used except by artizans and farmers. She had this sitting-room chiefly made at her own expense with these few comforts, in the way of easy folding-chairs, a vase of exquisite flowers on the table, a few delicate carvings, an easel, and drawings of the mountain peaks and ravines suspended everywhere.

Besides this there were only the bedrooms, as small as

they well could be.

They were summoned down to the evening meal, and the maid Lenchen was left with Lady Northmoor. There was only one other guest, a spectacled and rather silent German, and Constance presently gathered that Mrs. Bury was trying to encourage and inspirit Lord Northmoor, but seemed to think there might be some delay before a move would be possible.

They sent her to bed, for she was really very tired after the long walk and ride, and she could not help sleeping soundly; but the first thing she heard in the morning was that the guide had been desired to send a doctor from Botzen, and the poor child spent a dreary morning of anxiety with nothing to do but to watch the odd figures disporting themselves or resting in the shade after their baths, to try a little sketching and a little letter-writing, but she was too restless and anxious to get on with either.

All the comfort she got was now and then Mrs. Bury telling her that she need not be frightened, and giving her a book to read; and after the midday meal her uncle was desired by Mrs. Bury, who had evidently assumed the management of him, to take the child out walking, for the doctor could not come for hours, and Lady Northmoor had better be left to sleep.

So they wandered out into the pinewoods, preoccupied and silent, gazing along the path, as if that would hasten the doctor. Constance had perceived that questions were discouraged, and did her best to keep from being troublesome by trying to busy herself with a bouquet of mountain flowers.

The little German doctor came so late that he had to remain all night, but his coming, as well as that of a brisk

American brother and sister, seemed to have cheered things up a good deal. Mrs. Bury talked to the German, and the Americans asked so many questions that answering them made things quite lively. Indeed, Constance was allowed to wish her aunt good-night, and seeing her look just like herself on her pillows, much relieved her mind.

Charlotte M. Yonge

CHAPTER XX

RATZES

Things began to fall into their regular course at Ratzes, Lady Northmoor was in a day or two able to come into Mrs. Bury's sitting-room for a few hours every day; but there she lay on a folding chaise-longue that had been arranged for her, languid but bright, reading, working, looking at Mrs. Bury's drawings, and keeping the diary of the adventures of the others.

Her husband would fain never have left her, but he had to take his baths. These were in the lower story of the larger chalet. They were taken in rows of pinewood boxes in the vault. He muttered that it felt very like going alive into his coffin, when, like others, he laid himself down in the rust-coloured liquid, 'each in his narrow cell' in iron 'laid,' with his head on a shelf, and a lid closing up to his chin, and he was uncheered by conversation, as all the other patients were Austrians of the lower middle class, and their Tyrolean dialect would have been hard to understand even by German scholars. However, the treatment certainly did him good, and entirely drove away his neuralgia, he walked, rode, and climbed a good deal with Constance and a lad attached to the establishment, whose German Constance could just understand. And while he stayed with his wife, Mrs. Bury took Constance out, showed her many delights, helped her crude notions of drawing, and being a good botanist herself, taught the whole party fresh pleasures in the wonderful flora of the Dolomites.

Now and then an English traveller appeared, and Lord Northmoor was persuaded to join in expeditions for his niece's sake, that took them away for a night or two. Thus they saw Caprile Cadore, St. Ulrich, that town of toys, full of dolls of every tone, spotted wooden horses, carts, and the like. They beheld the tall points of Monte Serrata, and the wonderful 'Horse Teeth,' with many more such marvels; and many were the curiosities they brought back, and the stories they had to tell, with regrets that Aunt Mary had not been there to enjoy and add to their enjoyment.

So the days went on, and the end of Constance's holidays was in view, the limit that had been intended for the Kur at Ratzes; but Aunt Mary had not been out of doors since their arrival, and seemed fit for nothing save lying by the window.

Constance had begun to wonder what would be done, when she was told that a good-natured pair of English travellers, like herself bound to school terms, would escort her safely to London and see her into the train for Colbeam, just in time for the High School term.

'This will be the best way,' said her aunt, kissing her. 'You have been a dear good girl, Conny, and a great pleasure and comfort to us both.'

'Oh, auntie, I have not done anything, Mrs. Bury has done it all.'

'Mrs. Bury is most kind, unspeakably kind, but, my dear dear girl, your companionship has been so much to your dear uncle that I have been most thankful to you. Always recollect, dearest Conny, you can be more comfort to your uncle than anybody else, whatever may come. You *will* always be a good girl and keep up your tone, and make him your great consideration—after higher things; promise me.'

'Oh yes, indeed, auntie dear,' said the girl, somewhat frightened and bewildered as the last kisses and good-byes were exchanged. Since the travellers were to start very early the next morning on their mules for Botzen, whither Mrs. Bury meant to accompany them in order to make some purchases, Lord Northmoor went with the party to the limits of his walking powers, and on the slope of the Alp, amid the fir-woods, took his leave, Mrs. Bury telling him cheerfully that she should return the next day, while he said that he could not thank her enough. He bade farewell to his niece, telling her that he hoped she would by and by be spending her holidays at Northmoor if all went well.

Constance had begun to grow alarmed, and watched for an opportunity of imploring Mrs. Bury to tell her whether Aunt Mary were really very ill.

Mrs. Bury laughed, and confided to her a secret, which made her at once glad, alarmed, and important.

'Oh, and is no one to know?' said little Constance, with rosy cheeks.

'Not till leave is given,' said Mrs. Bury. 'You see there is still so much risk of things going wrong, that they both wish nothing to be said at present. I thought they had spoken to you.'

'Oh no. But—but—' and Constance could not go on, as

her eyes filled with tears.

'Is there special cause for anxiety, you mean, my dear? Hardly for *her*, though it was unlucky that she was as unknowing as you, and I don't see how she is to be taken over these roads into a more civilised place. But I shall stay on and see them through with it, and I daresay we shall do very well. I am used enough to looking after my own daughters, and nobody particularly wants me at home.'

'That's what Aunt Mary meant by saying you were *so* very good!'

'Well, it would be sheer inhumanity to leave them to themselves, and the mercies of Ratzes, and there seems to be no one else that could come.'

'I'm glad I know!' said Constance, with a long breath. 'Only what shall I do if any one asks me about her?'

'Say she had a nasty fall, which makes it undesirable to move her just yet. It is the simple truth, and what you would have naturally said but for this little communication of mine.'

'I suppose,' said Constance, in a tone Mrs. Bury did not understand, 'it will be all known before my Christmas holidays?'

'Oh yes, my dear, long before that. I'll write to you when I have anything to tell.'

For which Constance thanked her heartily, and thenceforth felt a great deal older for the confidence, which delighted as well as made her anxious, for she was too fond of her uncle and aunt, as well as too young and simple, for it to have occurred to her how the matter might affect her brother.

After seeing much more on her road than she had done before, and won golden opinions from her escort for intelligence and obligingness, she was safely deposited in the train for Colbeam, without having gone home.

She had made up her mind to pass Sunday at her boarding-house, and was greatly surprised when Lady Adela called on Saturday to take her to Northmoor for the Sunday.

'Now tell me about your uncle and aunt,' the good lady began, when Constance was seated beside her. 'Yes, I have heard from Mrs. Bury, but I want to know whether the place is tolerably comfortable.'

'Mrs. Bury has made it much better,' said Constance. 'And it is so beautiful, no one would care for comfort who was quite well.'

'And is your uncle well? Has he got over his headaches?' she asked solicitously.

In fact, the absence of Lord and Lady Northmoor had done more than their presence to make Lady Adela feel their value. She was astonished to find how much she missed the power of referring to him and leaning on his support in all questions, small or great, that cropped up; and she had begun to feel that the stick might be a staff; besides which, having imbibed more than an inkling of the cause of detention, she was anxious to gather what she could of the circumstances.

She was agreeably surprised in Constance, to whom the journey had been a time of development from the mere school girl, and who could talk pleasantly, showing plenty of intelligence and observation in a modest ladylike way. Moreover, she had a game in the garden which little Amice enjoyed extremely, and she and her little Sunday class were delighted to see one another again. It resulted in her Sundays being spent at Northmoor as regularly as before, and in Amice, a companionless child, thinking Saturday brought the white afternoon of the week.

CHAPTER XXI

THE HEIR-APPARENT

'MY DEAR ADDIE,

'You have no doubt ceased from your exertions in the way of finding nurses, since the telegram has told you that the son and heir has considerately saved trouble and expense by making his appearance on Michaelmas morning. It was before there was time to fetch anybody but the ancient village Bettina. Everything is most prosperous, and I am almost as proud as the parents—and to see them gloat over the morsel is a caution. They look at him as if such a being had never been known on the earth before; and he really is a very fine healthy creature, most ridiculously like the portrait of the original old Michael Morton Northmoor in the full-bottomed wig. He seems to be almost equally marvellous to the Ratzes population, being the first infant seen there unswaddled—or washed. Bettina's horror at the idea of washing him is worth seeing. Her brown old face was almost convulsed, and she and our Frau-wirthin concurred in assuring me that it would be fatal to *der kleine baron* if he were washed, except with white wine and milk at a fortnight old; nor would they accept my assurance that my three daughters and seven grandchildren had survived the process. I have to do it myself, and dress him as I can, for his wardrobe as made here is not complete, and whatever you can send us will be highly acceptable. It is lucky that Northmoor is a born nurse, for the women's fear of breaking the child is really justifiable, as they never handled anything not made up into a mummy; moreover, they wish to let all the world up into Mary's room to behold the curiosity, I met the priest upon his way and turned him back! So we have pretty well all the nursing on our hands, and happily it is of the most satisfactory kind, with the one drawback that we have to call in the services of a 'valia'; but on the other hand we have all been so much interested in a poor little widow, Hedwig Grantzen, whose husband was lost last spring in a snow-storm, that it is pleasant to have some employment for her. Such a creature as came over on chance and speculation—a great coarse handsome girl, in exaggerated costume, all new, with lacy ribbons down her back; but I rode over to Botzen, and interviewed her parish priest about her, and that was enough to settle her. Every one is asleep except myself, and Mary's face is one smile as she sleeps.

'This is going to be posted by the last of the tourists, luckily a clergyman, whom we begged to baptize the boy, as there is a possibility that snows may close us in before we can get away.

'So he is named Michael Kenton, partly after my own dear brother as well as the old founder, partly in honour of the day and of Sir Edward Kenton, who, they say, has been their very kind friend. It really is a feast to see people so wonderingly happy and thankful. The little creature has all the zest of novelty to them, and they coo and marvel over it in perfect felicity. When you will be introduced to the hero, I cannot guess, for though he has been an earlier arrival than his mother's inexperience expected, I much doubt her being able to get out of this place while the way to Botzen is passable according to the prognostics of the sages. What splendid studies of ice peaks I shall have! Your affectionate cousin,

'L. BURY.'

A telegram had preceded the letter. One soon followed by Mrs. Bury's promised note had filled Constance's honest little heart with rapture, another had set all the bells in Northmoor Church ringing and Best rejoicing that 'that there Harbut's nose was put out of joint,' a feeling wherein Lady Adela could not but participate, though, of course, she showed no sign of it to Constance. A sharply-worded letter to the girl soon came from her mother, demanding what she had known beforehand. Mrs. Morton had plainly been quite unprepared for what was a severe blow to her, and it was quite possible to understand how, in his shyness, Lord Northmoor had put off writing of the hope and expectation from day to day till all had been fulfilled sooner than had been expected.

It was the first thing that brought home to Constance that the event was scarcely as delightful to her family as to herself. She wrote what she knew and heard no more, for none of her home family were apt to favour her with much correspondence. Miss Morton, however, had written to her sister-in-law.

'Poor Herbert! I am sorry for him, though you won't be. He takes it very well, he really is a very good sort at bottom, and it really is the very best thing for him, as I have been trying to persuade him.'

Bulletins came with tolerable frequency from Ratzes, with all good accounts of mother and child, and a particular description of little Michael's beauties; but it was only too soon announced that snow was falling, and this was soon followed by another letter saying that consultation with the best authorities within reach had decided that unless the weather were extraordinarily mild, the journey, after November set in, was not to be ventured by Lady Northmoor or so young a child. There would be perils for any one, even the postmen and the guides, and if it were mild in one valley it might only render it more dangerous over the next Alp. Still Mrs. Bury, a practised and enterprising mountaineer, might have attempted it; but though Mary was rapidly recovering and the language was no longer utterly impracticable, the good lady could not bear to desert her charges, or to think what might happen to them, if left alone, in case of illness or accident, so she devoted herself to them and to her studies of ice and snow, and wrote word to her family that they were to think of her as hibernating till Easter, if not Whitsuntide.

Charlotte M. Yonge

CHAPTER XXII

OUT OF JOINT

Constance had, of course, to spend her Christmas holidays at home, where she had not been for nine months.

Her brother met her at the London terminus to go down with her, and there, to her great joy, she also saw Rose Rollstone on the platform. Herbert, whose dignity had first prompted him to seek a smoking carriage apart from his sister, thereupon decided to lay it aside and enter with them, looking rather scornful at the girls' mutual endearments.

'Come, Conny, Miss Rollstone has had enough of that,' he said, 'and here are a lot going to get in. Oh my, the cads! I shall have to get into the smoking carriage after all.'

'No, don't. Sit opposite and we shall do very well.'

Then came the exchange of news, and—'You've heard, of course, Rosie?'

'I should think I had,' then an anxious glance at Herbert, who answered—

'Oh yes, mother and Ida have been tearing their hair ever

since, but it is all rot! The governor's very welcome to the poor little beggar!'

'Oh, that's right! That's very noble of you, Herbert,' said both the girls in a breath.

'Well, you see, old Frank is good to live these thirty or forty years yet, and what was the good of having to wait? Better have done with it at once, I say, and he has written me a stunning jolly letter.'

'Oh, I was sure he would!' cried Constance.

'I'm to go on just the same, and he won't cut off my allowance,' pursued Herbert.

'It is just as my papa says,' put in Rose, 'he is always the gentleman. And you'll be in the army still?'

'When I've got through my exams; but they are no joke, Miss Rose, I can tell you. It is Conny there that likes to sap. What have you been doing this time, little one?'

'I don't know yet, but Miss Astley thinks I have done well and shall get into the upper form,' said Constance shyly. 'I got on with my German while I was abroad, trying to teach Uncle Frank.'

At which Herbert laughed heartily, and demanded what sort of scholar he made.

'Not very good,' owned Constance; 'he did forget so from day to day, and he asked so many questions, and was always wanting to have things explained. But it made me know them better, and Mrs. Bury had such nice books, and she helped me. If you want to take up French and German, Bertie—

Charlotte M. Yonge

He shrugged his shoulders.

'Don't spoil the passing hour, child. I should think you would be glad enough to get away from it all.'

'I do want to get on,' said Constance. 'I must, you know, more than ever now.'

'Oh, you mean that mad fancy of going and being a teacher?'

'It is not a bit mad, Herbert. Rose does not think it is, and I want you to stand by me if mamma and Ida make objections.'

'Girls are always in such a hurry,' grumbled Herbert. 'You need not make a stir about it yet. You won't be able to begin for ever so long.'

Rose agreed with him that it would be much wiser not to broach the subject till Constance was old enough to begin the preparation, though, with the impatience of youth to express its designs and give them form, she did not like the delay.

'I tell you what, Con,' finally said Herbert, 'if you set mother and Ida worrying before their time, I shall vote it all rot, and not say a word to help you.'

Which disposed of the subject for the time, and left them to discuss happily Constance's travels and Herbert's new tutor and companions till their arrival at Westhaven, where Constance's welcome was quite a secondary thing to Herbert's, as she well knew it would be, nor felt it as a grievance, though she was somewhat amazed at seeing him fervently embraced, and absolutely cried over, with 'Oh, my poor injured boy!'

Herbert did not like it at all, and disengaging himself rapidly, growled out his favourite expletive of 'Rot! Have done with that!'

He was greatly admired for his utter impatience of commiseration, but there was no doubt that the disappointment was far greater to his mother and Ida than to himself. He cared little for what did not make any actual difference to his present life, whereas to them the glory and honour of his heirship and the future hopes were everything—and Constance's manifest delight in the joy of her uncle and aunt, and her girlish interest in the baby, were to their eyes unfeeling folly, if not absolute unkindness to her brother.

'Dear little baby, indeed!' said Ida scornfully. 'Nasty little wretch, I say. One good thing is, up in that cold place all this time he's sure not to live.'

Herbert whistled. 'That's coming it rather strong.' And Constance, with tears starting to her eyes, said, 'For shame, Ida, how can you be so wicked! Think of Uncle Frank and Aunt Mary!'

'I believe you care for them more than for your own flesh and blood!' exclaimed her mother.

'Well, and haven't they done a sight deal more for her?' said Herbert.

'You turning on me too, you ungrateful boy!' cried Mrs. Morton.

Herbert laughed.

'If it comes to gratitude,' he said, and looked significantly at the decorations.

Charlotte M. Yonge

'And what is it but the due to his brother's widow?' said Mrs. Morton. 'Just a pittance, and you may depend that will be cut down on some pretext now!'

'I should think so, if they heard Ida's tongue!' said Herbert.

'And Constance there is spitefulness enough to go and tell them—favourite as she is!' said Ida.

'I should think not!' said Constance indignantly. 'As if I would do such a mean thing!'

'Come, come, Ida,' said her mother, 'your sister knows better than that. It's not the way when she is only just come home, so grown too and improved, "quite the lady."'

Mrs. Morton had a mother's heart for Constance, though only in the third degree, and was really gratified to see her progress. She had turned up her pretty brown hair, and the last year had made her much less of a child in appearance; her features were of delicate mould, she had dark eyes, and a sweet mouth, with a rose-blush complexion, and was pleasing to look on, though, in her mother's eyes, no rival to the thin, rather sharply-defined features, bright eyes, and pink-and-white complexion that made Ida the belle of a certain set at Westhaven. The party were more amicable over the dinner-table—for dinner it was called, as an assertion of gentility.

'Are you allowed to dine late,' asked Ida patronisingly of her sister, 'when you are not at school?

'Lady Adela dines early,' said Constance.

'Oh, for your sake, I suppose?'

'Always, I believe,' said Constance.

'Yes, always,' said Herbert. 'Fine people needn't ask what's genteel, you see, Ida.'

That was almost the only breeze, and after dinner Herbert rushed out for a smell of sea, interspersed with pipe, and to 'look up the inevitable old Jack.'

Constance was then subjected to a cross-examination on all the circumstances of the detention at Ratzes, and all she had heard or ought to have heard about the arrival of the unwelcome little Michael, while her mother and sister drew their own inferences.

'Really,' said Ida at last, 'it is just like a thing in a book.'

Constance was surprised.

'Because it was such a happy surprise for them,' she added hastily.

'No, nonsense, child, but it is just what they always do when they want a supposititious heir.'

'Ida, how can you say such things?'

'But it is, Conny! There was the wicked Sir Ronald Macronald. He took his wife away to Belgrade, right in the Ukraine mountains, and it—'

'Belgrade is in Hungary, and the Cossacks live in the Ukraine in Russia,' suggested Constance.

'Oh, never mind your school-girl geography, it was Bel something, an out-of-the-way place in the mountains anyway, and there he pretended she had a child, just out of malice to the right heiress, that lovely Lilian, and he got killed by a stag, and then she confessed on her death-bed. I declare it is just like—'

'My dear, don't talk in that way, your sister is quite shocked. Your uncle never would—'

'Bless me, ma, I was only in fun. I could tell you ever so many stories like that. There's Broughton's, on the table there. I knew from the first it was an impostor, and the old nurse dressed like a nun was his mother.'

'I believe you always know the end before you are half through the first volume,' said her mother admiringly; 'but of course it is all right, only it is a terrible disappointment and misfortune for us, and not to be looked for after all these years.'

The last three Christmastides had been spent at Northmoor, where it had been needful to conform to the habits of the household, which impressed Ida and her mother as grand and conferring distinction, but decidedly dull and religious.

So as they were at Westhaven, perforce, they would make up for it, Christmas Eve was spent in a tumult of prepa-ration for the diversions of the next day. Mrs. Morton had two maids now, but to her they were still 'gals,' not to be trusted with the more delicate cookeries, and Ida was fully engaged in the adornment of the room and herself, while Constance ran about and helped both, and got more thanks from her mother than her sister.

Ida was to end the day with a dance at a friend's house, but she was not desirous of taking Constance with her, having been accustomed to treat her as a mere child, and Constance, though not devoid of a wish for amusement, knew that her uncle and aunt would have taken her to church, where she would have enjoyed the festal service.

Her mother would not let her go out in the dark alone, and was too tired to go with her, so she had to stay at home, while Herbert disported himself elsewhere, and Constance underwent another cross-examination over the photographs she had brought home, but Mrs. Morton was never unkind when alone with her, and she had all the natural delight of youth in relating her adventures. Mrs. Morton, however, showed offence at not having been sent for instead of Mrs. Bury.—'So much less of a relation,' and Constance found herself dwelling on the ruggedness of the pass, and the difficulties of making oneself understood, but Mrs. Morton still persisted that she 'could not understand why they should have got into such a place at all, when there were plenty of fashionable places in the newspaper where they could have had society and attendance and everything.'

'Ah, but that was just what Uncle Frank didn't want.'

'Well, if they choose to be so eccentric, and close and shy, they can't wonder that people talk.'

'Mamma, you can't mean that horrid nonsense that Ida talked about! It was only a joke!'

'Oh, my dear, I don't say that I suspect anything—oh no,—only, if they had not been so close and queer, one would have been able to contradict it. I like people to be straightforward, that's all I have to say. And it is terribly hard on your poor brother to be so disappointed, after having his expectations so raised!' and Mrs. Morton melted into tears, leaving Constance with nothing to say, for in the first place, she did not think Herbert, as yet at least, was very sensible of his loss, and in the next, she did not quite venture to ask her mother whether she thought little Michael should have been sacrificed to Herbert's expectations. So she took the wiser course of producing a photograph of Vienna.

CHAPTER XXIII

VELVET

Constance created quite a sensation when she came down dressed for church on Christmas Day in a dark blue velvet jacket, deeply trimmed with silver fox, and a hat and muff *en suite*, matching with her serge dress, and though unpretending, yet very handsome.

Up jumped Ida, from lacing her boots by the fire. 'Well, I never! They are spoiling you! Real velvet, I declare, and real silk-wadded lining. Look, ma. What made them dress you like that?'

'It wasn't them,' said Constance, 'it was Lady Adela. One Sunday in October it turned suddenly cold, and I had only my cloth jacket, and she sent up for something warm for me. This was just new before she went into black, when husband died, and she had put it away for Amice, but it fitted me so well, and looked so nice, that she was so kind as to wish me to keep it always.'

'Cast-off clothes! That's the insolence of these swells,' said Ida. 'I wonder you had not the spirit to refuse.'

'Sour grapes,' muttered Herbert; while her mother sighed —'Ah, that's what we come to!'

Charlotte M. Yonge

'Must not I wear it, mamma?' said Constance, who had a certain attachment to the beautiful and comfortable garment. 'She told me she had only worn it once in London, and she was so very kind.'

'Oh, if you call it kindness,' said Ida, 'I call it impertinence.'

'If you had only heard—' faltered Constance.

'No, no,' said their mother, 'you could not refuse, of course, my dear, and no one here will know. It becomes her very well too. Doesn't it, Ida?'

Ida made a snort. 'If people choose to make a little chit of a schoolgirl ridiculous by dressing her out like that!' she said.

'There isn't time now before church,' said Constance almost tearfully, 'or I would take it off.'

'No such thing,' said Herbert. 'Come on, Conny. You shall walk with me. You look stunning, and I want Westhaven folk to see for once what a lady is like.'

Constance was very glad to be led away from Ida's comments, and resolved that her blue velvet should not see the light again at Westhaven; but she did not find this easy to carry out; for, perhaps for the sake of teasing Ida, Herbert used to inquire after it, and insist on her wearing it, and her mother liked to see her, and to show her, in it. It was only Ida who seemed unable to help saying something disagreeable, till, almost in despair, Constance offered to lend the bone of contention; but Lady Adela was a small woman, and Constance would never be on so large a scale as her sister, so that the jacket refused to be transferred except at the risk of being spoilt by alteration;

and here Mrs. Morton interfered, 'It would never do to have them say at Northmoor that "Lady Morton's" gift had been spoilt by their meddling with it.' Constance was glad, though she suspected that Lady Adela would never have found it out.

Then Ida consulted Sibyl Grover, who was working with a dressmaker, and with whom she kept up a sort of patronisingly familiar acquaintance, as to making something to rival it, and Sibyl was fertile in devices as to doing so cheaply, but when she consulted her superior, she was told that without the same expensive materials it would evidently be only an imitation, and moreover, that the fashion was long gone out of date. Which enabled Ida to bear the infliction with some degree of philosophy.

This jacket was not, however, Constance's only trouble. Her conscience was already uneasy at the impossibility of getting to evensong on Christmas Day. She had been to an early Celebration without asking any questions, and had got back before Herbert had come down to breakfast, and very glad she was that she had done so, for she found that her mother regarded it as profane 'to take the Sacrament' when she was going to have a party in the evening, and when Constance was in the midst of the party she felt that—if it were to be—her mother might be right.

It was a dinner first—at which Constance did not appear—chiefly of older people, who talked of shipping and of coals. Afterwards, if they noticed the young people, joked them about their imaginary lovers—beaux, as the older ladies called them; young men, as the younger ones said. One, the most plain spoken of all, asked Herbert how he felt, at which the boy wriggled and laughed sheepishly, and his mother had a great confabulation with various of the ladies, who were probably condoling with her.

Later, there were cards for the elders, and sundry more young people came in for a dance. The Rollstones were considered as beneath the dignity of the Mortons, but Herbert had loudly insisted on inviting Rose for the evening and had had his way, but after all she would not come. Herbert felt himself aggrieved, and said she was as horrid a little prig as Constance, who on her side felt a pang of envy as she thought of Rose going to church and singing hymns and carols to her father and mother, while she, after a struggle under the mistletoe, which made her hot and miserable, had to sit playing waltzes. One good-natured lady offered to relieve her, but she was too much afraid of the hero of the mistletoe to stir from her post, and the daughter of her kindly friend had no scruple in exclaiming—

'Oh no, ma, don't! You always put us out, you know, and Constance Morton is as true as old Time.'

'I am sure Constance is only too happy to oblige her friends,' said Mrs. Morton. 'And she is not out yet,' she added, as a tribute to high life.

If Constance at times felt unkindly neglected, at others she heard surges of giggling, and suppressed shrieking and protests that made her feel the piano an ark of refuge.

The parting speech from a good-natured old merchant captain was, 'Why, you demure little pussy cat, you are the prettiest of them all! What have yon lads been thinking about to let those little fingers be going instead of her feet? Or is it all Miss Ida's jealousy, eh?'

All this, in a speaking-trumpet voice, put the poor child into an agony of blushes, which only incited him to pat her on the cheek, and the rest to laugh hilariously, under the influence of negus and cheap champagne.

Constance could have cried for very shame, but when she was waiting on her mother, who, tired as she was, would not go to bed without locking up the spoons and the remains of the wine, Mrs. Morton said kindly, 'You are tired, my dear, and no wonder. They were a little noisy to-night. Those are not goings-on that I always approve, you know, but young folk always like a little pleasure extra at Christmas. Don't you go and get too genteel for us, Conny. Come, come, don't cry. Drink this, my love, you're tired.'

'Oh, mamma, it is not the being genteel—oh no, but Christmas Day and all!'

'Come, come, my dear, I can't have you get mopy and dull; religion is a very good thing, but it isn't meant to hinder all one's pleasure, and when you've been to church on a Christmas Day, what more can be expected of young people but to enjoy themselves? Come, go to bed and think no more about it.'

To express or even to understand what she felt would have been impossible to Constance, so she had to content herself with feeling warm at her heart, at her mother's kind kiss.

All the other parties she saw were much more decorous, even to affectation, except that at the old skipper's, and he was viewed by the family as a subject for toleration, because he had been a friend and messmate of Mrs. Morton's father. All the good side of that lady and Ida came out towards him and his belongings. He had an invalid granddaughter, with a spine complaint and feeble eyesight, and Ida spent much time in amusing her, teaching her fancy works and reading to her. Unluckily it was only trashy novels from the circulating library that they read; Ida had no taste for anything else, and protested

Charlotte M. Yonge

that Louie would be bored to death if she tried to read her the African adventures which were just then the subject of enthusiasm even with Herbert! Ida was not a dull girl. Unlike some who do not seem to connect their books with life, she made them her realities and lived in them, and as she hardly ever read anything more substantial her ideas of life and society were founded on them, though in her own house she was shrewd in practical matters, and though not strong was a useful active assistant to her mother whenever there was no danger of her being detected in doing anything derogatory to one so nearly connected with the peerage.

Indeed, she seemed to regard her sister's dutiful studies as proofs of dulness and want of spirit. She was quite angry when Constance objected to *The Unconscious Impostor*, —very yellow, with a truculent flaming design outside— that 'she did not think she ought to read that kind of book—Aunt Mary would not like it.'

'Well, if I would be in bondage to an old governess! You are not such a child now.'

'Don't, Ida. Uncle Frank would not like it either.'

'Perhaps not,' said Ida, with an ugly, meaning laugh as she glanced again at the title.

Constance might really have liked to read more tales than she allowed herself. *The House on the Marsh* tempted her, but she was true to the advice she had received, and Rose Rollstone upheld her in her resolution.

Ida thought it rather 'low' in Herbert and Constance to care for the old butler's daughter, but their mother had a warm spot in the bottom of her heart, and liked a gossip with Mrs. Rollstone too much to forbid the house to her daughter, besides that she shrank from inflicting on her so much distress.

So during the fortnight that Rose spent at home the girls were together most of the morning. After Constance, well wrapped up, had practised in the cold drawing-room, where economy forbade fires till the afternoon, she sped across to Rose in the little stuffy parlour where Mr. Rollstone liked to doze over his newspaper to the lullaby of their low-voiced chatter. Often they walked together, and were sometimes joined by Herbert, who on these occasions always showed that he knew how to behave like a gentleman.

Herbert was faithfully keeping his promise not to bet, though, as he observed, he had not expected to be in for it so long. But it was satisfactory to hear that his present fellow-pupils did not go in for that sort of thing, and Constance felt sure that her uncle and aunt would be pleased with him and think him much improved.

CHAPTER XXIV

THE REVENGE OF SORDID SPIRITS

'I am quite convinced,' said Ida Morton, 'it is quite plain why we are not invited.'

'My dear, you see what your aunt says; that Mrs. Bury's daughter's husband is ordered to India, and that having the whole family to stay at Northmoor gives them the only chance of being all together for a little while, and after their obligations to Mrs. Bury—'

'Ma, how can you be so green? Obligations, indeed! It is all a mere excuse to say there is not room for us in that great house. I see through it all. It is just to prevent us from being able to ask inconvenient questions of the German nurse and Mrs. Bury and all!'

'Now, Ida, I wish you would put away that fancy. Your uncle and aunt were always such good people! And there was Mrs. Bury—'

'Mother, you will never understand the revenge of sordid souls,' said Ida tragically, quoting from *The Unconscious Impostor*.

'Revenge! What can you mean?'

'Of course, you know, Mrs. Bury never forgave Herbert's taking her for a tramp, and you know how nasty uncle was about that white rook and the bets. Oh, it is quite plain. He was to be deprived of his rights, and so this journey was contrived, and they got into this out-of-the-way, inaccessible place, and sent poor Conny away, and then had no doctor or nurse—exactly as people always do.'

'Oh, Ida, only in stories! Your novels are turning your head.'

'Novels are transcripts of life,' again said Ida, solemnly quoting.

'I don't believe it if they put such things into your head,' said her mother. 'Asking Herbert to be godfather too! Such a compliment!'

'An empty compliment, to hoodwink us and the poor boy,' said Ida. 'No, no, ma, the keeping you away settles it in my mind, and it shall be the business of my life to unmask that!'

So spoke Ida, conscious of being a future heroine.

It was quite true that Herbert had been asked to stand godfather to his little cousin's admission into the Church, after, of course, a very good report had been received from his tutor. 'You are the little fellow's nearest kinsman,' wrote Lord Northmoor, 'and I trust to you to influence him for good.' Herbert wriggled, blushed, thought he hated it, was glad it had been written instead of spoken, but was really touched.

His uncle had justly thought responsibility would be wholesome, and besides, Herbert represented to him his brother, for whom he had a very tender feeling.

It was quite true that Northmoor was as full as it would hold. Mrs. Bury's eldest daughter was going out to India, and another had a husband in the Civil Service; the third lived in Ireland, and the only way of having the whole family together for their last fortnight was to gather them at Northmoor, as soon as its lord and lady returned, nor had they been able to escape from their Dolomite ravine till the beginning of May, for the roads were always dangerous, often impassable, so that there had been weeks when they were secluded from even the post, and had had difficulties as to food and fire.

However, it had done them no harm, and was often looked back upon as, metaphorically as well as literally, the brightest and whitest time in their lives. Frank had walked and climbed both with Mrs. Bury and on his own account, and had drunk in the wild glories of the mountain winter, and the fantastic splendours of snow and ice on those wondrous peaks. And, with that new joy and delight to be found in the queer wooden cradle, his heart was free to bound as perhaps it had never done before, in exulting thankfulness, as he looked up to those foretastes of the Great White Throne.

Never had he had such a rest before from toil, care, and anxiety as in those months in the dry, bracing air, and it was the universal remark that Lord Northmoor came back years younger and twice the man he had been before, with a spirit of cheerfulness and enterprise such as had always been wanting; while as to his wife, she was less strong than before, but there was a certain peaceful, yet exulting happiness about her, and her face had gained wonderfully in sweetness and expression.

The child was a fine plump little fellow, old enough to

laugh and respond to loving faces and gestures. Mary had feared the sight might be painful to Lady Adela, and was gratified to find her too true a baby-lover and too generous a spirit not to worship him almost as devotedly as did Constance.

Perhaps the heads of the family had never seen or participated in anything like the domestic mirth and enjoyment of that fortnight's visit; Bertha was with Lady Adela, and the intimacy and confidence in which Frank and Mary had lived with Mrs. Bury had demolished many barriers of shyness, and made them hosts who could be as one with their guests—guests with whom the shadow of parting made the last sunshine seem the more bright.

'I did not know what I was letting you in for,' said Bertha, in apology to Mrs. Bury.

'My dear, I would not have been without the experience on any account. I never saw such a refreshing pair of people.'

'Surely it must have been awfully slow—regular penal servitude!'

'You confuse absence of small talk with absence of soul, Birdie. When we had once grown intimate enough to hold our tongues if we had nothing to say, we got on perfectly.'

'And what you had to say was about Master Michael?'

'Not entirely; though I must say the mingled reverence and curiosity with which they regard the little monster, and their own fear of not bringing up their treasure properly, were a very interesting study.'

'More so than your snowy peaks! Ah, if the proper study

of mankind is man, the proper study of womankind is babe.'

'Well, it was not at all an unsatisfactory study, in this case. And let me tell you, Miss Birdie, it is no bad thing to be shut in for a few months with a few good books and a couple of thoroughly simple-hearted people, who have thought a good deal in their quiet humdrum way.'

'Why, Lettice, you must have been quite an education to them!'

'I hope they were an education to me.'

'I hope your conscience is not going to be such a rampant and obstructive thing as that which they possess in common,' said Bertha.

'I wish it had been,' said Mrs. Bury gravely.

'At any rate, the deadly lively time has brisked you all up,' said Bertha, laughing.

Constance, on her Saturdays and Sundays, looked on with a kind of wonder. She was not exactly of either set. The children were all so young as to look on her as a grown-up person, though willing to let her play with them; and she was outside the group of young married people, and could not enter into their family fun; but this kind of playfulness and merriment was quite a revelation to her. She had never before seen mirth, except, of course, childish and schoolgirl play, that had not in it something that hurt her taste and jarred on her feeling as much as did Ida's screeching laughter in comparison with the soft ripplings of these young matrons.

Still, little Michael was her chief delight, and she could

hardly be detached from him. She refreshed her colloquial German (or rather Austrian) with his nurse, who had much to say of the goodness of *die Gnadigen Frauen.* Poor thing, she was the youthful widow of a guide, and the efforts of the two Frauen had been in vain to keep alive her only child, after whose death she had found some consolation in taking charge of Lady Northmoor's baby on the way home. Constance hoped Ida might never hear this fact.

Some degree of prosperity was greeting the little heir. A bit of moorland, hitherto regarded as worthless, had first been crossed by a branch line, and the primary growth of a station had been followed by the discovery of good building stone, and the erection of a crop of houses of all degrees, which promised to set the Northmoor finances on a better footing than had been theirs for years, and set their conscientious landlord to work at once on providing church room and schools.

All this, and that most precious possession at home, combined to give Lord Northmoor an amount of spirit and life that enabled him to take his place in the county, emancipate himself from the squire, show an opinion of his own, and open his mouth occasionally. As Bertha observed, no one would ever have called him a stick if he had begun like this. To people like these, humbled and depressed in early life, a little happiness was a great stimulus.

CHAPTER XXV

THE LOVE

It was not till Christmas that Ida had the opportunity of making her observations. By that time 'Mite,' as he was supposed to have named himself, had found the use of his feet, and was acquiring that of his tongue. In fact, he was a very fine forward child, who might easily have been supposed to be eighteen months old instead of fifteen, as Ida did not fail to remark.

He was a handsome little creature, round and fair, with splendid sturdy legs and mottled arms, hair that stood up in a pale golden crest, round blue eyes and a bright colour, without much likeness as yet to either parent, though Lord Northmoor declared that there was an exact resemblance to his own brother, Charles, Herbert's father, as he first remembered him. Ida longed to purse up her lips but did not dare, and was provoked to see her mother taken completely captive by his charms, and petting him to the utmost extent.

Indeed, Lady Northmoor, who was very much afraid of spoiling him, was often distressed when such scenes as this took place. 'Mite! Mite, dear, no!' when his fat little hands had grasped an ivory paper-cutter, and its blade was on the way to the button mouth. 'No!' as he paused and looked at her. 'Here's Mite's ball! poor little dear, do let him have it'—and Mite, reading sympathy in his aunt's face, laughed in a fascinating triumphant manner, and took a bite with his small teeth.

'Mite! mother said no!' and it was gently taken from his hand, but before the fingers had embraced the substituted ball, a depreciating look and word of remonstrance gave a sense of ill-usage and there was a roar.

'Oh, poor little dear! Here—auntie's goody goody—'

'No, no, please, Emma, he has had quite as many as he ought! No, no, Mite—' and he was borne off sobbing in her arms, while Ida observed, 'There! is that the way people treat their own children?'

'Some people never get rid of the governess,' observed Mrs. Morton, quite unconscious that but for her interference there would have been no contest and no tears.

But she herself had no doubts, and was mollified by Mary's plea on her return. 'He is quite good now, but you see, there is so much danger of our spoiling him, we feel that we cannot begin too soon to make him obedient.'

'I could not bear to keep a poor child under in that way.'

'I believe it saves them a great deal if obedience is an instinct,' said Mary.

It had not been Mrs. Morton's method, and she was perfectly satisfied with the result, so she only made some inarticulate sound; but she thought Frank quite as unnatural, when he kept Michael on his knee at breakfast, but with only an empty spoon to play with! All the tossing and playing, the radiant smiles between the two did not in her eyes atone for these small beginnings of discipline, even though her brother-in-law's first proceeding, whenever he came home, was to look for his son, and if the child were not in the drawing-room, to hurry up to the nursery and bring him down, laughing and shouting.

The Tyrolean nurse had been sacrificed to those notions of training which the Westhaven party regarded as so harsh. Her home sickness and pining for her mountains had indeed fully justified the 'rampant consciences,' as to the humanity as well as the expedience of sending her home before her indulgence of the Kleiner Freiherr had had time to counteract his parents' ideas, and her place had been supplied by the nurse whom Amice was outgrowing, so that Ida was disappointed of her intentions of examining her, and laid up the circumstances as suspicious, though, on the other hand, her mother was gratified at exercising a bit of patronage by recommending a nursery girl from Westhaven. The next winter, however, was not marked by a visit to Northmoor. Ida had been having her full share of the summer and early autumnal gaieties of Westhaven, and among the yachts who were given to putting in there was a certain *Morna*, belonging to Sir Thomas Brady, who had become a baronet by force of success in speculation. His son, who chiefly used it, showed evident admiration of Miss Morton's bright cheeks and eyes, and so often resorted to Westhaven, and dropped in at what she had named Northmoor cottage, that there was fair reason for supposing that this might result in more than an ordinary flirtation.

However, at the regatta, when she had looked for distinguished attention on his part, she felt herself absolutely neglected, and the very next day the *Morna* sailed away, without a farewell.

Ida at first could hardly believe it. When she did, the conviction came upon her that his son's attachment had been reported to Sir Thomas, and that the young man had been summoned away against his will. It would have been different, no doubt, had Herbert still been heir-presumptive.

'That horrid little Mite!' said she.

Whether her heart or her ambition had been most affected might be doubtful. At any rate, the disappointment added to the oppression of a heavy cold on the chest, which she had caught at the regatta, and which became severe enough to call for the doctor.

Thus the mother and daughter did not go to Northmoor. At a ball given on board a steam yacht just before Christmas Ida caught a violent cold on the chest, the word congestion was uttered, and an opinion was pronounced that as she had always weak lungs, a spring abroad would be advisable.

Mrs. Morton wrote a letter with traces of tears upon it, appealing to her brother-in-law to assist her as the only hope of saving her dearest child, and the quarries had done so well during the last year that he was able to respond with a largesse sufficient for her needs, though not for her expectations.

Mrs. Morton would have liked to have taken Constance as interpreter, and general aid and assistant; but Constance was hard at work, aspiring to a scholarship, at a ladies' college, and it was plain that her sister was not so desirous of her company as to make her mother overrule her wishes as a duty.

In fact, Ida had found a fellow-traveller who would suit

Charlotte M. Yonge

her much better than Constance. Living for the last year in lodgings near at hand was a Miss Gattoni, daughter of an Italian courier and French lady's maid. As half boarder at a third-rate English school, she had acquired education enough to be first a nursery-governess, and later a companion; and in her last situation, when she had gone abroad several times with a rheumatic old lady, she had recommended herself enough to receive a legacy which rendered her tolerably independent. She was very good-natured, and had graduated in the art of making herself acceptable, and, as she really wished to go abroad again, she easily induced Mrs. Morton and Ida to think it a great boon that she should join forces with them, and as she was an experienced traveller with a convenient smattering of various tongues, she really smoothed their way considerably and lived much more at her ease than she could have done upon her own resources, always frequenting English hotels and boarding-houses.

Mrs. Morton and Ida were of that order of tourists who do not so much care for sights as for being on a level with those who have seen them; and besides, Ida was scarcely well or in spirits enough for much exertion till after her first month at Nice, which restored her altogether to her usual self, and made her impatient of staying in one place.

It is not, however, worth while to record the wanderings of the trio, until in the next summer they reached Venice, where Ida declared her intention of penetrating into the Dolomites. There was an outcry. What could she wish for in that wild and savage country, where there was no comfortable hotel, no society, no roads—nothing in short to make life tolerable, whereas an hotel full of Americans of extreme politeness to ladies, and expeditions in gondolas, when one could talk and have plenty of attention, were only too delightful?

That peaks should be more attractive than flirtations was inexplicable, but at last in secret confabulation Ida disclosed her motive, and in another private consultation Mrs. Morton begged Miss Gattoni to agree to it, as the only means of satisfying the young lady, or putting her mind at rest about a fancy her mother could not believe in; though even as she said, 'it would be so very shocking, it is perfectly ridiculous to think my brother Lord Northmoor would be capable,' the shrewd confidante detected a lingering wish that it might be so!

Maps and routes were consulted, and it was decided that whereas to go from Venice through Cadore would involve much mule-riding and rough roads, the best way would be to resort to the railway to Verona, and thence to Botzen as the nearest point whence Ratzes could be reached.

Charlotte M. Yonge

CHAPTER XXVI

IDA'S WARNING

Botzen proved to be very hot and full of smells, nor did Mrs. Morton care for its quaint old medieval houses, but Ida's heart had begun to fail her when she came so near the crisis, and on looking over the visitors' book she gave a cry. 'Ah, if we had only known! It is all of no use.'

'How?' she was asked.

'That horrid Mrs. Bury!'

'There?'

'Of course she is. Only a week ago she was here. If she is at Ratzes, of course we can do nothing.'

'And the road is *affreux*, perfectly frightful,' said Mademoiselle. 'I have been inquiring about it. No access except upon mules. A whole day's journey—and the hotel! Bah, it is *vilain*!'

'If Ida is bent on going she must go without me,' said Mrs. Morton. 'I—I have had enough of those horrid beasts. Ida's nonsense will be the death of me.'

'I don't see much good in going on with that woman there,' said Ida gloomily. 'She would be sure to stifle all inquiry.'

'A good thing too,' muttered poor, weary Mrs. Morton.

Ida turned the leaves of the visitors' book till she found the names of Lord and Lady Northmoor, and then, growing more eager as obstructions came in her way, and not liking to turn back as if on a fool's errand, she suggested to Miss Gattoni that questions might be asked about their visit. The Tyrolean patois was far beyond her, and not too comprehensible to her friend, but there was a waiter who could speak French, and the landlady's German was tolerable.

The milord and miladi were perfectly remembered, as well as their long detention, but the return had been by way of Italy, so they had not revisited Botzen with their child the next spring.

'But,' said the hostess, 'there is a young woman in the next street who can tell you more than I. She offered herself as a nurse.'

This person was at once sent for. She was the same who had been mentioned by Mrs. Bury, but she had exchanged the peasant costume, which had, perhaps, only been assumed to please the English ladies, for the towns-woman's universal endeavour at French fashion, which by no means enhanced her rather coarse beauty, which was more Italian than Austrian.

Italian was the tongue which chiefly served as a medium between her and Miss Gattoni, though hers was not pure enough to be easily understood. Mrs. Morton and Ida put questions which Miss Gattoni translated as best she could, and made out as much as possible of the answers. It was elicited that she had not been allowed to see the English miladi. All had been settled by the signora who came yearly, and they had rejected her after all her trouble; the doctor had recommended her, and though her *creatura* would have been just the right age, and that little *ipocrila's* child was older, ever so much older—she spread out her hands to indicate infinity.

'Ah!' said Ida, 'I always thought so.'

'Ask her how much older,' demanded Mrs. Morton.

The replies varied from nearly *un sanestre* to *tre settimane*—and no more could be made of that question.

'Where was the foster-child?'

Again the woman threw up her hands to indicate that she had no notion—what was it to her? She could not tell if it were alive or dead; but (upon a leading question) it had not been seen since Hedwige's departure nor after return. Was it boy or girl? and, after some hesitation, it was declared to have been *un maschio*.

There was more, which nobody quite understood, but which sounded abusive, and they were glad to get rid of her with a couple of *thalers*.

'Well?' said Ida triumphantly.

'Well?' echoed her mother in a different tone. 'I don't know what you were all saying, but I'm sure of this, that that woman was only looking to see what you wanted her to say. I watched the cunning look of her eyes, and I would not give that for her word,' with a gesture of her fingers.

'But, ma, you didn't understand! Nothing could be plainer. The doctor recommended her, and sent her over in proper time, but she never saw any one but Mrs. Bury, who, no doubt, had made her arrangements. Then this other woman's child was older—nobody knows how much— but we always agreed that nobody could believe Mite, as they call him, was as young as they said. And then that other child was a boy, and it has vanished.'

'I don't believe she knew.'

'No, I do not think she did,' chimed in Miss Gattoni. 'This *canaille* will say anything!'

'I believe the woman,' said Ida obstinately. 'Her evidence chimes in with all my former conclusions.'

The older ladies both had a strong misgiving that the conclusions had formed the evidence, and Mrs. Morton, though she had listened all along to Ida's grumbling, was perfectly appalled at the notion of bringing such a ridiculous accusation against the brother-in-law, against whom she might indeed murmur, but whom she knew to be truthful and self-denying. She ventured to represent that it was impossible to go upon this statement without ascertaining whether the Grantzen child was alive, or really dead and buried at Ratzes, and that the hostess of the inn would have been better evidence, but—

He that of purpose looks beside the mark,
Might as well hoodwinked shoot as in the dark,

and Ida was certain that all the people at Ratzes had been bribed, and that no one would dare to speak out while Mrs. Bury kept guard there. Indeed, for that lady to guess at such suspicions and inquiries would have been so dreadful that Ratzes was out of the question, much to the

Charlotte M. Yonge

relief of the elders, dragged along by the masterful maiden against their better judgment, though indeed Miss Gattoni gave as much sympathy in her *tete-a-tetes* with Ida as she did to her mother in their consultations.

They were made to interview the doctor, but he knew as little about the matter as the disappointed *balia*, and professed to know much less. In point of fact, though he had been called in after the accident, Mrs. Bury had not thought much of his skill, and had not promoted after-visits. There had not been time to summon him when the birth took place, and Mrs. Bury thought her experience more useful afterwards than his treatment was likely to be. So he was a slighted and offended man, whose testimony, given in good German, only declared the secretiveness, self-sufficiency, and hard-neckedness of Englander!

And Ida's state of mind much resembled that of the public when resolved to believe in the warming-pan.

CHAPTER XXVII

THE YOUNG PRETENDER

The denunciation of the Young Pretender was not an easy matter even in Ida's eyes. It was one thing to have a pet grievance and see herself as a heroine, righting her dear injured brother's wrongs, and another to reproach two of the quietest most matter-of-fact people in the world with the atrocious frauds of which only a wicked baronet was capable.

She was not sorry that the return to England was deferred by the tenants of the house at Westhaven wanting to stay on; and when at length a Christmas visit was paid at Northmoor, Mite was an animated little personage of three and a quarter, and, except that he could not accomplish a *k*, perfect in speaking plainly and indeed with that pretty precision of utterance that children sometimes acquire when baby language has not been foolishly fastened. Indeed, his pet name of Mite was only for strictly private use. Except to his nearest relatives, he was always Michael.

Mrs. Morton was delighted with him, and would have liked to make up for her knowledge of Ida's suspicions by extra petting, and by discovering resemblances to all the family portraits as well as to his parents, none of which

Charlotte M. Yonge

any one else could see. She lived upon thorns lest Ida should burst out with some accusation, but Ida had not the requisite impudence, and indeed, in sight of the boy with his parents, her 'evidence' faded into such stuff as dreams are made of.

There was some vexation, indeed, that Louisa the nursery-maid, whom Mrs. Morton had recommended, had had to be dismissed.

'I am sorry,' said Mrs. Morton, 'for, as I told you, her father was the mate aboard the *Emma Jane*, my poor father's ship, you know, and went down with poor pa and my poor dear Charlie. And her mother used to char for us, which was but her due.'

'Yes, I know,' said Mary; 'Frank and I were both very sorry, and we would have found her another place, but she would go home. You see, we could not keep her in the nursery, for we must have a thoroughly trustworthy person to go out with Michael.'

'What! Can't your fine nurse?'

'Eden? It is her one imperfection. It is some weakness of the spine, and neither she nor I can be about with Michael as long as it is good for him. I thought he must be safe in the garden, but it turned out that Louisa had been taking him down to the village, and there meeting a sailor, who I believe came up in a collier to Colbeam.'

'Oh, an old friend from Westhaven?'

'Sam Rattler,' suggested Ida. 'Don't you remember, mamma, Mrs. Hall said they were sweethearting, and she wanted to get her out of the way of him.'

'Perhaps,' said Lady Northmoor, 'but I should have forgiven it if she had told me the truth and not tempted Mite. She used to make excuses to Eden for going down to the village, and at last she took Mite there, and they gave him sweets at the shop not to tell!'

'Did he?' said Ida, rather hoping the model boy would have failed.

'Oh yes. The dear little fellow did not understand keeping things back, and when his papa was giving him his nightly sugar-plum, he said, "Blue man gave me a great striped sweet, and it stuck in my little teeth"; and then, when we asked when and where, he said, "Down by Betty's, when I was out with Cea and Louie"; and so it came out that she had taken him into the village, met this man, brought him into the grounds by the little gate, and tried to bribe Mite to say nothing about it. Cea told us all about it,—the little girl who lives with Miss Morton. Of course we could never let him go out with her again, and you would hardly believe what an amount of falsehoods she managed to tell Eden and me about it.'

'Ah, if you had lived at Westhaven you would have found out that to be so particular is the way to make those girls fib,' said Mrs. Morton.

'I hope not. I think we have a very good girl now, trained up in an orphanage.'

'Oh, those orphanage girls are the worst of all. I've had enough of them. They break everything to pieces, and they run after the lads worst of all, because they have never seen one before!'

To which Mary answered by a quiet 'I hope it may not turn out so.'

Charlotte M. Yonge

There were more agitating questions to be brought forward. Herbert had behaved very fairly well ever since the escapade of the pied rook; the lad kept his promise as to betting faithfully in his uncle's absence, and though it had not been renewed, he had learnt enough good sense to keep out of mischief.

Unfortunately, however, he had not the faculty of passing examinations. He was not exactly stupid or idle, but any kind of study was a bore to him, and the knowledge he was forced to 'get up' was not an acquisition that gave him the slightest satisfaction for its own sake, or that he desired to increase beyond what would carry him through. Naturally, he had more cleverness than his uncle, and learning was less difficult to him, but he only used his ability to be sooner done with a distasteful task, which never occupied his mind for a moment after it was thrown aside. Thus time after time he had failed in passing for the army, and now only one chance remained before being reduced to attempting to enter the militia. And suppose that there he failed?

He remained in an amiable, passive, good-humoured state, rather amused than otherwise at his mother's impression that it was somehow all his uncle's fault, and ready to be disposed of exactly as they pleased provided that he had not the trouble of thinking about it or of working extra hard.

Mrs. Morton was sure that something could be done. Could not his uncle send him to Oxford? Then he could be a clergyman, or a lawyer or anything. Oh dear, were there those horrid examinations there too? And then those gentlemen that belonged to the ambassadors and envoys—she was sure Mr. Rollstone had told her any one who had connection could get that sort of appointment to what they called the Civil Service. What, examinations again? connection no good? Well, it was shame! What would things come to? As Mr Rollstone said, it was mere ruin!

Merchant's office? Bah! such a gentleman as her Herbert was, so connected! What was his uncle thinking of, taking him up to put him down in that way? It was hard.

And Lord Northmoor was thankful to the tears that as usual choked her, while he begged her at present to trust to that last chance. It would be time to think what was to come next if that failed.

Wherewith the victim passed the window whistling merrily, apparently perfectly regardless of his doom, be it what it might, and with Mite clinging to his hand in ecstatic admiration.

Constance too was in question. Here she was at eighteen, a ladylike, pleasant, good girl, very nice-looking, sweet-faced, and thoughtful, having finished her course at the High School with great credit, but alas! it was not in the family to win scholarships. She did things well, but not so brilliantly as cleverer girls, having something of her uncle's tardiness of power.

Her determination to be a governess was as decided as ever, and it was first brought before her mother by an offer on Lady Adela's part to begin with her at once for Amice, who was now eleven years old.

'Really, now!' said Mrs. Morton, stopping short to express her offence.

'That is—' added Ida, equally at a loss.

'But what do you mean, mamma?' said Constance. 'I

Charlotte M. Yonge

always intended to be a teacher; I think it noble, useful work.'

'Oh, my poor child! what have they brought you to? Pretending such affection, too!'

'Indeed, mamma, I have meant this always. I could not be dependent all my life, you know. Do listen, mamma; don't Ida—'

'That my Lady Adela should insult us that way, when you are as good as she!'

'Nonsense, Ida! That has nothing to do with it. It is the greatest possible compliment, and I am very much pleased.'

'Just to live there, at her beck and call, drudging at that child's lessons!' sneered Ida.

'Yes, and when I made sure, at least after all the fuss they have made with you, that your aunt would present you at Court, and make you the young lady of the house, and marry you well, but there's no trust to be placed in them— none!'

'Oh, mamma, don't cry. I should not feel it right, unless Aunt Mary really needed me, and, though she is so kind and dear, she does not really. My only doubt is—'

'You have a doubt, then?'

'Yes. I should be so much fitter if I could go to one of the ladies' colleges, and then come back to dear little Amice, but now I have failed, I don't like to let Uncle Frank spend all that money on me, when I might be earning eighty pounds for myself.'

'Well, you are a strange girl, with no proper pride for your family,' said her mother.

And Ida chimed in: 'Yes. Do you think any one will be likely to marry you? or if you don't care about yourself, you might at least think of me!'

Mrs. Morton shed her ready tears when talking it over with Lady Northmoor.

'You see,' said Mary gently, 'I should like nothing better than to have dear little Conny to live with me like a daughter, but, for one thing, it would not be fair towards Ida, and besides, it would not be good for her in case she did not marry to have wasted these years.'

Mrs. Morton by no means appreciated the argument. However, Lord Northmoor put off the matter by deciding to send Constance to St. Hugh's Hall, thinking she really deserved such a reward to her diligence.

Charlotte M. Yonge

CHAPTER XXVIII

TWO BUNDLES OF HAY

Ida was, as all agreed, much improved in looks, style, and manners by her travels. Her illness had begun the work of fining her down from the bouncing heartiness of her girlhood, and she really was a handsome creature, with dark glowing colouring; her figure had improved, whether because or in spite of her efforts in that way might be doubtful; and she had learnt how to dress herself in fairly good taste.

Though neither Mademoiselle Gattoni nor the boarding-house society she had frequented was even second-rate in style, still there was an advance over her former Westhaven circle, with a good deal more restraint, so that she had almost insensibly acquired a much more ladylike air and deportment.

Moreover, the two years' absence had made some changes. The young men who had been in the habit of exchanging noisy jests with Ida had mostly drifted away in different directions or sobered down; girl companions had married off; and a new terrace had been completed with inhabitants and sojourners of a somewhat higher grade, who accepted Mrs. and Miss Morton as well connected.

Mr. Rollstone's lodgings were let to Mr. Deyncourt, a young clergyman who had come full of zeal to work up the growing district. He had been for a short time in the Northmoor neighbourhood, and had taken the duty there for a few weeks, so that he heard the name of Morton as prominent in good works, and had often seen Lady Adela and Constance with the Sunday-school. As Mr. Rollstone was not slow to mention the connection, he was not slow to call on Mrs. Morton and Miss Morton, in hopes of their co-operation, and as Mr. Rollstone had informed them that he was of 'high family' and of good private means, Mrs. Morton had a much better welcome for him than for his poor little predecessor, who lived over a shoemaker's shop, and, as she averred, never came except to ask subscriptions for some nonsense or other.

Mr. Deyncourt was a tall fine-looking man, and did not begin by asking subscriptions, but talked about Northmoor, Constance, and Lady Adela, so that Ida found herself affecting much closer knowledge of both than she really had.

'I found,' he said, 'that your sister is most valuable in the Sunday-school. I wonder if you would kindly assist us.'

Mrs. Morton began, 'My daughter is not strong, Mr. Deyncourt.'

And Ida simpered and said, hesitating, 'I—I don't know.'

If poor Mr. Brown had ever been demented enough even to make the same request, he would have met with a very different answer.

'I do not think it will be very fatiguing,' said Mr. Deyncourt. 'Do you know Mrs. Brandon? No! I will ask her to call and explain our plans. She is kind enough to let me meet the other teachers in her dining-room once a week to arrange the lessons for the Sunday. There are Miss Selwood and Mrs. and Miss Hume.'

These were all in the social position in which Ida was trying to establish her footing, and though she only agreed to 'think about it,' her mind was pretty well made up that it would be a very different thing from the old parish school where Rose Rollstone used to work among a set of small tradesmen's daughters.

When she found herself quite the youngest and best-looking of the party, she was entirely won over. There was no necessity for speaking so as to betray one's ignorance during Mr. Deyncourt's instructions, and she was a person of sufficient force and spirit to impose good order on her class; and thus she actually obtained the gratitude of the young clergyman as an efficient assistant.

Their domiciles being so near together, there were many encounters in going in and out, nor were these avoided on either side. Ida had a wonderful amount of questions to ask, and used to lie in wait to get them solved. It was very interesting to lay them before a handsome young clergy-man with a gentle voice, sweet smile, and ready attention, and religion seemed to have laid aside that element of dulness and moping which had previously repelled her.

She was embroidering a stole for Easter, and wanted a great deal of counsel for it; and she undertook to get a basket of flowers for Easter decorations from Northmoor, where her request caused some surprise and much satis-faction in the simple pair, who never thought of connec-ting the handsome young mission priest with this sudden interest in the Church.

And Mr. Deyncourt had no objection to drop in for

afternoon tea when he was met on the sands and had to be consulted about the stole, or to be asked who was worthy of broth, or as time went on to choose soup and practise a duet for the mission concert that was to keep people out of mischief on the Bank-holiday.

Ida had a voice, and music was the one talent she had cared to cultivate; she had had good lessons during her second winter abroad, and was an acquisition to the amateur company. Besides, what she cared for more, it was a real pleasure and rest to the curate to come in and listen to her or sing with her. She had learnt what kind of things offended good taste, and she set herself to avoid them and to school her mother into doing the same.

What Mr. Deyncourt thought or felt was not known, though thus much was certain, that he showed himself attentive enough to this promising young convert, and made Mrs. Brandon and other prudent, high-bred matrons somewhat uneasy.

And in the midst the *Morna* put in at Westhaven, and while Ida was walking home from Mrs. Brandon's, she encountered Mr. Brady, looking extremely well turned-out in yachting costume and smoking a short pipe.

There was something very flattering in the sound of the exclamation with which he greeted her; and then, as they shook hands, 'I should not have known you, Miss Morton; you are—' and he hesitated for a compliment—'such a stunner! What have you been doing to yourself?'

At the gate of the narrow garden, Mr. Deyncourt overtook them, carrying Ida's bag of books for her. She introduced them, and was convinced that they glared at each other.

And there ensued a time of some perplexity, but much

enjoyment, on Ida's part. Mr. Brady reviled the parson and all connected therewith in not very choice language, and the parson, on his side, though saying nothing, seemed to her to be on the watch, and gratified, if not relieved, when she remained steady to her parochial work.

And what was her mind? Personally, she had come to like and approve Mr. Deyncourt the most, and to have a sense that there was satisfaction in that to which he could lead her, while the better taste that had grown in her was sometimes offended, almost insulted, by Tom Brady's tendency to coarseness, and to treating her not as a lady, but as the Westhaven belle he had honoured with his attentions two years before. Yet she had an old kindness for him as her first love. And, moreover, he could give her eventually a title and very considerable wealth, a house in London, and all imaginable gaiety. While, as to Mr. Deyncourt, he was not poor and had expectations, but the utmost she could look to for him with confidence was Northmoor Vicarage after Mr. Woodman's time, and any-where the dull, sober, hard-working life of a clergyman's wife!

Which should she choose—that is, if she had her choice, or if either were in earnest? She was not sure of the curate, and therefore perhaps longed most that he should come to the point, feeling that this would anyway increase her self-esteem, and if she hesitated to bind herself to a life too high, and perhaps too dull, there was the dread, on the other hand, that his family, who, she understood, were very grand people, would object to a girl with nothing of her own and a governess sister.

On the other hand, the Bradys were so rich that they had little need to care for fortune—only, the richer people were, the greater their expectations—and she was more at ease with Tom than with Mr. Deyncourt. They would probably condone the want of fortune if she could write 'Honourable' before her name, or had any prospect of so doing, and the governess-ship might be a far greater drawback in their eyes than in those of the Deyncourts. 'However, thank goodness,' said she to herself, 'that won't begin for two or three years, and one or other will be hailed long before that—if—Oh, it is very hard to be kept out of everything by an old stick like Uncle Frank and a little wretch like Mite, who, after all, is a miserable Tyrolese, and not a Morton at all! It really is too bad!'

Charlotte M. Yonge

CHAPTER XXIX

JONES OR RATTLER

When Lord Northmoor had occasion to be in London he usually went alone, for to take the whole party was too expensive, and not good for little Michael. Besides, Bertha Morton had so urgently begged him to regard her house as always ready for him, that the habit had been established of taking up his quarters there.

Some important measures were coming on after Easter, and he had some other business, so that, in the form of words of which she longed to cure him, he told her that he was about to trespass on her hospitality for a week or fortnight.

'As long as ever you please,' she said. 'I am glad to have some one to sit opposite to me and tell me home news,' and they met at the station, she having been on an expedition on her own account, so that they drove home together.

No sooner were they within the house door than the parlour-maid began, 'That man has been here again, ma'am.'

'What, Jones?' said Bertha, in evident annoyance.

'Yes, ma'am, and I am sorry to say he saw little Cea. The child had run down after me when I answered the door, and he asked her if she did not know her own father, and if she would come with him. "No," she says, "I'm Miss Morton's," and he broke out with his ugly laugh, and says he, "You be, be you, you unnatural little vagabond?"— those were his very words, ma'am—"but a father is a father, and if he gives up his rights he must know the reason why." He wanted me, the good-for-nothing, to give him half a sovereign at once, or he would take off the child on the spot, but, by good luck, she had been frightened and run away, the dear, and I had got the door between me and him, so I told him to be off till you came home, or I would call for the police. So he was off for that time.'

'Quite right, Alice,' said Miss Morton, and then, leading the way upstairs and throwing herself down on a chair, she exclaimed, 'There, it ought to be a triumph to you, Northmoor! You told me that I should have trouble about poor little Cea's father, the brute!'

'Is he levying blackmail on you?'

'Yes. It is horribly weak of me, I know, and I can scarcely believe it of myself, but one can't abandon a child to a wretch like that, and he has the law on his side.'

'Are you quite sure of that? He deserted her, I think you said. If you could establish that, or prove a conviction against him—'

'Oh, I know she might be sent to an industrial school if I took it before a magistrate, but if the other alternative would be destruction, that would be misery to her. See—' and there was a little tap at the door. 'Come in, Cea. There, make your curtsey to his lordship.'

A pretty little fair-haired pale-cheeked girl, daintily but simply dressed, came in and made her curtsey very prettily, and replied nicely to Lord Northmoor's good-natured greeting and information that Michael had sent her a basket of primroses and a cowslip ball, which she would find in the hall.

'What do you say, Cea?' said Bertha, anxious to demonstrate her manners.

'Thank you, my lord, and Master Michael,' she uttered, but she was evidently preoccupied with what she had to tell Miss Morton. 'Oh'm, there was such a nasty man here! And he wanted me, and said he was my father, but he wasn't. He was the same man that gave Master Mite and me the bull's-eyes when we were naughty and Louisa went away.'

'Are you sure, Cea?' both exclaimed, but to the child of six the very eagerness of the question brought a certain confusion, and though more gently Lord Northmoor asked her to describe him, she could not do it, and indeed she had been only five when the encounter had taken place. The urgency of the inquiry somehow seemed to dispose her to cry, as if she thought she had been naughty, and she had to be dismissed to the cowslip ball.

'If the child is right, that man cannot be her father at all,' said Lord Northmoor. 'That man's name is Rattler, and he is well known at Westhaven.'

'Should you know him?'

'I never saw him, but I could soon find those who have done so.'

'If we could only prove it! Oh, what a relief it would be! I dare not even send the child to school—as I meant to do, Northmoor, for indeed we don't spoil her—for fear she should be kidnapped; and I don't know if the school-board officer won't be after her, and I can't give as a reason "for fear she should be stolen by her father."'

'Not exactly. It ought to be settled once for all. Perhaps the child will tell more when you have her alone.'

'Is not Rattler only too like a nickname, or is he a native of Westhaven?'

This Lord Northmoor thought he could find out, but the dinner was hardly over before a message came that the man Jones had called again.

'Perhaps I had better see him alone,' said the guest, and Bertha was only too glad to accept the offer, so he proceeded to the little room opening into the hall, where interviews with tradesfolk or petitioners were held.

The man had a blue jersey, a cap, and an evidently sailor air, or rather that of the coasting, lower stamp of seaman; but he was tall, rather handsome, and younger-looking than would have been expected of Cea's father. He looked somewhat taken aback by the appearance of a gentleman, but he stood his ground.

'So I understand that you have been making demands upon Miss Morton,' Lord Northmoor began.

'Well, sir, my lord, a father has his feelings. There is a situation offered me in Canada, and I intend to take the little girl with me.'

'Oh, indeed!' And there was a pause.

'Or if the lady has taken a fancy to her, I'd not baulk her for a sum down of twenty or five-and-twenty, once for all.'

'Oh, indeed!' again; then 'What do you say is the child's name?'

'Jones, my lord.'

'Her Christian name, I mean?'

He scratched his head. 'Cissy, my lord—Celia—Cecilia. Blest if I'm sure!' as he watched the expression of the questioner. 'You see, the women has such fine names, and she was always called Baby when her poor mother was alive.'

'Where was she baptized?'

'Well, you see, my lord, the women-folk does all that, and I was at sea; and by and by I comes home to find my poor wife dead, and the little one gone.'

'I suppose you are aware that you can have no legal claim to the child without full proof of her belonging to you— the certificate of your marriage and a copy of the register of her birth?'

The man was scarcely withheld from imprecations upon the work that was made about it, when Miss Morton had been quite satisfied on a poor fellow's word.

'Yes, ladies may be satisfied for a time, but legally more than your word is required, and you will remember that unless you can bring full proof that this is your child, there is such a thing as prosecution for obtaining money on false pretences.'

'And how is a poor fellow to get the fees for them register clerks and that?' said the man, in a tone waxing insolent.

'I will be answerable for the fees, if you will tell me where the certificates are to be applied for.'

'Well, how is a cove to know what the women did when he was at sea? She died at Rotherhithe, anyway, so the child will be registered there.'

'And the marriage? You were not at sea then, I suppose?'

But the man averred that there were so many churches that there was no telling one from another, and with a knowing look declared that the gals were so keen after a man that they put up the banns and hauled him where they would.

He was at last got rid of, undertaking to bring the proofs of his paternity, without which Lord Northmoor made it clear to him that he was to expect neither child nor money.

'I greatly doubt whether you will see any more of him,' said Lord Northmoor when describing the interview.

'Oh, Frank,' cried Bertha, calling him thus for the first time, 'I do not know how to thank you enough. You have done me an infinite kindness.'

'Do not thank me yet,' he answered, 'for though I do not in the least believe that this fellow is the child's father, he may find his way to the certificates or get them forged; and it would be well to trace what has become of the real Jones, as well as to make out about this Rattler. Is it true that the wife died at Rotherhithe?'

Charlotte M. Yonge

'Quite true, poor thing. I believe they had lived there since the marriage.'

'I will run down there if you can give me the address, and see if I can make out anything about her husband, and see whether any one can speak to his identity with this man.'

'You are a man of gold! To think of your taking all this trouble!'

'I only hope I may succeed. It is a return to old habits of hunting up evidence.'

Bertha was able to give the address of the lodging-house where poor Mrs. Jones had died, and the next morning produced another document, which had been shut up in the Bible that had been rescued for the child, namely the marriage lines of David Jones and Lucy Smith at the parish church of the last Lord Northmoor's residence in town.

To expect a clergyman or clerk to remember the appearance of a bridegroom eight years ago was too much, even if they were the same who had officiated; but Bertha undertook to try, and likewise to consult a former fellow-servant of poor Lucy, who was supposed to have abetted her unfortunate courtship. Frank, after despatching a letter of inquiry to his sister-in-law about 'Sam Rattler,' set forth by train and river steamer for Rotherhithe.

When they met again in the evening, Bertha had only made out from the fellow-servant that the stoker was rather small, and had a reddish beard and hair, wherewith Cea's complexion corresponded.

The Rotherhithe discoveries had gone farther. Lord Northmoor had penetrated to the doleful den where the poor woman had died, and no wonder! for it seemed, as Bertha had warned him, a nest of fever and horrible smells. The landlady remembered her death, which had been made memorable by Miss Morton's visits; but knew not whence she had come, though, stimulated by half-a-crown, she mentioned a small grocery shop where more might be learnt. There the woman did recollect Mrs. Jones as a very decent lady, and likewise her being in better lodgings until deserted by her husband, the scamp, who had gone off in an Australian steamer.

At these lodgings the inquiry resulted in the discovery of the name of the steamer; and there was still time to look up the agent and the date approximately enough to obtain the list of the crew, with David Jones among them. It further appeared that this same David Jones had fallen overboard and been drowned, but as he had not entered himself as a married man, his wife had remained in ignorance of his fate. It was, however, perfectly clear that the little girl was an orphan, and that Bertha might be quite undisturbed in the possession of her.

And thus Lord Northmoor came home a good deal fagged, and shocked by the interior he had seen at Rotherhithe, but quite triumphant.

Bertha was delighted, and declared herself eternally grateful to him; and she could not but entertain the hope that the *soi-disant* parent would make another application, in which case she was quite prepared to give him into custody; and she proceeded to reckon up the number of times that he had applied to her, and the amount that he had extracted, wondering at herself for not having asked for proofs, but owning that she had been afraid of being thus compelled to give up the child to perdition.

The applications had all been within the last year, so that

Charlotte M. Yonge

the man had probably learnt from Louisa Hall, the nursery-maid, that Cea was the child of a deserted wife.

A letter from Mrs. Morton gave some of the antecedents of Sam Rattler, as learnt from Mrs. Hall, the charwoman, whose great dread he was. His real surname was Jones, and he was probably a Samuel Jones whose name Lord Northmoor had noted as a boy on board David's ship. He belonged to a decent family in a country village, but had run away to sea, and was known at Westhaven by this nickname. He had a brother settled in Canada, who had lately written to propose to him a berth on one of the Ontario steamers, and it was poor Mrs. Hall's dread that her daughter should accompany him, though happily want of money prevented it. As to his appearance, as to which there had been special inquiries, he was a tall fine-looking man, with a black beard, and half the girls at Westhaven were fools enough to be after him.

All this tallied with what had been gathered from the child, and this last had probably been a bold attempt to procure the passage-money for his sweetheart.

He never did call again, having probably been convinced of the failure of his scheme, and scenting danger, so that every day for a fortnight Bertha met her cousin with a disappointed 'No Rattler!'

CHAPTER XXX

SCARLET FEVER

There was a meeting of one of the many charitable societies to which Bertha had made Lord Northmoor give his name, and she persuaded him to stay on another day for it, though he came down in the morning with a sore throat and heavy eyes, and, contrary to his usual habits, lay about in an easy-chair, and dozed over the newspaper all the morning.

When he found himself unable to eat at luncheon, she allowed that he was not fit for the meeting, but demurred when he declared that he should go home at once that afternoon to let Mary nurse his cold. The instinct of getting back to wife and home were too strong for Bertha to contend with, and he started, telegraphing to Northmoor to be met at the station.

Perhaps there were delays, as in his oppressed and dazed state he had mistaken the trains, for he did not arrive at home till nine o'clock instead of seven, and then he looked so ill as he stumbled into the hall, dazzled by the lights, that Mary looked at him in much alarm.

'Yes,' he said hoarsely, 'I have a bad cold and sore throat, and I thought I had better come home at once.'

Charlotte M. Yonge

'Indeed you had! If only you have not made it worse by the journey!'

Which apparently he had done, for he could scarcely swallow the warm drinks brought to him, and had such a night, that when steps were heard in the house, he said—

'Mary, dear, don't let Mite come in. I am afraid it is too late to keep you away, but if I had felt like this yesterday, I would have gone straight to the fever hospital.'

'Oh no, no, what should you do but come home to me? Was it that horrible place at Rotherhithe?'

'Perhaps. It is just a fortnight since, and I felt a strange shudder and chill as I was talking. But it may be nothing; only keep Mite away till I have seen Trotman. My Mary, don't look like that! It may be nothing, and we have been very happy—thank God.'

Poor Mary, in a choking state, hurried away to send for the doctor, and to despatch orders to Nurse Eden to confine Master Michael to the nursery and garden for the present, her sinking and foreboding heart forbidding her to approach the child herself.

The verdict of the doctor confirmed these alarms, for all the symptoms of scarlet fever had by that time manifested themselves. Mary had gone through the disease long before, and had nursed through more than one outbreak at Miss Lang's, so her husband might take the comfort of knowing that there was little anxiety on her account, though the doctor, evidently expecting a severe attack, insisted on sending in a trained nurse to assist her.

As the little boy had fortunately been in bed and asleep long before his father came home, there was as yet no danger of infection for him, though he must be sent out of the house at once.

Lady Adela was not at home, and Mary would have doubted about sending him to the Cottage, even if she had been there; so she quickly made up her mind that Eden and the young nursery-maid should take him at once to Westhaven, to be either in the hotel or at Northmoor Cottage, according as his aunt should decide.

How little she had thought, when she heard him say his prayers, and exchanged kisses with him at the side of his little bed, that it was the last time for many a long day; and that her hungry spirit would have to feed itself on that last smile and kiss of the fat hand, as she looked out of her husband's window as the carriage drove away.

Lady Adela knew too well what it was to be desolate not to come home so as to be at hand, though she left her little daughter at her uncle's. Bertha came on the following day.

'I feel as if it were all my doing,' she said. 'I could not bear it, if it does not go well with him, after being the saving of poor little Cea.'

'There is nothing to reproach yourself with,' said sober-minded Lady Adela. 'Neither you nor he could guess that he was running into infection.'

'No,' said Bertha; 'of course, one never thinks of such things with grown-up people, especially one whom one has always thought of as a stick, and to whom perhaps ascribed some of its toughness,' she added, smiling; 'but he did come home looking very white and worn-out, and complained of horrible smells. No, dear man, he was far too punctilious to use the word, he only said that he should like to send the Sanitary Commission down the

Charlotte M. Yonge

alley. I ought to have dosed him with brandy on the spot, for of course he was too polite to ask for it, so I only gave him a cup of *tea*,' said Bertha, with an infinite tone of scorn in the name of the beverage.

'Will it be any comfort to tell you that most likely it would have been too late even if he would have accepted it? Come, Bertha, how often are we told that we are not to think so much of consequences as of actions, and there was nothing blameworthy in the whole business.'

'Except that I was such a donkey as not to have begun by asking for the man's proofs, but I was so much afraid that he would pounce on the child that I only thought of buying him off from time to time. I did not know I was so weak. Well, at any rate, with little Mite to the fore, the place will be left in good hands. I like Herbert on the whole, but to have that woman reigning as Madame Mere would be awful.'

'Nay, I trust we are not coming to that! Trotman says it is a thoroughly severe attack, but not abnormally malignant, as he calls it. It is a matter of nursing, he tells me, and that he has of the best—a matter of nursing and of prayer, and that,' added Adela, her eyes filling with tears, 'I am sure he has.'

'And yet—and yet,' Bertha broke off.

'Ah, you are thinking how we prayed before! And yet, Birdie, after these six years of seeing his rule and recognising what mine would have been, I see it was for the best that my own little Michael was taken to his happy home.'

'You'll call it for the best now,' said Bertha grimly.

'If it be so, it will prove itself; but I really do not see any special cause for extra fear.'

Lady Adela and Bertha both thought themselves as far safe as any one can be with scarlet fever, and would gladly have taken a share in the nursing. Bertha, however, had far too much of the whirlwind in her to be desirable in a sick house, and on the principle that needless risk was wrong, was never admitted within the house doors, but Lady Adela insisted on seeing Mary every day, and was assured that she should be a welcome assistant in case of need; but at present there was no necessity of calling in other help, the form of fever being lethargic with much torpidity, but no violence of delirium, and requiring no more watching than the wife and nurse could give.

Frank never failed to know his Mary, and to respond when she addressed him; but she was told never to attempt more than rousing him when it was needful to make him take food. He had long ago, with the precaution of his legal training, made every needful arrangement for her and for his son; and even on the first day, he had not seemed to trouble himself on these points, being too heavy and oppressed for the power of looking forward. So the days rolled on in one continual watch on Mary's part, during which she seemed only to live in the present, and, secure that her boy was safe, would not risk direct communication with him or with his nurse.

Lady Adela had undertaken to keep Constance, the person who really loved her uncle best, daily informed, and she also wrote at intervals to Mrs. Morton, by special desire of Lady Northmoor, and likewise to her own old servant, Eden, the nurse. She wrote cheerfully, but Eden had other correspondents in the servants' hall, who dwelt sensationally on the danger, as towards Whitsun week the fever began to run higher towards the crisis, the strength was

Charlotte M. Yonge

reduced, the torpor became heavier; and anxiety increased as to whether there would be power of rally in a man who, though healthy, had never been strong.

The anxiety manifested by the entire neighbourhood was a notable proof of the estimation in which the patient was held, and was very far from springing only from pity or humanity. Half the people who came to Lady Adela for further information had some cause going on in which 'That Stick' was one of the most efficient of props.

CHAPTER XXXI

MITE

Little Michael Morton was in the meantime installed in his aunt's house. For him to be anywhere else was not to be thought of, and Mrs. Morton was soft-hearted enough to be very fond of such a bright little boy, so much in her own hands, and very amusing with the old-fashioned formal ways derived from chiefly consorting with older people.

Besides, the pretty little fellow was an object of great interest to all her acquaintances, especially as it was understood at Westhaven that it was only too possible that he might any day become Lord Northmoor; and never had Mrs. Morton's drawing-room been so much resorted to by visitors anxious for bulletins, or perhaps more truly for excitement. Mite was a young gentleman of some dignity. He sat elevated on a hassock upon a chair to dine at luncheon-time, comporting himself most correctly; but his aunt was sorely chafed at Eden's standing behind his chair, like Sancho's physician, to regulate his diet, and placing her veto upon lobsters, cucumbers, pastry, and glasses of wine with lumps of sugar in them.

It amounted to a trial of strength between aunt and nurse. Michael submitted once or twice, when told that his

Charlotte M. Yonge

mamma would not approve, but the lobster struck him with extreme amazement and admiration, and he could not believe but that the red, long-whiskered monster was not as good as he was beautiful.

'He has got a glove like what Peter wears to cut the holly hedge,' exclaimed the boy, to the general amusement. 'Where's his hand?'

'My Mite shall have a bit of his funny hand,' said Mrs. Morton, and Ida was dealing with the claw, when Eden interposed and said she did not think her ladyship would wish Master Michael to have any.

'Just a taste, nurse, with some of the cream,' said Mrs. Morton. 'Here, Mitey dear.'

'No, Master Michael, mamma would say no,' said Eden.

'Really, Eden, you might let Mrs. Morton judge in her own house,' said Ida.

'Master Morton is under my charge, ma'am, and I am responsible for him,' said Eden, respectfully but firmly. But Ida held out the claw, and Michael made a dart at it.

Eden again said 'No,' but he looked up at her with an exulting roguish grin, and clasped it, whereupon she laid hold of him by the waist, and bore him off, kicking and roaring, amid the pitiful and indignant exclamations of his aunt and cousin.

It may be that the faithful Eden was somewhat wanting in tact, by her determined attention to the routine that chafed her hosts; but she had been forced to come away without directions, and could only hold fast to the discipline of her well-ordered nursery under all obstacles.

Master Michael was to have his cup of milk and run on the beach with the nursery-maid long before the usual awakening of the easy-going household, which regarded late hours as belonging to gentility; then, after the general breakfast, his small lessons, over which there often was a battle, first, because he felt injured by not doing them with his mother, and next, because his hostesses regarded them as a hardship, and taught him to cry over 'Reading without tears,' besides detaining him as late as they could over the breakfast, or proposing to take him out at once, without waiting for that quarter of an hour's work. Or when out-of-doors, they would not bring him home for the siesta, on which his nurse insisted, though it was often only lying down in the dark; nor had Mrs. Morton any scruple in breaking it, if she wanted to exhibit him to her friends, though if it were interrupted or omitted, the child's temper was the worse all the afternoon.

'That nurse is a thorough tyrant over the poor little darling, and a very impertinent woman besides,' said Mrs. Morton.

'A regular little spoiled brat,' Ida declared him.

While certainly the worse his father was said to be, the more his aunt tried to spoil and indulge him, as a relief to her pity and grief.

He had missed his home and parents a good deal at first, had cried at his lessons, and cried more at not having father to carry him to the nursery, nor mother to hear him say his prayers and kiss him at night; but time wore off the association, and he was full of delight at the sea, the ships, the little crabs, and all the other charms of the shore.

Above all, he was excited about the little boys. His own

kind had never come in his way before, his chief playfellow being Amice, who was so much older as to play with him condescendingly and always give way to him. There was a large family in a neighbouring lodging containing what he respectfully called 'big knicker-bocker boys,' who excited his intense admiration, and drew him like a magnet.

For once Mrs. Morton and Eden were agreed as to the propriety of the companionship, since Rollstone had pronounced them of 'high family,' and the governess who was in charge of them was quite ready to be interested in the solitary little stranger, even if he had not been the Honourable Michael. So was the elder girl of the party, but, unluckily, Michael was just of the age to be a great nuisance to children who played combined and imaginative games which he could not yet understand.

When they were making elaborate approaches to a sand fortification, erected with great care and pains, he would dash on it with a *coup de main*, break it down at once with his spade, and stand proudly laughing and mixing up the ruins together, heedless of the howls of anger of the besiegers, and believing that he had done the right thing.

And once, when a wrathful boy of eight had shaken the troublesome urchin as he would have done his own junior, had this last presumed to stir up his clear pool of curiosities, most of the female portion of the family had taken the part of the intruder, and cried shame on any one who could hurt or molest a poor dear little boy away from a father who was so ill!

Thus the Lincoln family, for the sake of peace and self-defence, used sedulously to flee at the approach of Mite, and seek for secluded coves to which he was not likely to penetrate.

Mr. Rollstone was Eden's great solace. They discovered that they had once been staying in the same country-house, and had a great number of common acquaintances in the upper-servant world, and they entirely agreed in their estimate of Mrs. Morton and Ida, whom Mr. Rollstone pronounced to be neither fish, flesh, nor fowl, though as for Miss Constance, she was a lady all over, and always had been, and there might have been hopes for Mr. Herbert, if only he could have got into the army.

To sit with Mr. Rollstone, whom the last winter's rheumatics had left very infirm, was Eden's chief afternoon employment, as she could not follow her charge's wanderings on the beach, but had to leave him to the nursery-maid, Ellen. The old butler wanted much to show 'Miss Eden' his daughter, who took advantage of Whit-Sunday and the Bank-holiday to run down and see her parents, though at the next quarter she was coming home for good, extremely sorry to leave her advantages in London, and the friends she had made there, but feeling that her parents needed her so much that she must pursue her employment at home.

They were all very anxious on that Whit-Sunday, and Rose carried with her something of Constance's feeling, as with tears in her eyes she looked at the little fellow at the children's service, standing by his nurse, with wide open, inquiring eyes, chiefly fixed upon Willie Lincoln in satisfaction whenever an answer proceeded from that object of his unrequited attachment. With the young maiden's love of revelling in supposed grief, Rose already pitied the fair-faced, unconscious child as fatherless, and weighted with heavy responsibilities.

Another pair of eyes looked at the boy, not with pity, but indignant impatience.

Perhaps even already that little pretender was the only obstacle between Herbert and the coronet that was his by right, between Ida herself and—

Ida had walked from the school to the church with Mr. Deyncourt, and he had talked so gently and pitifully of the family distress, and assumed so much grief on her part, that his sympathy made her heart throb; above all, when he told her that his two sisters were coming to stay with him, Mrs. Rollstone had contrived to make room for them, and they would show her, better than he could, some of the plans he wished to have carried out with the little children.

So he wished to introduce her to his sisters! What did that mean? If the Deyncourts were ever so high they could not sneer at Lord Northmoor's sisters.

Then she thought of many a novel, and in real life, of what she believed respecting that lost lover of Miss Morton's. And later in the day Tom Brady lounged up to Northmoor Cottage, and leaning with one elbow on the window-sill, while the other arm held away the pipe he had just taken from his lips, he asked if they would give him a cup of tea, the whole harbour was so full of such beastly, staring cads that there was no peace there. One ought to give such places a wide berth at Whitsuntide.

'I wonder you did not,' said Ida, as she hastened to compound the tea.

'Forgot it,' he lazily droned, 'forgot it. Attractions, you know,' and, as she brought the cup to the window, with a lump of sugar in the tongs, 'when sugar fingers are—' and the speech ended in a demonstration at the fingers that made Ida laugh, blush, and say, 'Oh, for shame, Mr. Brady!'

'You had better come in, Mr. Brady,' called Mrs. Morton. 'You can't drink it comfortably there, and you'll be upsetting it. We are down in the dining-room to-day, because—'

The cause, necessary to her gentility, was lost, as Ida proceeded to let him in at the front door, and he presently deposited himself on the sofa, grumbling complacently at the bore of holidays, especially bank holidays. His crew would have been ready to strike, he declared, if he had taken them out of harbour, or he would have asked the ladies to come on a cruise out of the way of it all.

'Why, thank you very much, Mr. Brady, but, really in my poor brother, Lord Northmoor's state, I don't know that it would be etiquette.'

'Ah, yes. By the bye, how's the governor?'

'Very sad, strength failing. I hardly expect to hear he is alive to-morrow,' and Mrs. Morton's handkerchief was raised.

'Oh ay, sad enough, you know! I say, will it make any difference to you?'

'My poor, dear brother! Well, it ought, you know. Indeed it would if it had not been for that dear little boy. My poor Herbert!'

'It must have been an awful sell for him.'

'Yes,' said Ida, 'and some people think there was something very odd about it all—the child being born out in the Dolomites, with nobody there!'

'Don't, Ida, I can't have you talk so,' protested her mother.

'Supposititious, by all that's lucky! I should strangle him!' and Mr. Brady put back his head and laughed a loud and hearty laugh, by no means elegant, but without much sound of truculent intentions.

CHAPTER XXXII

A SHOCK

It was on the Thursday of Whitsun-week when Lady Adela and Bertha came down from their visit of inquiry, a little more hopeful than on the previous day, though they could not yet say that recovery was setting in.

But a great shock awaited them. The parlour-maid met them at the door, pale and tearful. 'Oh, my lady, Mrs. Eden's come, and—'

Poor Eden herself was in the hall, and nothing was to be heard but 'Oh, my lady!' and another tempest of sobs.

'Come in, Eden,' scolded Bertha, in her impatience. 'Don't keep us in this way. What has happened to the child? Let us have it at once! The worst, or you wouldn't be here.'

For all answer, Eden held up a little wooden spade, a sailor hat, and a shoe showing traces of sand and sea-water.

'It is so then,' said Lady Adela. 'Oh, his mother! But,' after that one wail, she thought of the poor woman before her, 'I am sure you are not to blame, Eden.'

Charlotte M. Yonge

'Oh, my lady, if I could but feel that! But that I should have trusted the darling out of my sight for a moment!'

Presently they brought her to a state in which she could tell her lamentable history.

She had been spending the afternoon at Mr. Rollstone's, leaving Master Michael as usual in the care of the underling, Ellen, and after that she knew no more till neither child nor maid came home at his supper-time, and Mrs. Morton was slowly roused to take alarm, while Eden, half distracted, wandered about, seeking her charge, and found Ellen, calling and shouting in vain for him. Ellen confessed that she had seen him running after the Lincoln children, and supposing him with them, had given herself up to the study of a penny dreadful in company with another young nursemaid. When they had awakened to real life, the first idea had been that he must be with these children; but they were gone, and Ellen, fancying that he might have gone home with them, asked at their lodging, but no, he was not there.

The tide was by this time covering the beach, and driving away the miserable maids, with the aunt, cousin and others who had been on the fruitless quest. No more could be done then, and they went home with desolation in their hearts. Miss Ida, as Eden declared, stayed out long after everybody else when it was clearly of no use, and came back so tired and upset that she went up straight to bed. There was still a hope that some one might have met the little boy and taken him home, unable clearly to make out to whom he belonged, more especially as the Lincolns in terror and compunction had confessed that they had seen him and his nurse from a distance, and had rushed headlong round a projecting rock into a cove, hoping that he had not seen them, because he was so tiresome and spoilt all their games. And when that morning the spade, hat, and shoe were discovered upon the shore, not far from the very rock, the poor children had to draw plenty of morals on the consequences of selfishness. No doubt that poor little Michael had pursued them barefooted and gone too near the waves!

There was nothing more but the forlorn hope that the waves would restore the little body they had carried off, and Mrs. Morton was watching for that last sad satisfaction. In case of that contingency, Ellen, as the last person known to have seen the boy, had been left at Westhaven, in agonies of despair, vowing that she would never speak to any one, nor look at a story-book again in her life. She had attempted the excuse that she thought she saw Miss Ida going in that direction, but the young lady had declared that she had never been on the beach at all that afternoon till after the alarm had been given; and had been extremely angry with Ellen for making false excuses and trying to shift off the blame, and the girl had been much terrified, and owned that she was not at all sure.

'And oh, my lady,' entreated Eden, 'don't send me up to the House! Don't make me face her ladyship! I should die of it!'

'We must think what is to be done about that,' said Lady Adela. 'Can you tell whether any one from the House has seen you?'

Eden thought not, and after she had been consigned to her friend, Lady Adela's maid, to be rested, fed, and comforted as far as might be possible, the sisters-in-law held sad counsel, and agreed that it was not safe to keep back the terrible news from the poor mother who expected daily tidings of her child, and might hear some report, in spite of her shut-up state.

Charlotte M. Yonge

'Poor Adela, I pity you almost as much as her,' said Bertha.

'Oh, I know now how much I have to be thankful for! No uncertainty—and my little one's grave.'

'Besides Amice. Let me drive you up, Addie. Your heart is beating enough to knock you down.'

'Well, I believe it is. But not up to the front door. I will go in by the garden. Oh, may he be spared to her at least!'

Very pale then Lady Adela crept in, meeting a weeping maid who was much relieved to see her, but was hardly restrained from noisy sobs. Mr. Trotman, she said, had come just before the garden boy had inevitably dashed up with the tidings, and the household had been waiting till he came out, to secure that he should be near when Lady Northmoor was told.

Adela felt that this might be the safest opportunity, and sent a message to the door to beg that her ladyship would come and speak to her for a few minutes in the study.

Mary's soft step was soon there, and her lips were framing the words, 'No ground lost,' when at sight of Adela's face the light went out of her eyes, and setting herself firmly on her feet, she said, 'You have bad news. My boy!'

Adela came near and would have taken her hand, saying—'My poor Mary'—but she clasped them both as if to hold herself together, and said, 'The fever!'

'No, no—sadder still! Drowned!'

'Ah, then there was not all that suffering, and without me! Thankworthy— Oh no, no, please'—as Lady Adela, with eyes brimming over, would have pressed her to her bosom—'don't—don't upset me, or I could not attend to Frank. It all turns on this one day, they say, and I must—I must be as usual. There will be time enough to know all about it—if'—with a long oppressed gasp—'he is saved from the hearing it.'

'I think you are right, dear,' said Adela, 'if you keep him—' but she could not go on.

'Well, any way,' said Mary, 'either he will be given back, or he will be saved this. Let me go back to him, please.' Then at the door, putting her hand to her head—'Who is here?'

'Poor Eden.'

'Ah, let her and Emma know that I am sure it is not their fault. Come again to-morrow, please; I think he will be better.'

She went away in that same gliding manner, perfectly tearless. Adela waited to see the doctor, who assured her that the patient had rather gained than lost during the last twenty-four hours, and that if he could be spared from any shock or agitation he would probably recover. Lady Northmoor seemed so entirely absorbed by his critical state, that she was not likely to betray the sad knowledge she had put aside in the secret chamber of her heart, more especially as her husband was still too much weighed down, and too slumberous to be observant, or to speak much, and knowing the child to be out of the house, he did not inquire for him.

Nevertheless, Mr. Trotman gladly approved of Lady Adela's intention of sleeping in the house in case of any sudden collapse; and the servants, who were not to let

Charlotte M. Yonge

Lady Northmoor know, evidently felt this a great relief.

'Yes, it is a comfort to think some one will be within that poor thing's reach,' said Bertha, as they went back together, 'and, if you can bear it, you are the right person.'

'She will not let herself dwell on it. She never even looked at Mrs. Morton's letter.'

'And I really hope they won't find the poor little dear, to have all the fuss and heart-rending.'

'Oh, Birdie!'

'There's only one thing that would make me wish it. I'm quite sure that that Miss Ida knows more about it than she owns. No, you need not say, "Oh, Birdie" again; I don't suspect her of the deed, but I do believe she saw the boy and kept out of his way, and now wants that poor Ellen to have all the blame!'

'You will believe nothing against a girl out of an orphanage!'

'I had rather any day believe Ellen Mole than Ida Morton. There's something about that girl which has always revolted me. I would never trust her farther than I could see her!'

'Prejudice, Birdie; because she is in bad style.'

'You to talk of prejudice, Addie, who hardly knew how to go on living here under the poor stick!'

'Don't, Birdie. He has earned esteem by sheer goodness. Poor man, I don't know what to wish for him when I think of the pang that awaits him.'

'You know what to wish for yourself and Northmoor! Not but that Herbert may come to good if he doesn't come into possession for many a long year.'

'And now I must write to that poor child, Constance. But oh, Bertha, don't condemn hastily! Haven't I had enough of that?'

Charlotte M. Yonge

CHAPTER XXXIII

DARKNESS

Full a week later, Frank looked up from his pillow, and said, 'I wonder when it will be safe to have Mite back. Mary, sweet, what is it? I have been sure something was burthening you. Come and tell me. If he has the fever, you must go to him. No!' as she clasped his hand and laid her face down on the pillow.

'Ah, Frank, he does not want us any more!'

'My Mary, my poor Mary, have you been bearing such knowledge about with you? For how long?'

'Since that worst day, yesterday week. Oh, but to see you getting better was the help!'

'Can you tell me?'

She told him, in that low, steady voice, all she knew. It was very little, for she had avoided whatever might break the composure that seemed so needful to his recovery; and he could listen quietly, partly from the lulling effect of weakness, partly from his anxiety for her, and the habit of self-restraint, in which all the earlier part of their lives had been passed, made utterance come slowly to them.

'Life will be different to us henceforth,' he once said. 'We have had three years of the most perfect happiness. He gave and He hath taken away. Blessed—'

And there he stopped, for he saw the working of her face. Otherwise they hardly spoke of their loss even to one another. It went down deeper than they could bear to utter, and their hearts and eyes met if their lips did not. Only Lord Northmoor lay too dejected to make the steps expected in the recovery of strength for a few days after the grievous revelation, and on the day when at last he was placed on a couch by the window, his wife collapsed, and, almost unconscious, was carried to her bed.

It was not a severe or alarming attack, and all she wanted was to be let alone; but there was enough of sore throat and other symptoms to prolong the quarantine, and Lady Adela could no longer be excluded from giving her aid. She went to and fro between the patients, and comforted each with regard to the other, telling the one how her husband's strength was returning, and keeping the other tranquil by the assurance that what his wife most needed was perfect rest, especially from the necessity of restraining herself. Those eyes showed how many tears were poured forth when they could have their free course. Lady Adela had gone through enough to feel with ready tact what would be least jarring to each. She had persuaded Bertha to go back to London, both to her many avocations and to receive Amice, who must still be kept at a distance for some time.

Lord Northmoor, as soon as he had strength and self-command for it, read poor Mrs. Morton's letters, and also saw Eden, for whom there was little fear of infection. She managed to tell her history and answer all his questions in detail, but she quite broke down under his kind tone of forgiveness and assurance that no blame attached to her, and that he was only grateful to her for her tender care of his child, and she went away sobbing pitifully.

Adela came back, after taking her from the room, where Frank was sitting in an easy-chair by the window, and looking out on the summer garden, which seemed to be stripped of all its charm and value for him.

'Poor thing,' she said, 'she is quite overcome by your kindness.'

'I do not think any one is more to be pitied,' said he.

'No, indeed, but she wishes you would have heard what she had to say about the supposing Ida to have gone in that direction.'

'I thought it better not. It would not have exonerated the poor little maid from carelessness, and there is no use in fostering a sense of injury or suspicion, when what is done cannot be undone,' he said wearily.

'Indeed you are quite right,' said Adela earnestly. 'You know how to be in charity with all men. Oh, the needless misery of hasty unjust suspicions!' Then as he looked up at her—'Do you know our own story?'

'Only the main facts.'

'I think you ought to know it. It accounts for so much!' said she, moved partly by the need of utterance, and partly by the sense that the turn of his thoughts might be good for him. 'You know what a passion for horses there has always been in this family.'

'I know—I could have had it if my life had begun more prosperously.'

'And you have done your best to save Herbert from it. Well, my Arthur had it to a great degree; and so indeed had Bertha. They were brought up to nothing else; Bertha was, I really think, a better judge than her brother, she was not so reckless. They became intimate with a Captain Alder, who was in the barracks at Copington—much the nicest, as I used to think, of the set, though I was not very glad to see an attachment growing up between him and Bertha. There was always such a capacity of goodness in her that I longed to see her in the way of being raised altogether.'

'She has always been most kind to us. There is much to admire in her.'

'Her present life has developed all that is best; but—' She hesitated, wondering whether the good simple man were sensible of that warp in the nature that she had felt. She went on, 'Then she was a masterful, high-spirited girl, to whom it seemed inevitable to come to high words with any one about whom she cared. And I must say—she and my husband, while they were passionately fond of one another, seemed to have a sort of fascination in provoking one another, not only in words but in deeds. Ah, you can hardly believe it of her! How people get tamed! Well, Arthur bought a horse, a beautiful creature, but desperately vicious. Captain Alder had been with him when he first saw it, and admired it; but I do not think gave an opinion against it. Bertha, however, from the moment she saw its eyes and ears, protested against it in her vehement way. I remember imploring her not to make Arthur defy her; but really when they got into those moods, I don't think they could stop themselves, and she thought Captain Alder encouraged him. So Arthur went out on that fatal drive in the dog-cart, and no sooner were they out on the Colbeam road than the horse bolted, they came into collision with a hay waggon. And—'

Charlotte M. Yonge

'I know!'

'Captain Alder was thrown on the top of the hay and not hurt. He came to prepare me to receive Arthur, and then went up to the house. Bertha, poor girl, in her wild grief almost flew at him. It was all his doing, she said; he had egged Arthur on; she supposed Arthur had bets. In short, she knew not what she said; but he left the house, and never has been near her again.'

'Were they engaged?'

'Not quite formally, but they understood one another, and were waiting for a favourable moment with old Lord Northmoor, who was not easy to deal with, and it was far from being a good match anyway. We all thought, I believe, that the drive was the fault or rather the folly of Captain Alder, and Arthur was too ill to explain— unconscious at first—then not rousing himself. At last he asked for his friend, and then he told me that Captain Alder had done all in his power to prevent his taking the creature out—had told him he had no right to endanger his life; and when only laughed at, had insisted on going with him, in hopes, I suppose, of averting mischief. I wrote—Lord Northmoor wrote to him at his quarters; but our letters came back to us. We had kept no watch on the gazette, and he had retired and left no address with his brother-officers. Bertha knew that his parents were dead, and that he had a sister at school at Clifton. I wrote to her, but the mistress sent back my letter; and we found that he had fetched away his sister and gone. Even his money was taken from Coutts's, as if to cut off any clue.'

'He should not have so attended to a girl in her angry grief.'

'No, but I think there was some self-blame in him, though

not about that horse. I believe he thought he might have checked Arthur more. And he had debts which he seems to have paid on selling out his capital. So, as I have told poor Bertha whenever she would let me, there may have been other reasons besides her stinging words.'

'And it has preyed on her?'

'More than any one would guess who had not known her in old times. I was glad that you secured that child, Cea, to her. She seems to have fastened her affections on her.'

'Alder,' presently repeated Frank. 'Alder—I was thinking how the name had come before me. There were some clients of ours—of Mr. Burford's, I mean—of that name; I think they sold an estate. Some day I will find out whether he knows anything about them, and I shall remember more by and by.'

'It would be an immense relief if you could find out anything good about the poor fellow,' said Adela, very glad to have found any topic of interest, and pleased to find that it occupied his thoughts afterwards, when he asked whether she knew the Christian name of *this* young man, without mentioning any antecedent, as if he had been going on with the subject all the time.

In a few days the pair were able to meet, and to take up again the life over which a dark veil had suddenly descended, contrasting with the sunshine of those last few years. To hold up one another, and do their duty on their way to the better world, was evidently the one thought, though they said little.

Still neither was yet in a condition to return to ordinary life, and it was determined that as soon as they were disinfected, they should leave the house to undergo the

Charlotte M. Yonge

same process, and spend a few weeks at some health resort. Only Mary shuddered at the notion of hearing the sound of the sea, and Malvern was finally fixed upon. Lady Adela would go with them, and she wrote to beg that Constance, so soon as her term was over, might bring Amice thither, to be in a separate lodging at first, till there had been time to see whether the little girl's company would be a solace or a trial to the bereaved parents.

Bertha, as soon as the chief anxiety was over, joined Mrs. Bury in a mountaineering expedition. She declared that she had never dared to leave Cea before, lest the wretched father, now proved to be a myth, should come and abstract the child.

CHAPTER XXXIV

THE PHANTOM OF THE STATION

There was a crash in Mrs. Morton's kitchen, where an elegant five o'clock tea was preparing, not only to greet Herbert, who had just come home to await the news of his fate after the last military examination open to him, but also for a friend or two of his mother's, who, to his great annoyance, might be expected to drop in on any Wednesday afternoon.

Every one ran out to see what was the matter, and the maid was found picking up Mrs. Morton's silver teapot, the basket-work handle of which had suddenly collapsed under the weight of tea and tea-leaves. The mistress's exclamations and objurgation of the maid for not having discovered its frail condition need not be repeated. It had been a wedding-present, and was her great pride. After due examination to see whether there were any bruises or dents, she said—

'Well, Ida, we must have yours; run and fetch it out of the box. You have the key of it.' And she held out the key of the cupboard where the spoons were daily taken out by herself or Ida.

The teapot had been left to Ida by a godmother, who had

Charlotte M. Yonge

been a farmer's wife, with a small legacy, but was of an unfashionable make and seldom saw the light.

'That horrid, great clumsy thing!' said Ida. 'You had much better use the blue china one.'

'I'll never use that crockery for company when there's silver in the house! What would Mrs. Denham say if she dropped in?'

'I won't pour out tea in that ugly, heavy brute of a thing.'

'Then if you won't, I will. Give me the key this instant!'

'It is mine, and I am not going to give it up!'

'Come, Ida,' said Herbert, weary of the altercation; 'any one would think you had made away with it! Let us have it for peace's sake.'

'It's no business of yours.'

He whistled. However, at that moment the door-bell rang.

It was to admit a couple of old ladies, whom both the young people viewed as very dull company; and the story of the illness of 'my brother, Lord Northmoor,' as related by their mother, had become very tedious, so that as soon as possible they both sauntered out on the beach.

'I wonder when uncle will send for you!' Ida said. 'He must give you a good allowance now.'

'Don't talk of it, Ida; it makes me sick to think of it. I say—is that the old red rock where they saw the last of the poor little kid?'

'Yes; that was where his hat was.'

'Did you find it? Was it washed up?'

'Don't talk of such dreadful things, Bertie; I can't bear it! And there's Rose Rollstone!'

Ida would have done her utmost to keep her brother and Rose Rollstone apart at any other time, but she was at the moment only too glad to divert his attention, and allowed him, without protest, to walk up to Rose, shake hands with her, and rejoice in her coming home for good; but, do what Ida would, she could not keep him from recurring to the thought of the little cousin of whom he had been very fond.

'Such a jolly little kid!' he said; 'and full of spirit! You should have seen him when I picked him up before me on the cob. How he laughed!'

'So good, too,' said Rose. 'He looked so sweet with those pretty brown eyes and fair curls at church that last Sunday.'

'I can't make out how it was. The tide could not have been high enough to wash him off going round that rock, or the other children would not have gone round it.'

'Oh, I suppose he ran after a wave,' said Ida hastily.

'Do you know,' said Rose mysteriously, 'I could have declared I saw him that very evening, and with his nursery-maid, too!'

'Nonsense, Rose! We don't believe in ghosts!' said Ida.

'It was not like a ghost,' said Rose. 'You know I had come

Charlotte M. Yonge

down for the bank-holiday, and went back to finish my quarter at the art embroidery. Well, when we stopped at the North Westhaven station, I saw a man, woman, and child get in, and it struck me that the boy was Master Michael and the woman Louisa Hall. I think she looked into the carriage where I was, and I was going to ask her where she was taking him.'

'Nonsense, Rose! How can you listen to such folly, Herbert?'

'But that's not all! I saw them again under the gas when I got out. I was very near trying to speak to her, but I lost sight of her in the throng; but I saw that face so like Master Michael, only scared and just ready to cry.'

'You'll run about telling that fine ghost-story,' said Ida roughly.

'But Louisa could not have been a ghost,' said Rose, bewildered. 'I thought she was his nursery-maid taking him somewhere! Didn't she—' then with a sudden flash— 'Oh!'

'Turned off long ago for flirting with that scamp Rattler,' said Herbert. 'Now she has run off with him.'

'There was a sailor-looking man with her,' said Rose.

'I never heard such intolerable nonsense!' burst out Ida. 'Mere absurdity!'

Herbert looked at her with surprise at the strange passion she exhibited. He asked—

'Did you say the Hall girl had run away?'

'Oh, never mind, Herbert!' cried Ida, as if unable to command herself. 'What is it to you what a nasty, horrid girl like that does?'

'Hold your tongue, Ida!' he said resolutely. 'If you won't speak, let Rose.'

'She did,' said Rose, in a low, anxious, terrified voice. 'I only heard it since I came home. She was married at the registrar's office to that man Jones, whom they call the Rattler, and went off with him. It must have been her whom I saw, really and truly; and, oh, Herbert, could she have been so wicked as to steal Master Michael!'

'Somebody else has been wicked then,' said Herbert, laying hold of his sister's arm.

'I don't know what all this means,' exclaimed Ida, in great agitation; 'nor what you and Rose are at! Making up such horrible, abominable insinuations against me, your poor sister! But Rose Rollstone always hated me!'

'She does not know what she is saying,' sighed Rose; and, with much delicacy, she moved away.

'Let me go, Herbert!' cried Ida, as she felt his grip on her hand.

'Not I, Ida—till you have answered me! Is this so—that Michael is not drowned, but carried off by that woman?' demanded Herbert, holding her fast and looking at her with manly gravity, not devoid of horror.

'He is a horrid little impostor, palmed off to keep you out of the title and everything! That's why I did it!' sobbed Ida, trying to wrench herself away.

'Oh, you did it, did you? You confess that! And what have you done with him?'

'I tell you he is no Morton at all—just the nurse-woman's child, taken to spite you. I found it all out at—what's its name?—Botzen; only ma would not be convinced.'

'I should suppose not! To think that my uncle and aunt would do such a thing—why, I don't know whether it is not worse than stealing the child!'

'Herbert! Herbert! do you want to bring your sister to jail, talking in that way?'

'It is no more than you deserve. I *would* bring you there if it is the only way to get back the child! I do not know what is bad enough for you. My poor uncle and aunt! To have brought such misery on them!' He clenched his hands as he spoke.

'Everybody said she didn't mind—didn't ask questions, didn't cry, didn't go on a bit like his real mother.'

'She could not, or it might have been the death of my uncle. Bertha wrote it all to me; but you—you would never understand. Ida, I can't believe that you, my sister, could have done such an awfully wicked thing!'

'I wouldn't, only I was sure he was not—'

'No more of that stuff!' said Herbert. 'You don't know what they are.'

'I do. So strict—not a bit like a mother.'

'If our mother had been like them, you might not have been such a senseless monster,' said Herbert, pausing for a word. 'Come, now; tell me what you have done with him, or I shall have to set on the police.'

'Oh, Herbert, how can you be so cruel?'

'It is not I that am cruel! Come, speak out! Did you bribe her with your teapot? Ah! I see: what has she done with him?'

He gripped her arm almost as he used to torture her when they were children, and insisted again that either she must tell him the whole truth or he should set the police on the track.

'You wouldn't,' she said, awed. 'Think of the exposure and of mother!'

'I can think of nothing but saving Mite! I say—my mother knows nothing of this?'

'Oh no, no!'

Herbert breathed more freely, but he was firm, and seemed suddenly to have grown out of boyishness into manly determination, and gradually he extracted the whole story from her. He would not listen to the delusion in which she had worked herself into believing, founded upon the negations for which she had sedulously avoided seeking positive refutation, and which had been bolstered up by her imagination and wishes, working on the unsubstantial precedents of novels. She had brought herself absolutely to believe in the imposture, and at a moment when her uncle's condition seemed absolutely to place within her grasp the coronet for Herbert, with all possibilities for herself.

Then came the idea of Louisa Hall, inspired by seeing her

speak to little Michael on the beach, and obtain his pretty smiles and exclamation of 'Lou, Lou! mine Lou!' for he had certainly liked this girl better than Ellen, who was wanting in life and animation. Ida knew that Sam Jones, alias Rattler, was going out to join his brother in Canada, and that Louisa was vehemently desirous to accompany him, but had failed to satisfy the requirements of Government as to character, so as to obtain a free passage, and was therefore about to be left behind in desertion and distress. She might beguile Michael away quietly and carry him to Canada, where, as it seemed, there were any amount of farmers ready to adopt English children—a much better lot, in Ida's eyes, than the little Tyrolese impostor deserved. She even persuaded herself that she was doing an act of great goodness, when, at the price of her teapot, she obtained that Louisa should be married by the registrar to Sam Jones, and their passage paid, on condition of their carrying away Michael with them. The man was nothing loth, having really a certain preference for Louisa, and likewise a grudge against Lord Northmoor for having spoilt that game with Miss Morton, which might have brought the means for the voyage.

They were married on Whit Monday, and Ida was warned that if she and Louisa could not get possession of the child by Wednesday, he would be left behind. Louisa was accordingly on the watch, and Ida hovered about, just enough completely to put the nurses off their guard. They heard Michael's imploring call of 'Willie! Willie!' and then Louisa descended on him with coaxings and promises, and Ida knew no more, except that, as she had desired, a parcel had been sent her containing the hat and shoes. The spade she had herself picked up.

When Rose had seen them, they had no doubt been on their way to Liverpool.

It seemed to be Herbert's horror-stricken look that first showed his sister the enormity of what she had done, and when she pleaded 'for your sake,' he made such a fierce sound of disgust, that she only durst add further, 'Oh, Herbert, you will not tell?'

'Not find him?' he thundered.

'No, no; I didn't mean that! But don't let them know about me! Just think—'

'I must think! Get away now; I can't bear you near!'

And just then a voice was heard, 'Miss Hider, Miss Hider, your ma wants you!'

CHAPTER XXXV

THE QUEST

Herbert had made no promises, but as he paced up and down the shingle after his sister had gone in, he had time to feel that, though he was determined to act at once, the scandal of her deed must be as much as possible avoided. Indeed, he believed that she might have rendered herself amenable to prosecution for kidnapping the child, and he felt on reflection that his mother must be spared the terror and disgrace. His difficulties were much increased by the state of quarantine at Northmoor, for though the journey to Malvern had been decided upon, neither patient was yet in a state to attempt it, and as one of the servants had unexpectedly sickened with the disease, all approach to the place was forbidden; nor did he know with any certainty how far his uncle's recovery had advanced, since Bertha, his chief informant, had gone abroad with Mrs. Bury, and Constance was still at Oxford.

He went home, and straight up to his room, feeling it intolerable to meet his sister; and there, the first sleepless night he had ever known, convinced him that to the convalescents it would be cruelty to send his intelligence, when it amounted to no more than that their poor little boy had been made over to an unscrupulous woman and a violent, good-for-nothing man.

'No,' said Herbert, as he tossed over; 'it would be worse than believing him quietly dead, now they have settled down to that. I must get him back before they know anything about it. But how? I must hunt up those wretches' people here, and find where they are gone; if they know—as like as not they won't. But I'll throw everything up till I find the boy!' He knelt up in his bed, laid his hand on his Bible—his uncle's gift—and solemnly swore it.

And Herbert was another youth from that hour.

When he had brought his ideas into some little order, the foremost was that he must see Rose Rollstone, discover how much she knew or guessed, and bind her to silence. 'No fear of her, jolly little thing!' said he to himself; but, playfellows as they had been, private interviews were not easy to secure under present circumstances.

However, the tinkling of the bell of the iron church suggested an idea. 'She is just the little saint of a thing to be always off to church at unearthly hours. I'll catch her there—if only that black coat isn't always after her!'

So Herbert hurried off to the iron building, satisfied himself with a peep that Rose's sailor hat was there, and then—to make sure of her—crept into a seat by the door, and found his plans none the worse for praying for all needing help in mind, body, or estate. Rose came out alone, and he was by her side at once. 'I say, Rose, you did not speak about *that* last night?'

'Oh no, indeed!'

'You're a brick! I got it all out of that sister of mine. I'm only ashamed that she is my sister!'

Charlotte M. Yonge

'And where is the dear little boy?'

'That's the point,' and Herbert briefly explained his difficulties, and Rose agreed that he must try to learn where the emigrants had gone, from their relations. And when he expressed his full intention of following them, even if he had to work his passage, before telling the parents, she applauded the nobleness of the resolution, and all the romance in her awoke at the notion of his bringing home the boy and setting him before his parents. She was ready to promise secrecy for the sake of preventing the prosecution that might, as Herbert saw, be a terrible thing for the whole family; and besides, it must be confessed, the two young things did rather enjoy the sharing of a secret. Herbert promised to meet her the next morning, and report his discoveries and plans, as in fact she was the only person with whom he could take counsel.

He did meet her accordingly, going first to the church. He had to tell her that he had been able to make nothing of Mrs. Hall. He was not sure whether she knew where her daughter had gone; at any rate, she would not own to any knowledge, being probably afraid. Besides, when acting as charwoman, Master Herbert had been such a torment to her that she was not likely to oblige him.

He had succeeded better with the Jones family, and perhaps had learnt prudence, for he had not begun by asking for the Rattler, but for the respectable brother who had invited him out, and had thus learnt that the destination of the emigrant was Toronto, where the elder brother was employed on the *British Empress*, Ontario steamer. Mrs. Jones, the mother, and her eldest son were decent people, and there was no reason to think they were aware of the encumbrances that their scapegrace had taken with him.

So Herbert had resolved, without delay, to make his way to Toronto; where he hoped to find the child, and maybe, bring him back in a month's time.

'Only,' said Rose timidly, 'did you really mean what you said about working your way out?'

'Well, Rose, that's the hitch. I had to pay up some bills after I got my allowance, and unluckily I changed my bicycle, and the rascals put a lot more on the new one, and I haven't got above seven pounds left, and I must keep some for the rail from New York and for getting home, for I can't take the kid home in the steerage. The bicycle's worth something, and so is my watch, if I put them in pawn; so I think I can do it that way, and I'm quite seaman enough to get employment, only I don't want to lose time about it.'

'I was thinking,' said Rose shyly; 'they made me put into the Post Office Savings Bank after I began to get a salary. I have five-and-twenty pounds there that I could get out in a couple of days, and I should be so glad to help to bring that dear little boy home.'

'Oh, Rose, you *are* a girl! You see, you are quite safe not to lose it, for my uncle would be only too glad to pay it back, even if I came to grief any way, and it would make it all slick smooth. I would go to Liverpool straight off, and cross in the first steamer, and the thing's done. And can you get at it at once with nobody knowing?'

'Yes, I think so,' said Rose. 'My father asked to see my book when first I came home, and he is not likely to do so again, till I can explain all about it, and I am sure it cannot be wrong.'

'Wrong—no! Right as a trivet! Rose, Rose, if ever that

Charlotte M. Yonge

poor child sees his father and mother again, it is every bit your doing! No one can tell what I think of it, or what my uncle and aunt will say to you! You've been the angel in this, if Ida has been the other thing!'

But Rose found difficulties in the way of her angelic part, for her father addressed her in his most solemn and sententious manner: 'Rose, I have always looked on you as sensible and discreet, but I have to say that I disapprove of your late promenades with a young man connected with the aristocracy.'

Rose coloured up a good deal, but cried out, 'It's not that, papa, not that!'

'I do not suppose either you or he is capable at present of forming any definite purpose,' said Mr. Rollstone, not to be baulked of his discourse; 'but you must bear in mind that any appearance of encouragement to a young man in his position can only have a most damaging effect on your prospects, and even reputation, however flattering he may appear.'

'I know it, papa, I know it! There has been nothing of the kind, I assure you,' said Rose, who during the last discourse had had time to reflect; 'and he is going away to-morrow or next day, so you need not be afraid, though I must see him or send to him once more before he goes.'

'Well, if you are helping him to get some present for his sisters, I do not see so much objection for this once; only it must not occur again.'

Rose was much tempted to let this suggestion stand, but truth forbade her, and she said, 'No, papa, I cannot say it is that; but you will know all about it before long, and you will not disapprove, if you will only trust your little Rose,' and she looked up for a kiss.

'Well, I never found you not to be trusted, though you are a coaxing puss,' said her father, and so the matter ended with him, but she had another encounter with her mother.

'Mind, Rose, if that churching—which Sunday was enough for any good girl in my time—is only to lead to walking with young gents which has no call to you, I won't have it done.'

Mrs. Rollstone was not cultivated up to her husband's mark, neither had she ever inspired so much confidence, and Rose made simple answer, 'It is all right, mamma; I have spoken to papa about it.'

'Oh, if your pa knows, I suppose he is satisfied; but men aren't the same as a mother, and if that there young Mr. Morton comes dangling and gallanting after you, he is after no good.'

'He is doing no such thing,' said Rose in a resolutely calm voice that might have shown that she was with difficulty controlling her temper; 'and, besides, he is going away.'

Wherewith Mrs. Rollstone had to be satisfied.

Rose took a bold measure when she had taken her five five-pound notes from the savings bank. She saw her father preparing to waddle out for his daily turn on the beach, and she put the envelope containing them, addressed to H. Morton, Esq., into his hand, begging him to give it to Mr. Morton himself.

Which he did, when he met Herbert trying to soothe his impatience with a cigar.

Charlotte M. Yonge

'Here, sir,' he said, 'my daughter wishes me to give you this. I don't ask what it is, mind; but I tell you plainly, I don't like secrets between young people.'

Herbert tried to laugh naturally, then said, 'Your daughter is no end of a trump, Mr. Rollstone.'

'Only recollect this, sir—I know my station and I know yours, and I will have no nonsense with her.'

'All right!' said Herbert shortly, with a laugh, his head too full of other matters to think what all this implied.

He wished to avoid exciting any disturbance, so he told his mother that he should be off again the next day.

'It is very hard,' grumbled Mrs. Morton, 'that you can never be contented to stay with your poor mother! I did hope that with the regatta, and the yachts, and Mr. Brady, you would find amusement enough to give us a little of your company; but nothing is good enough for you now. Which of your fine friends are you going to?'

Herbert was not superior to an evasion, and said, 'I'm going up to town first, and shall see Dacre, and I'll write by and by.'

She resigned herself to the erratic movements of the son, who, being again, in her eyes, heir to the peerage, was to her like a comet in a higher sphere.

CHAPTER XXXVI

IDA'S CONFESSION

The move to Malvern was at last made, and the air seemed at once to invigorate Lord Northmoor, though the journey tried his wife more than she had expected, and she remained in a very drooping state, in spite of her best efforts not to depress him. Nothing seemed to suit her so well as to lie on a couch in the garden of their lodging, with Constance beside her, talking, and sometimes smiling over all her little Mite's pretty ways; though at other times she did her best to seem to take interest in other matters, and to persuade her husband that his endeavours to give her pleasure or interest were success-ful, because the exertions he made for her sake were good for him.

He was by this time anxious—since he was by the end of three weeks quite well, and fairly strong—to go down to Westhaven, and learn all he could about the circum-stances of the fate of his poor little son; and only delayed till he thought his wife could spare him. Lady Adela urged him at last to go. She thought that Mary lived in a state of effort for his sake, and that there was a certain yearning and yet dread in the minds of both for these further details, so that the visit had better be over.

Charlotte M. Yonge

Thus it was about six weeks after Herbert's departure that Mrs. Morton received a note to tell her that her brother-in-law would arrive the next evening. It was terrible news to Ida, and if there had been time she would have arranged to be absent elsewhere; but as it was she had no power to escape, and had to spend her time in assisting in all the elaborate preparations which her mother thought due to the Baron—a very different personage in her eyes from the actual Frank.

He did not come till late in the day, and then Mrs. Morton received him with a very genuine gush of tears, and anxious inquiries. He was thin, and looked much older; his hair was grayer, and had retreated from his brow, and there was a bent, worn, dejected air about the whole man, which, as Mrs. Morton said, made her ready to cry whenever she looked at him; but he was quite composed in manner and tone, so as to repress her agitation, and confirm Ida's inexperienced judgment in the idea that Michael was none of his. He was surprised and concerned at Herbert's absence, which was beginning to make his mother uneasy, and he promised to write to some of the boy's friends to inquire about him. To put off the evil day, Ida had suggested asking Mr. Deyncourt to meet him, but that gentleman could not come, and dinner went off in stiff efforts at conversation, for just now all the power thereof, that Lord Northmoor had ever acquired, seemed to have forsaken him.

Afterwards, in the August twilight, he begged to hear all. Ida withdrew, glad not to submit to the ordeal, while her mother observed, 'Poor, dear Ida! She was so fond of her dear little cousin, she cannot bear to hear him mentioned! She has never been well since!'

Then, with copious floods of tears, and all in perfect good faith, she related the history of the loss, as she knew it, with—on his leading questions—a full account of all the child's pretty ways during his stay, and how he had never failed to say his prayer about making papa better, and how he had made friends with Mr. Deyncourt, in spite of having pronounced his church like a big tin box all up in frills; and how he had admired the crabs, and run after the waves, and had been devoted to the Willie, who had thought him troublesome—giving all the anecdotes, to which Frank listened with set face and dry eyes, storing them for his wife. He thanked Mrs. Morton for all her care and tenderness, and expended assurances that no one thought her to blame.

'It is one of those dispensations,' he said, 'that no one can guard against. We can only be thankful for the years of joy that no one can take from us, and try to be worthy to meet him hereafter.'

Mrs. Morton had wept so much that she was very glad to seize the first excuse for wishing good-night. She said that she had put all Michael's little things in a box in his father's room, for him to take home to his mother, and bade Frank—as once more she called him—good-night, kissing him as she had never done before. The shock had brought out all that was best and most womanly in her.

That box had an irresistible attraction for Frank. He could not but open it, and on the top lay the white woolly, headless dog that had been Mite's special darling, had been hugged by him in his slumbers every night, and been the means of many a joyous game when father and mother came up to wish the noisy creature good-night, and 'Tarlo' had been made to bark at them.

Somehow the 'never more' overcame him completely. He had not before been beyond the restraint of guarding his feelings for Mary's sake; and, tired with the long day, and torn by the evening's narration, all his self-command gave way, and he fell into a perfect anguish of deep-drawn, almost hysterical sobbing.

Those sobs were heard through the thin partition in Ida's room. They were very terrible to her. They broke down the remnant of her excuse that the child was an imposition. They woke all her woman's tenderness, and the impulse to console carried her in a few moments to the door.

'Uncle! Uncle Frank!'

'I'm not ill,' answered a broken, heaving, impatient voice. 'I want nothing.'

'Oh, let me in, dear uncle—I've something to tell you!'

'Not now,' came on the back of a sob. 'Go!'

'Oh, now, now!' and she even opened the door a little. 'He is not drowned! At least, Rose Rollstone thinks—'

'What?' and he threw the door wide open.

'Rose Rollstone is sure she saw him with Louisa Hall in London that day,' hurried out Ida, still bent on screening herself. 'She's gone to Canada. It's there that Herbert is gone to find him and bring him home!'

'And why—why were we never told?'

'You were too ill, uncle, and Rose did not know about it till she came home. Then she told Herbert, and he hoped to find him and write.'

'When was this?'

'When Herbert came home—the 29th or 30th of June,' said Ida, trembling. 'He *must* find him, uncle; don't fear!'

It was a strange groaning sigh that answered; then, with a great effort—

'Thank you, Ida; I can't understand it yet—I can't talk! Good-night!' Then, with an afterthought, when he had almost shut his door, he turned the handle again to say, 'Who did you say saw—thought she saw—my boy? Where?'

'Rose Rollstone, uncle; first at the North Station—then at Waterloo! And Louisa Hall too!'

'I thank you; good-night!'

And for what a night of strange dreams, prayers, and uncertainties did Frank shut himself in—only forcing himself by resolute will into sleeping at last, because he knew that strength and coolness were needful for to-morrow's investigation.

Charlotte M. Yonge

CHAPTER XXXVII

HOPE

That last sleep lasted long, till the sound of the little tinkling bell came through the open window, and then the first waking thought that Mite was alive was at first taken for a mere blissful dream. It was only the sight of the woolly dog that recalled with certainty the conversation with Ida.

To pursue that strange hint was of course the one impulse. The bell had ceased before Frank had been able to finish dressing, but the house was so far from having wakened to full life, that remembering the lateness of the breakfast hour, he decided on hastening out to lay his anxious, throbbing feelings before his God, if only to join in the prayer that our desires may be granted as may be most expedient for us.

Nor was he without a hope that the girl whom Constance described as so devout and religious might be found there.

And she was; he knew her by sight well enough to accost her when she came out with 'Miss Rollstone, I believe?'

She bowed, her heart thumping almost as much as the father's, in the importance of what she had to tell, and the doubt how much she had a right to speak without betrayal.

'I am told,' Lord Northmoor said, with a tremble in his voice, 'that you think you saw my poor little boy.'

'I am almost sure I did,' said Rose.

'And when, may I ask?'

'On the evening of the Wednesday in Whitsun week,' said Rose.

'Just when he was lost—and where?'

'At the North Station. I had got into the train at the main station. I saw him put into the train at the North one, and taken out at Waterloo.'

'And why—why, may I ask, have we been left—have we never heard this before?'

His voice shook, as he thought of all the misery to himself and his wife that might have been spared, as well as the danger of the child. Rose hesitated, doubting how much she ought to say, and Mr. Deyncourt came out.

'May I introduce myself?' said Frank, hoping for an auxiliary,—'Lord Northmoor. I have just heard that Miss Rollstone thinks she saw my little boy in the London train the day he disappeared; and I am trying to understand whether there is really any hope that she is right, and that we can recover him.'

Mr. Deyncourt was infinitely surprised, and spoke a few words of wonder that this had not been made known. Rose found it easier to speak to him.

'I saw Louisa Hall with him; I did not know she was not still his maid. I thought she had been sent to take him somewhere. And when I heard from home that he—he was—drowned, I only thought the likeness had deceived me. It was not till Mr. Morton came home, and we talked it over, that I understood that Louisa Hall was dismissed long ago, and was eloping to Canada.

'And then,' for she had spoken falteringly, and with an effort, as their sounds of inquiry elicited each sentence— 'and then, Mr. Morton said he would follow her to Canada. He did not want Lady Northmoor to be tortured with uncertainty.'

'Very strange,' said the gentlemen one to the other, Lord Northmoor adding—

'Thank you, Miss Rollstone; I will not detain you, unless you can tell me more.'

Rose was glad to be released, though pained and vexed not to dare to express her reasons for full certainty.

'Is this only a girl's fancy?' sighed the father.

'I think she is a sensible girl.'

'And my nephew Herbert is a hard-headed fellow, not likely to fly off on a vague notion. Is this Hall girl's mother still living here?'

'Certainly. It has been a bad business, her going off with that Jones; but I ascertained that she was married to him.'

'Jones—Sam Jones, or Rattler?'

'Even so.'

'Ah! She was dismissed on his account. And I detected him in imposing on Miss Morton. Yet—where does this Mrs. Hall live?'

'Along this alley. Shall I come with you?'

'Thank you.'

'It may induce her to speak out, if there is anything to hear. I dare not hope! It is too incredible, and I don't understand those children's silence.'

He spoke it almost to himself, and the clergyman thought it kinder not to interrupt his thoughts during the few steps down the evil-smelling alley that led to the house, where Mrs. Hall was washing up her cup after breakfast. It was Mr. Deyncourt who spoke, seeing that the swelling hope and doubt were almost too much for his companion.

'Good morning, Mrs. Hall; we have come to you early, but Lord Northmoor is very anxious to know whether you can throw any light on what has become of his little boy.'

Mrs. Hall was in a very different state of mind from when she had denied all knowledge to Herbert, a mere boy, whom she did not like, and when she was anxious to shelter her daughter, whose silence had by this time begun to offend her. The sight of the clergyman and the other gentleman alarmed her, and she began by maundering out—

'I am sure, sir, I don't know nothing. My daughter have never writ one line to me.'

'He was with her!' gasped out Lord Northmoor.

'I am sure, sir, it was none of my doing, no, nor my

Charlotte M. Yonge

daughter wouldn't neither, only the young lady over persuaded her. 'Tis she as was the guilty party, as I'll always say.'

'She—who?'

'Miss Morton—Miss Hida, sir; and my gal wouldn't never have done it, sir, but for the stories she told, fictious stories they was, I'm sure, that the child wasn't none of my lady's, only a brat picked up in foreign parts to put her brother out of his chance.'

'What are you saying?' exclaimed Lord Northmoor. 'My niece never could have said any such thing.'

'Indeed, but she did, sir, my Lord, and that's what worked on my daughter, though I always told her not to believe any such nonsense; but then you see, she couldn't get her passage paid to go out with Rattler, and Miss Hida give her the money if so be she would take off the child to Canada with her.'

'And where?' hoarsely asked the father.

'That I can't tell, my Lord; Louey have never written, and I knows no more than nothing at all. She've not been a dutiful gal to me, as have done everything for her.'

There was no more to be made out of Mrs. Hall, and they went their way.

'There is no doubt that the little fellow is alive,' said Mr. Deyncourt.

'Who can guess what those wretches have done to him?' said Lord Northmoor under his breath. 'Not that I am unthankful for the blessed hope,' he added, uncovering his head, 'but I am astounded more than I can say, by *this*—'

'It must be invention of the woman,' said Mr. Deyncourt.

'I hope so,' was the answer.

'Could Miss Rollstone have suspected it? She was very unlike what I have seen of her before.'

They separated for breakfast, agreeing to meet afterwards to hunt up the Jones family.

Ida had suffered a good deal all the night and morning as she wondered what her confession might entail on her. Sometimes she told herself that since it would come out in Herbert's letters on the discovery of the child, it was well to have the honour of the first disclosure, and her brother was certain to keep her part in the matter a secret; but, on the other hand, she did not know how much Louisa might have told her mother, nor whether Mrs. Hall might persist in secrecy—nay, or even Rose. Indeed, she was quite uncertain how much Rose had understood. She could not have kept back guesses, and she did not believe in honour on Rose's part. So she was nervous on finding that her uncle was gone out.

When he came in to breakfast, he merely made a morning greeting. Afterwards he scarcely spoke, except to answer an occasional remark from her mother. To herself, he neither looked nor spoke, but when Mrs. Morton declared that he looked the better for his morning walk, there was a half smile and light in his eye, and the weight seemed gone from his brow. Mrs. Morton asked what he was going to do.

'I am going out with Mr. Deyncourt,' he answered.

And Ida breathed more freely when he was gone.

But she little knew that Mr. Deyncourt had gone to Rose Rollstone in her father's presence, and told her of Mrs. Hall's revelations, asking her if this had been the cause of her silence. She had to own how the truth had flashed at once on her and Mr. Morton.

'It would be so very dreadful for them if it were known,' she said. 'He thought if he brought back the boy, his sister's part need not be known.'

'Then that was the secret!' exclaimed Mrs. Rollstone. 'Well, I'll not blame you, child, but you might have told us.'

Secrets were safe with the ex-butler, but not quite so much so with his wife, though all three tried to impress on her the need of silence, before Mr. Deyncourt hastened out to rejoin Lord Northmoor. The inquiry took a much longer time than they had expected, for the family wanted did not live in Mr. Deyncourt's district, and they were misdirected more than once to people who disdained the notion of being connected with the Rattler, if they had ever heard of such a person. At last they did find a sister-in-law, who pronounced George Jones to be a good fellow, so far as she knew. He sent home to his mother regularly, and lately had had out his brother Sam, and a good job too, to have him out of the way, only what must he do but go and marry that there trollopy girl, as was no good.

Yes, George had written to say they had come safe to Toronto, but she did not hear as he said anything about a child. The letter was to his mother, who had taken it into the country when she went to stay with her daughter. This deponent didn't know the address, and her husband was out with a yacht.

Nothing could be done but to pursue the mother to a village about five miles off, where she was traced out with some difficulty, and persuaded to refer to her son George's letter, where he mentioned the safe arrival of Mr. and Mrs. Sam, but without a word about their bringing a child with them. This omission seemed to dash all former hopes, so as to show Frank how strong they had been, and besides, there had been more than time for Herbert to have written after reaching Toronto.

However, the one step of knowing George Jones's address had been gained, and with no more than this, they had to return, intending to see whether Ida had any notion as to what was to be done.

It was evening when Lord Northmoor came in. Mrs. Morton was alone, and as she looked up, was answered by his air of disappointment as he shook his head.

'Oh, it is so dreadful,' she exclaimed, 'it is all over the place! We met Mr. Brady and his sisters, and they cut Ida dead. She is quite broken-hearted, indeed, she is.'

'Then she has told you all?'

'She could not help it. Mrs. Rollstone came to ask me if it was true—as a friend, she said, I should say it was more like an enemy, and Mrs. Hall came too, wanting to see Ida, but I saw her instead. The wicked woman to have given in! And they have gone and told every one, and the police will be after my poor child.'

'No, they would not interfere unless I prosecuted, and that I certainly should not do unless it proved the only means of tracing my child. I came home intending to ask Ida if she gave any directions about him. It seems certain that he was not brought to Toronto.'

'Indeed! She made sure that he would be there!' exclaimed Mrs. Morton, much dismayed. 'Let me go and see. She is so much upset altogether that she declares that she cannot see you this evening.'

Mrs. Morton went, and presently brought word that Ida was horrified at hearing that little Michael was not with the Joneses. She had trusted Louisa to treat him kindly, and only dispose of him to some of those Canadian farmers, who seemed to have an unlimited appetite for adopted children, and the last hope was that this might have been the case, though opportunities could have been few on the way to Toronto.

Ida had cried over the tidings. It must have been worse than she had ever intended that the child should be treated; and the shock was great both to her and to her mother.

Mrs. Morton really seemed quite broken down, both by sorrow and fear for the boy, and by the shame, the dread of the story getting into the papers, and the sense that she could never go on living at Westhaven; and her brother-in-law quite overwhelmed her by saying that he should do all in his power to prevent publicity, and that he entirely exonerated her from all blame in the matter.

'Ah, Frank dear,' she said, 'you are so good, it makes me feel what a sinful woman I am! I don't mean that I ever gave in for a moment to that nonsense of poor Ida's which was her only bit of excuse. No one that had ever been a mother could, you know; but I won't say that I did not grumble at my boy losing his chances.'

'I don't wonder!'

'And—and I never would listen to you and Mary about poor Ida. I let her idle and dress, and read all those novels, and it is out of them she got that monstrous notion. You little know what I have gone through with that girl, Frank, so different from the other two. Oh! if I could only begin over again!'

'Perhaps,' said Frank, full of pity, 'this terrible shock may open her eyes, and by God's blessing be the beginning of better things.'

'Oh, Frank, you are a perfect angel ever to bear the sight of us again!' cried the poor woman, ever violent in her feelings and demonstrations. 'Hark! What's that?—I can't see any one.'

'Please, ma'am, it's Miss Rollstone, with a letter for his Lordship.'

Charlotte M. Yonge

CHAPTER XXXVIII

THE CLUE

'BEST OF ROSES,—

'I don't know where my uncle is, so please send him this. I got to Toronto all right, and had not much trouble in finding out the steady-going Jones, who is rather a swell, chief mate on board the *British Empress*. He was a good deal taken aback by my story, and said that his brother had come out with his wife, but no child. It was quite plain that he was a good deal disappointed in the Rattler, and not at all prepared for Mrs. Louisa, whom neither he nor his wife admired at all, at all. He had got his brother a berth on a summer steamer that had just been set up on Lake Winnipeg—being no doubt glad to get rid of such an encumbrance as the wife, and he looked very blue when he heard that I was quite certain that she had taken the kid away with her, and been paid for it. There was nothing for it but to go after them, and find out from them what they had done with poor little Mite. He is a right good fellow, and would have gone with me, but that he is bound to his boat, and a stunner she is; but he gave me a letter to Sam, so I had to get on the Canadian Pacific Railway, so that I should have been nonplussed but for your loan. Splendid places it goes through, you never saw such trees, nor such game.

'As good luck would have it, I was in the same car with an Englishman—a gentleman, one could see with half an eye, and we fraternised, so that I told him what I was come about. He was awfully good-natured, and told me he lived a mile or two out of Winnipeg, and had a share in the steam company, and if I found any difficulty I was to come to him, Mr. Forman, at Northmoor. I stared at the name, as you may guess! There was a fine horse and buggy waiting for him at the station, and off he went. I put up at the hotel—there's sure to be that whatever there is not—and went after the Joneses next. I got at the woman first, she looked ill and fagged, as if she didn't find life with Rattler very jolly. She cried bucketsful, and said she didn't know anything, since she put the poor little Mite to sleep after supper in a public-house at Liverpool. She was dead tired, and when she woke he was gone, and her husband swore at her, and never would tell her what he had done with the boy, except that he had not hurt him. Then I interviewed Sam Rattler himself. He cut up rough, as he said my Lord had done him an ill turn, and he had the game in his hands now, and was not going to let him know what was become of his child, without he came down handsome enough to make up for what he had done him out of. So then I had to go off to Mr. Forman. He has such a place, a house such as any one might be delighted to have—pine trees behind, a garden in front, no end of barns and stables, with houses and cows, fine wheat fields spreading all round, such as would do your heart good. That is what Mr. Forman and his brother-in-law, Captain Alder, have made, and there's a sweet little lady as ever you saw, Alder's sister. The Captain was greatly puzzled to hear it was Lord Northmoor's son I was looking for. He is not up in the peerage like your father, you see, and I had to make him understand. He thought Lord N. must be either the old man, or Lady Adela's little boy. He said some of his happiest days had been at Northmoor, and

Charlotte M. Yonge

he asked after Lady Adela, and if Miss Morton was married. He came with me, and soon made Mr. Rattler change his note, by showing him that it would be easy to give him the sack, even if he was not laid hold of by the law on my information for stealing the child. They are both magistrates and could do it. So at last the fellow growled out that he wasn't going to be troubled with another man's brat, and just before embarking, he had laid it down asleep at the door of Liverpool Workhouse! So no doubt poor little Michael is there! I would have telegraphed at once; but I don't know where my uncle is, or whether he knows about it, but you can find out and send him this letter at once. I have asked him to pay your advance out of my quarter; and as to the rest of it, it is all owing to you that the poor little kid is not to grow up a pauper.

'I am staying on at Northmoor—it sounds natural; they want another hand for their harvesting, so I am working out my board, as is the way here, at any rate till I hear from my uncle, and I shall ask him to let me stay here for good as a farming-pupil. It would suit me ever so much better than the militia, even if I could get into it, which I suppose I haven't done. It is a splendid country, big enough to stretch oneself in, and I shall never stand being cramped up in an island after it; besides that I don't want to see Ida again in a hurry, though there is some one I should like no end to see again. There, I must not say any more, but send this on to my uncle. I wish I could see his face. I did look to bring Mite back to him, but that can't be, as I have not tin enough to carry me home. I hope your loan has not got you into a scrape.

'Yours ever (I mean it),
'H. MORTON.'

The letter to Lord Northmoor, which the servant put into his hand, was shorter, and began with the more important sentence—'The rascal dropped Michael at Liverpool Workhouse.'

The father read it with an ejaculation of 'Thank God,' the aunt answered with a cry of horror, so that he thought for a moment she had supposed he said 'dropped him into the sea,' and repeated 'Liverpool Workhouse.'

'Oh, yes, yes; but that is so dreadful. The Honourable Michael Morton in a workhouse!'

'He is safe and well taken care of there, no doubt,' said Frank. 'I have no fears now. There are much worse places than the nurseries of those great unions.' Then, as he read on, 'There, Emma, your boy has acted nobly. He has fully retrieved what his sister has done. Be happy over that, dear sister, and be thankful with me. My Mary, my Mary, will the joy be too much? Oh, my boy! How soon can I reach Liverpool? There, you will like to read it. I must go and thank that good girl who found him the means.'

He was gone, and found Rose in the act of reading her letter aloud (all but certain bits, that made her falter as if the writing was bad) to her parents and Mr. Deyncourt. And there, in full assembly, he found himself at a loss for words. No one was so much master of the situation as Mr. Rollstone.

'My Lord, I have the honour to congratulate your Lordship,' he said, with a magnificence only marred by his difficulty in rising.

'I—I,' stammered his Lordship, with an unexpected choke in his throat, 'have to congratulate you, Mr. Rollstone, on having such a daughter.' Then, grasping Rose's hand as in a vice, 'Miss Rollstone, what we owe to you—is past expression.'

'I am sure she is very happy, my Lord, to have been of service,' said her mother, with a simper.

Mr. Deyncourt, to relieve the tension of feeling, said, 'Miss Rollstone was reading the letter about Mr. Morton's adventures. Would you not like her to begin again?'

And while Rose obeyed, Lord Northmoor was able to extract his cheque-book from his pocket-book, and as Rose paused, to say—

'I have a debt of which my nephew reminds me. Miss Rollstone furnished the means for his journey. Will you let me fill this up? This can be repaid,' he added, with a smile, 'the rest, never.'

Mr. Rollstone might have been distressed at the venture on which his daughter's savings had gone; but he was perfectly happy and triumphant now, except that, even more than Mrs. Morton, he suffered from the idea of the Honourable Michael being exposed to the contamination of a workhouse, and was shocked at his Lordship's thinking it would have been worse for him to be with the Rattler. Then, hastily looking at his watch, Lord Northmoor asked when the post went out, and hearing there was but half an hour to spare, begged Mr. Deyncourt to let him lose no time by giving him the wherewithal to write to his wife.

'She would miss a note and be uneasy,' he said. 'Yet I hardly know what I dare tell her. Only not mourning paper!' he added, with an exultant smile.

In the curate's room he wrote—

'DEAREST WIFE,—

'I have been out all day, and have only a moment to say that I am quite well, and trust to have some most thankworthy news for you. Don't be uneasy if you do not hear to-morrow.—Your own

'FRANK.'

There was still time to scribble—

'DEAR LADY ADELA,—

'I trust to you to prepare Mary for well-nigh incredible joy, but do not agitate her too soon. I cannot come till Friday afternoon.

'Yours gratefully,
'NORTHMOOR.'

Having sent this off, his next search was for a time-table. He would fain have gone by the mail train that very night, but Mr. Deyncourt and Mrs. Morton united in persuading him that his strength was not yet equal to such a pull upon it, and he yielded. They hardly knew the man, usually so equable and quiet as to be almost stolid.

He smiled, and declared he could neither eat nor sleep, but he actually did both, sleeping, indeed, better and longer than he had done since his illness, and coming down in the morning a new man, as he called himself, but the old one still in his kindness to Mrs. Morton. He promised to telegraph to her as soon as he knew all was well, assured her that he would do his best to keep the scandal out of the papers, that he would never forget his obligations to Herbert's generosity, and that if she made up her mind to leave Westhaven he would facilitate her so doing.

Ida was not up. She had had a very bad night, and indeed she had confessed that she had been miserable under dreams worse than waking, ever since the child was carried off. Her mother had observed her restlessness and nervousness, but had set a good deal down to love, and perhaps had not been entirely wrong. At any rate, she was now really ill, and could not bear the thought of seeing her uncle, though he sent a message to her that now he did not find it nearly so hard to forgive her, and that he felt for her with all his heart.

It was this gentleness that touched Mrs. Morton above all. Years had softened her; perhaps, too, his patience, and the higher tone of Mr. Deyncourt's ministry, and she was, in many respects, a different woman from her who had so loudly protested against his marrying Mary Marshall.

CHAPTER XXXIX

THE HONOURABLE PAUPER

Lord Northmoor's card was given to the porter with an urgent request for an interview with the Master of the workhouse.

He steadied his voice with difficulty when, on entering the office, he said that he had come to make inquiry after his son, a child of three and a half years old, who had been supposed to be drowned, but he had now discovered had been stolen by a former nurse, and left at the gate of the workhouse, and as the Master paused with an interrogative 'Yes, my Lord?' he added—'On the night between the Wednesday and Thursday of Whitsun week, May the—'

'Children are so often left,' said the Master. 'I will ascertain from the books as to the date.'

After an interval really of scarcely a minute, but which might have been hours to the father's feeling, he read—

'May 18th.—Boy, of apparently four years old, left on the steps, asleep, apparently drugged.'

'Ah!'

Charlotte M. Yonge

'Calls himself Mitel Tent—name probably Michael Trenton.'

'Michael Kenton Morton.' Then he reflected, 'No doubt he thought he was to say his catechism.'

'Does not seem to know parents' name nor residence. Dress—man's old rough coat over a brown holland pinafore—no mark—feet bare; talks as if carefully brought up. May I ask you to describe him.'

'Brown eyes, light hair, a good deal of colour, sturdy, large child,' said Lord Northmoor, much agitated. 'There,' holding out a photograph.

'Ah!' said the Master, in assent.

'And where—is he here?'

'He is at the Children's Home at Fulwood Lodge. Perhaps I had better ask one of the Guardians, who lives near at hand, to accompany you.'

This was done, the Guardian came, much interested in the guest, and a cab was called. Lord Northmoor learnt on the way that the routine in such cases, which were only too common, was the child was taken by the police to the bellman's office till night and there taken care of, in case he should be a little truant of the place, but being unclaimed, he spent a few days at the Union, and then was taken to the Children's Home at Fulwood. Inquiries had been made, but the little fellow had been still under the influence of the drug that had evidently been administered to him at first, and then was too much bewildered to give a clear account of himself. He was in confusion between his real home and Westhaven, and the difference between his appellation and that of his parents was likewise perplexing, nor could he make himself clear, even as to what he knew perfectly well, when interrogated by official strangers who alarmed him.

Lord Northmoor was himself a Poor Law Guardian, and had no vague superstitions to alarm him as to the usage of children in workhouses; but he was surprised at the pleasant aspect of the nursery of the Liverpool Union, a former gentleman's house and grounds, with free air and beautiful views.

The Matron, on being summoned, said that she had from the first been sure, in spite of his clothes, that little Mike was a well-born, tenderly-nurtured child, with good manners and refined habits, and she had tried in vain to understand what he said of himself, though night and morning, he had said his prayers for papa and mamma, and at first added that 'papa might be well,' and he might go home; but where home was there was no discovering, except that there had been journeys by puff puff; and Louey, and Aunt Emma, and Nurse, and sea, and North something, and 'nasty man,' were in an inextricable confusion.

She took them therewith into a large airy room, where the elder children, whole rows of little beings in red frocks, were busied under the direction of a lively young nurse, in building up coloured cubes, 'gifts' in Kindergarten parlance.

There was a few moments of pause, as all the pairs of eyes were raised to meet the new-comers. With a little sense of disappointment, but more of anxiety, Frank glanced over them, and encountered a rounded, somewhat puzzled stare from two brown orbs in a rosy face. Then he ventured to say 'Mite,' and there followed a kind of laughing yell, a leap over the structure of cubes, and the warm, solid, rosy boy was in his arms, on his breast, the head on his shoulder in indescribable ecstasy of content on both sides, of thankfulness on that of the father.

'No doubt there!' said the Guardian and the Matron to one another, between smiles and tears.

Mite asked no questions. Fate had been far beyond his comprehension for the last five months, and it was quite enough for him to feel himself in the familiar arms, and hear the voice he loved.

'Would he go to mamma?'

The boy raised his head, looked wonderingly over his father's face, and said in a puzzled voice—

'Louey said she would take me home in the puff puff.'

'Come now with father, my boy. Only kiss this good lady first, who has been so kind to you.

'Kiss Tommy too, and Fanny,' said Michael, struggling down, and beginning a round of embraces that sufficiently proved that his nursery had been a happy one, while his father could see with joy that he was as healthy and fresh-looking as ever, perhaps a little less plump, but with the natural growth of the fourth year, and he was much the biggest of the party, with the healthfulness of country air and wholesome tendance, while most of the others were more or less stunted or undergrown.

Lord Northmoor's longing was to take his recovered son at once to gladden his mother's eyes; but Michael's little red frock would not exactly suit with the manner of his travels.

So he accepted the Guardian's invitation to come to his house and let Michael be fitted out there, an invitation all the more warmly given because it would have been a pity to let wife and daughters miss the interest of the sight of the lost child and his father. So, all formalities being complied with and in true official spirit, the account for the boy's maintenance having been asked for, a hearty and cordial leave was taken of the Matron, and Michael Kenton Morton was discharged from Liverpool Union.

The lady and her daughters were delighted to have him, and would have made much of him, but the poor little fellow proved that his confidence in womankind had been shaken, by clinging tight to his father, and showing his first inclination to cry when it was proposed to take him into another room to be dressed. Indeed, his father was as little willing to endure a moment's separation as he could be, and looked on and assisted to see him made into a little gentleman again in outward costume.

After luncheon there was still time to reach Malvern by a reasonable hour of the evening, and Frank felt as if every moment of sorrow were almost a cruelty to his wife. The Guardian's wife owned that she ought not to press him to sleep at her house, and forwarded his departure with strong fellow-feeling for the mother's hungry bosom.

From the station Frank sent telegrams to Herbert, to Mrs. Morton, and to Rose Rollstone; besides one to Lady Adela, containing only the reference, Luke xv. 32.

People looked somewhat curiously at the thin, worn-looking, elderly man, with the travelling bag in one hand, and the little boy holding tight by the other, each with a countenance of radiant gladness; and again, to see how, when seated, he allowed himself to be climbed over and clasped by the sturdy being, who seemed almost overwhelming to one so slight.

When the September twilight darkened into night, Michael, who had been asleep, awoke with a scream and flung both arms round his father's neck, exclaiming—

'Oh, Louey, I'll not cry! Don't let him throw me out! Oh, the nasty man!'

And even when convinced that no nasty man was present, and that it was papa, not Louey, whom he was grappling, he still nestled as close as possible, while he was only pacified in recurring frights by listening to a story. Never good at story-telling, the only one that, for the nonce, his father could put together was that of Joseph, and this elicited various personal comparisons.

'Mine wasn't a coat of many colours, it was my blue frock! Did they dip it in blood, papa?'

'Not quite, my darling, but it was the same thing.'

Then presently, 'It wasn't a camel, but a puff puff, and *he* was so cross!'

By and by, 'I didn't tell anybody's dreams, papa. They didn't make me ride in a cha-rot, but nurse made me monitor, 'cause I knew all my letters. I should like to have a brother Benjamin. Mayn't Tommy be my brother? Wasn't Joseph's mamma very glad?'

Michael's Egypt had not been a very terrible house of bondage, and the darker moments of his abduction did not dwell on his memory; but years later, when first he tasted beer, he put down the glass with a shudder, as the smell and taste brought back a sense of distress, confusion, and horror in a gas-lit, crowded bar, full of loud-voiced, rough figures, and resounding with strange language and fierce threats to make him swallow the draught which, no doubt, had been drugged.

Charlotte M. Yonge

CHAPTER XL

JOY WELL-NIGH INCREDIBLE

The midday letters were a riddle to the ladies at Malvern.

'Out all day,' said Mary, 'that is well. He will get strong out boating.'

'I hope Herbert has come home to take him out,' said Constance.

'Or he may be yachting. I wonder he does not say who is taking him out. I am glad that he can feel that sense of enjoyment.'

Yet that rejoicing seemed to be almost an effort to the poor mother who craved for a longer letter, and perhaps almost felt as if her Frank were getting out of sympathy with her grief—and what could be the good news?

'Herbert must have passed!' said Constance.

'I hope he has, but the expression is rather strong for that,' said Lady Adela.

'Perhaps Ida is engaged to that Mr. Deyncourt? Was that his name?' said Lady Northmoor languidly.

'Oh! that would be delicious,' cried Constance, 'and Ida has grown much more thoughtful lately, so perhaps she would do for a clergyman's wife.'

'Is Ida better?' asked her aunt, who had been much drawn towards the girl by hearing that her health had suffered from grief for Michael.

'Mamma does not mention her in her last letter, but poor Ida is really much more delicate than one would think, though she looks so strong. This would be delightful!'

'Yet, joy well-nigh incredible!' said her aunt, meditatively. 'Were not those the words? It would not be like your uncle to put them in that way unless it were something— even more wonderful, and besides, why should he not write it to me?'

'Oh—h!' cried Constance, with a leap, rather than a start. 'It can be only one thing.'

'Don't, don't, don't!' cried poor Mary; 'you must not, Constance, it would kill me to have the thought put into my head only to be lost.'

Constance looked wistfully at Lady Adela; but the idea she had suggested had created a restlessness, and her aunt presently left the room. Then Constance said—

'Lady Adela, may I tell you something? You know that poor dear little Mite was never found?'

'Oh! a boat must have picked him up,' cried Amice; 'and he is coming back.'

'Gently, Amy; hush,' said the mother, 'Constance has more to tell.'

Charlotte M. Yonge

'Yes,' said Constance. 'My friend, Rose Rollstone, who lives just by our house at Westhaven, and was going back to London the night that Mite was lost, wrote to me that she was sure she had seen his face just then. She thought, and I thought it was one of those strange things one hears of sights at the moment of death. So I never told of it, but now I cannot help fancying—'

'Oh! I am sure,' cried Amice.

Lady Adela thought the only safe way would be to turn the two young creatures out to pour out their rapturous surmises to one another on the winding paths of the Malvern hills, and very glad was she to have done so, when by and by that other telegram was put into her hands.

Then, when Mary, unable to sit still, though with trembling limbs, came back to the sitting-room, with a flush on her pale cheek, excited by the sound at the door, Lady Adela pointed to the yellow paper, which she had laid within the Gospel, open at the place.

Mary sank into a chair.

'It can't be a false hope,' she gasped.

'He would never have sent this, if it were not a certainty,' said Adela, kneeling down by her, and holding her hands, while repeating what Constance had said.

A few words were spent on wonder and censure on the girl's silence, more unjust than they knew, but hardly wasted, since they relieved the tension. Mary slid down on her knees beside her friend, and then came a silence of intense heart-swelling, choking, and unformed, but none the less true thanksgiving, and ending in a mutual embrace and an outcry of Mary's—

'Oh, Adela! how good you are, you with no such hope'—
and that great blessed shower of tears that relieved her
was ostensibly the burst of sympathy for the bereaved
mother with no such restoration in view. Then came
soothing words, and then the endeavour with dazed eyes
and throbbing hearts to look out the trains from Liverpool,
whence, to their amazement, they saw the telegram had
started, undoubtedly from Lord Northmoor. There was
not too large a choice, and finally Lady Adela made the
hope seem real by proposing preparations for the child's
supper and bed—things of which Mary seemed no more
to have dared to think than if she had been expecting a
little spirit; but which gave her hope substance, and
inspired her with fresh energy and a new strength, as she
ran up and downstairs, directing her maid, who cried for
joy at the news, and then going out to purchase those
needments which had become such tokens of exquisite
hope and joy. After this had once begun, she seemed
really incapable of sitting still, for every moment she
thought of something her boy would want or would like,
or hurried to see if all was right.

Constance begged again and again to run on the
messages, but she would not allow it, and when the girl
looked grieved, and said she was tiring herself to death,
Lady Adela said—

'My dear, sitting still would be worse for her. However it
may turn out, fatigue will be best for her.'

'Surely it can't mean anything else!' cried Constance.

'I don't see how it can. Your uncle weighs his words too
much to raise false hopes.'

Charlotte M. Yonge

So, dark as it was by the time the train was expected, Adela promoted the ordering a carriage, and went herself with the trembling Mary to the station, not without restoratives in her bag, in case of, she knew not what. Not a word was spoken, but hands were clasped and hearts were uplifted in an agony of supplication, as the two sat in the dark on the drive to the station. Of course they were too soon, but the driver manoeuvred so as to give them a full view of the exit—and then came that minute of indescribable suspense when the sounds of arrival were heard, and figures began to issue from the platform.

It was not long—thanks to freedom from luggage—before there came into full light a well-known form, with a little half-awake boy holding his hand.

Then Adela quietly let herself out of the brougham, and in another moment her clasping hand and swimming eyes had marked her greeting. She pointed to the open door and the white face in it, and in one moment more a pair of arms had closed upon Michael, and with a dreamy murmur, 'Mam-mam, mam-ma,' the curly head was on her bosom, the precious weight on her lap, her husband by her side, the door had closed on them, they were driving away.

'Oh! is it real? Is he well?'

'Perfectly well! Only sleepy. Strong, grown, well cared for.'

'My boy, my boy,' and she felt him all over, gazed at the rosy face whenever a tantalising flash of lamplight permitted, then kissed and kissed, till the boy awoke more fully, with another 'Mamma! Mamma,' putting his hand to feel for her chain, as if to identify her. Then with a coo of content, 'Mite has papa and mamma,' and he seemed under the necessity of feeling them both.

Only at their own door did those happy people even recollect Lady Adela, with shame and dismay, which did not last long, for she came on them, laughing with pleasure, and saying it was just what she had intended, while Mite was recognising his Amy and his Conny, and being nearly devoured by them.

He still was rather confused by the strange house. 'It's not home,' he said, staring round, and blinking at the lights; 'and where's my big horse?'

'You shall soon go home to the big horse—and Nurse Eden, poor nurse shall come to you, my own.'

To which Michael responded, holding out a plump leg and foot for admiration. 'I can do mine own socks and bootses now, and wash mine own hands and face.'

Nevertheless, he was quite sleepy enough to be very happy and content to be carried off to his mother's bedroom, where he sat enthroned on her lap, Constance feeding him with bread and milk, while Amice held the bowl, and the maid, almost equally blissful, hovered round, and there again he sat with the two admiring girls one at each foot, disrobing him, as best they might.

Nearly asleep at last, he knelt at his mother's knee with the murmured prayer, but woke just enough to say, 'Mite needn't say "make papa better," nor "bring Mite home."'

'No, indeed, my boy. Say Thank God for all His mercy.'

He repeated it and added of himself, 'Bless nursey, and let Tommy and Fan have papas and mammas again. Amen.'

Charlotte M. Yonge

He was nodding again by that time, but he held his mother's hand fast with 'Don't go, Mam!' Nor did she. She had asked no questions. To be alone with her boy and Him, whom she thanked with her whole soul, was enough for her at present.

CHAPTER XLI

THE CANADIAN NORTHMOOR

It was not till Lord Northmoor began to answer in detail the questions that were showered on him as he ate his late dinner, that he fully realised the history of his recovered son even to himself. 'Liverpool Workhouse,' and 'all owing to Herbert,' were his first replies, and he had eaten his soup before Adela and Constance had discovered the connection between the two; nay, they were still more bewildered when Constance asked, 'Then Herbert found him there?'

'Herbert? Oh no, good fellow. He is in Canada, he went after him there.'

'To Canada?'

'Yes; that woman, the nursery girl Hall, kidnapped the child, Herbert followed her there, and found he had been dropped at Liverpool.'

Then on further inquiries, Frank became sensible that he must guard the secret of Ida's part in the transaction. He hoped to conceal it from all, except his wife, for it was hardly injustice to the Jones pair in another hemisphere to let their revenge bear the whole blame. Indeed, he did not

Charlotte M. Yonge

himself know that it was Ida's passion or Rose's mention of having seen Michael's face that had roused Herbert's suspicion.

He had heard Herbert's account of his adventures in the letter to Rose with mere impatience to come to what related to his son, and it had made no impression on his mind; but when he took out his own much briefer letter, the address at Northmoor, and the sentences that followed, the brief explanation where to seek for Michael suggested much.

'I doubt whether I could ever have got the rascal to speak out if it had not been for Captain Alder, with whose brother-in-law, Mr. Forman, I had the luck to meet on the way. They were some of the first settlers here, and have a splendid farm, export no end of wheat and ice, and have a share in the steam company. I am working out my board here for them till you are good enough to send me my quarter's allowance, deducting the 25 pounds that Miss Rollstone helped me to, as there was no one else to whom I could apply. I should like to stay here for good and all, and they would take me for a farming-pupil for less than you have been giving to my crammers, all in vain, I am afraid. The life would suit me much better; they let me live with the family, and they are thorough right sort of people, religious, and all that—and Alder seemed to take an interest in me from the time he made out who I was, and, indeed, the place is named after our Northmoor, where he says he spent his happiest days. If you can pacify my mother, and if you would consent, I am sure I could do much better here than at home, and soon be quite off your hands.'

For the present, Lord Northmoor, who could only feel that he owed more than he could express to his nephew, sent the youth a bill such as to cover his expenses, with permission, so far as he himself was concerned, to remain with these new friends, at least until there was another letter and time to consider this proposal.

At the same time, he wrote to Rose Rollstone, not only the particulars of Michael's history, but a request for those details about Herbert's friends to which he had scarcely listened when she read them. He sent likewise a paragraph to several newspapers, explaining that the Honourable M. K. Morton, whose 'watery grave' had been duly recorded, had in fact been only abducted by a former maid-servant, and bestowed in Liverpool Workhouse, where he had been discovered by the generous exertions of his cousin, Herbert Morton, Esquire. It was hoped that this would obviate all suspicion of Ida, who was reported as still so unwell that her mother was anxious to carry her abroad at once to try the effect of change of scene. Upon which Frank consulted Mr. Hailes, as to whether the prosperity that had begun to flow in upon Northmoor would justify him in at once taking the house at Westhaven off her hands, and making it a thank-offering as a parsonage for the district of St. James. This break-up seemed considerably to lessen her reluctance to the idea of Herbert's remaining in Canada, as in effect, neither she nor Ida felt inclined as yet to encounter his indignation, or to let him hear what Westhaven said. There would be no strong opposition on her part, except the tears which he would not see; and she was too anxious to carry Ida away to think of much besides.

Frank had, however, made up his mind that he could not let the son of his only brother, the youth whom he had regarded almost as a son, and who had lost so much by the discovery of the child, drift away into expatriation, without being personally satisfied as to these new companions. This was ostensible reason enough for a resolution to go out himself to the transatlantic Northmoor to make

Charlotte M. Yonge

arrangements for his nephew. Moreover, he was bent on doing so before the return of Mrs. Bury and Bertha, from whom the names of Alder and Northmoor were withheld in the joyful letters.

From Mr. Hailes he obtained full confirmation of what he had heard from Lady Adela—a story which the old gentleman's loyalty had withheld as mere gossip—about the young people who had been very dear to him.

He confessed that poor Arthur Morton had a bad set about him—indeed, his father's tastes had involved him in the kind of thing, and Lady Adela had been almost a child when married to him by relations who were much to blame. Captain Alder had belonged to the set, but had always seemed too good for them, and as if thrown among them from association. There was no doubt that he and Bertha were much in love, but there was sure to be strong opposition from her father, and even her brother had shown symptoms of thinking his friend had no business to aspire to his sister's hand. Moreover, it appeared afterwards that the Captain was heavily in debt to Arthur Morton. It was under these circumstances that the accident occurred. Bertha had mistrusted the horse's eye and ear, and implored her brother not to venture on driving it, and had been bantered good-humouredly on her unusual fears. At the first shock, the untamed girl had spoken bitter words, making Captain Alder accountable for the accident. What they were, neither Mr. Hailes nor any one else exactly knew, but they had cut deep.

When, on poor Arthur's recovery of consciousness, there was an endeavour to find Captain Alder, he had left the army; and though somewhat later the full amount of the debt was paid, it was conveyed in a manner that made the sender not easily traceable, and as it came just when Arthur was again past communication, and sinking fast, no great effort was made to seek one who was better forgotten.

It had not then been known how Bertha's life would be wrecked by that sense of injustice and cruelty—nor what a hold the love of that man had taken on her; but like Lady Adela, Mr. Hailes averred that she had never been the same since that minute of stormy grief and accusation; and that he believed that, whatever might come of it, the being able to confess her wrongs, and to know the fate of her lover, was the only thing that could restore the balance of her spirits or heal the sore.

From his own former employer, Mr. Burford, Frank procured that other link which floated in his memory when Lady Adela spoke. The name had come into Mr. Burford's office because he had been engaged on the part of one of his clients in purchasing an estate of the Alder family, at a time which corresponded with Arthur Morton's death, and the payment of the debt. There was a second instalment of the price which had to be paid to a Quebec bank.

This was all that could be learnt; but it confirmed Lord Northmoor's impression that it would be right to see him, and as far as explanation could go, to repair the injustice which had stung him so deeply. A letter could not do what an interview could, and Herbert's plans were quite sufficient cause for a journey to Winnipeg.

Of course it was a wrench to leave his wife and newly-recovered son; but he had made up his mind that it was right, both as an act of justice to an injured man, incumbent upon him as head of the family, and likewise as needful in his capacity of guardian to Herbert, while the possibility of bringing healing to Bertha also urged him.

Charlotte M. Yonge

However, Frank said little of all this, only quite simply, as if he were going to ride to the petty sessions at Colbeam, mentioned that he thought it right to go out to Canada to see about his nephew.

And as soon as he had brought the party home, and seen his boy once more in his own nursery, he set forth, leaving Mary to talk and wonder with Lady Adela over the possible consequences.

CHAPTER XLII

HUMBLE PIE

Bertha had just arrived from her tour, having rushed home on the tidings of a quarrel between the doctors and the lady nurses of her pet hospital; and she had immediately dashed down to Northmoor to secure her cousin as one of the supporters. She sat by Lady Adela's fire, very much disconcerted at hearing that he was not come home yet, though expected every day.

'What should he have gone off to Canada for? He might have been contented to stay at home, after having lost all this time by his illness. Oh, yes, I know that sounds ungrateful, when it was all in the cause of my little Cea. I shall be thankful to him all my life, but all the same, he ought to be at home when he is wanted, and I wonder he liked to fly off just when he had got his dear little boy back again.'

'He did not like it, but thought it his duty.'

'Duty—what, to Herbert? Certainly the boy has come out very well in this matter, considering that the finding Mite was to his own detriment; but probably he has found his vocation as a colonist. Still Northmoor might have let him find that for himself.'

'Do you know where the home he found is, Bertha?'

'Somewhere about Lake Winnipeg, isn't it?'

'Yes; and the name is Northmoor.'

'Named by Herbert, eh? Or didn't John Tulse go out? Did he name the place in loyalty to us?'

'Not John Tulse, but one who told Herbert that his happiest days were spent here.'

'Adela, you mean something. Don't tantalise me. Is it Fred Alder? And was he kind to the boy for old sake's sake, because he bore the old name? Did he think he was your Mike?'

Bertha was leaning forward now, devouring Adela with her eyes.

'He was much puzzled to understand who Herbert was, but he gave him great help. The man could hardly have been made to speak if he had not brought him to his bearings. Herbert has been living with him and his brother-in-law ever since, and is going to remain as a farming-pupil.'

'Married of course to a nasal Yankee?'

'No.'

There was a pause. Bertha drew herself back in her chair, Adela busied herself with the tea-cups. Presently came the question—

'Did Northmoor know?'

'Yes, he did.'

'And was that the reason of his going out?'

'Herbert was one motive, but I do not think he would have gone if there had not been another reason.'

'You did not ask him?' she said hotly.

'Certainly not.'

'I don't want any one to interfere,' said Bertha, in a suddenly changed mood, 'especially not such a stick as that. He might have let it alone.'

'And if you heard that Captain Alder was—'

'A repentant prodigal, eh? A sober-minded, sponsible, easy-going, steady money-making Canadian,' interrupted Bertha vehemently, 'such as approved himself to his Lordship's jog-trot mind. Well, what then?'

'Oh, Birdie, perverse child as ever.'

'And so you actually despatched my Lord to eat humble pie in my name. You might have waited to see what I thought of the process.'

Bertha jumped up, as if to go and take off her hat, but just at that moment some figures crossed the twilight window, and in another second Adela had sprung into the hall, meeting Mary and Frank, whom she beckoned into the dining-room.

Bertha had followed as far as the room door, when, in the porch, she beheld a tall large form, and bearded countenance. One moment more and those two were shut into the drawing-room.

Mary, Frank, and Adela stood together over the dining-room fire, all smiles and welcome.

'Doesn't he look well?' was Mary's cry, as she displayed her husband.

'Better than ever. Nothing like bracing air. Oh! I am glad you brought *him*' indicating the other room, 'down at once; she might have had a naughty fit, and tormented herself and everybody.'

'You think it will be all right?' said Frank anxiously. 'It was a venture, but when he heard that she was at the Dower House, there was no holding him. He thinks she has as much to forgive as he has.'

'You wrote something of that—though the actual misery and accident were no fault of his, poor fellow, and yet—yet all that self-acted and re-acted on one another, and did each other harm,' said Adela.

'Yes,' said Frank; 'harm that he only fully understood gradually, after he had burst away from it all in the shock, and was living a very different life with his little sister, and afterwards with her husband, a thoroughly good man.'

'To whom you have trusted your nephew?'

'Entirely. Herbert is very happy there, much more so than ever before, useful and able to follow his natural bent.'

'I am very glad he will do well there.'

A sudden interruption here came on them in the shape of Amice, who had not been guarded against. She flew into the room in a fright, exclaiming—

'Mamma, mamma, there's a strange man like a black bear in the drawing-room, and he has got his arm round Aunt Bertha's waist.'

'Oh!' as she perceived Lord Northmoor.

'A Canadian bear I have just brought home, eh, Amy?' said he, exhilarated into fun for once, while Lady Adela indulged in a quiet smile at the manner of partaking of humble pie.

Amice had, however, broken up the *tete-a-tete*, and all were soon together again, Lady Adela greeting Captain Alder as an old friend, and he, in the restraint of good breeding, betraying none of his feeling at the contrast between the girlish wife and the faded widow, although perhaps in very truth Adela Morton was a happier, certainly a more peaceful woman now than in those days.

All must spend the evening together. Where? The Northmoors carried the day, Adela and Bertha must come up to dinner, yes, and Amice too. It was fine moonlight and the Captain would stay and escort them.

Meantime Lord and Lady Northmoor revelled in a moonlight walk together exactly as they had done seven years before as a bride and bridegroom, but with that further ingredient in joy before them—that nightly romp with their Mite, to which Frank had been looking forward all through his voyage. Their Mite all the happier because his Tom and Fanny were at the keeper's lodge, and allowed to play with him in the garden, and on the heath.

Six weeks later, Lord Northmoor acted as father at Bertha's wedding, a quiet one, with Constance and Amice

Charlotte M. Yonge

as bridesmaids, with, as supernumerary, little Boadicea, who was to share the new Canadian home.

Michael was there in the glory of his first knickerbockers, and Mrs. Bury was there, and her last words ere the bride came down dressed for the journey were, 'How about "that stick," my dear?'

'Ah! sticks are sometimes made of good material.'

'There is a tree that groweth by the Water Side,' said Adela.

CHAPTER XLIII

THE STAFF

Five years later almost all the members of the Morton family were met once more at Westhaven.

Ida was slowly dying. She had always been more or less delicate, and she had never entirely recovered the effect of the distress she had brought upon herself by that foolish crime towards her little cousin. Her mother had joined Miss Gattoni, and they had roamed about the Continent in the various resorts of seekers of health and of pleasure, hoping to distract her mind and restore her strength and spirits. For a time this sometimes seemed to succeed, and she certainly became prettier; but disappointment always ensued; a little over-exertion or excitement was sure to bring on illness, and there were even more painful causes for her collapses. Her uncle's care had not been entirely able to prevent the publication of such a sensational story, known, as it was, to most people at Westhaven; in fact, he was only able to reach the more respectable papers; and the society to which Miss Gattoni introduced them was just that which revelled in the society papers. So every now and then whispers would go about that Miss Morton was the heroine—or rather the villain—of the piece, and these were sure ultimately to reach Miss Gattoni. And at Genoa they had actually been at the same *table-d'hote*

Charlotte M. Yonge

with Tom Brady's sister—nay, they had seen the *Morna* in the harbour.

Gradually each summer brought less renovation; each winter, wherever spent, brought Ida lower, till at length she was ill enough for her mother thankfully to reply to Constance's entreaty to come out to them at Biarritz.

Constance had grown to be in her vacation more and more the child of the house at Northmoor, and since her college career had ended with credit externally, and benefit inwardly, she had become her aunt's right hand, besides teaching Amice music and beginning Michael's Latin; but it was plain that her duty lay in helping to nurse her sister, and her uncle escorted her. They were greatly shocked at the change in the once brilliant girl, and her broken, dejected manner, apparently incapable of taking interest in anything. She would scarcely admit her uncle at first, but when she discovered that even Constance was in perfect ignorance of her part in the loss of Michael, she was overcome with the humiliation of intense gratitude, and the sense of a wonderful forgiveness and forbearance.

He never exactly knew what he had said to her; but for the two days that he was able to remain, she wished for him to sit with her as much as possible, though often in silence; and she let him bring her the English chaplain.

No one expected her to live through the spring, but with it came another partial revival, and therewith a vehement desire to see Westhaven again. It was as if her uncle had extracted the venom of the sting of remorse, and when that had become repentance, the old affection for the home of her childhood was free to revive. Good Mr. Rollstone was dead, but his wife and daughter kept on the lodging-house, and were affectionately glad to welcome their old friends. Herbert, who had been happily farming for two years on his own account, on an estate that his uncle had purchased for him, came for the first time on a visit from the Dominion—tall, broad, bearded, handsome, and manly, above all, in his courtesy and gentleness to the sick sister who valued his strong and tender help more than any other care. Mary came with her husband and boy from Northmoor for the farewell. When Ida tearfully asked her forgiveness, the injury was so entirely past that it was not hard to say, in the spirit of Joseph—

'Oh, my poor child, do not think of that! No one has suffered from it so much as you have. It really did Michael no harm at all, only making a little man of him; and as to Herbert, his going out was the best thing in the world for him, dear, noble, generous fellow. And after all, Ida,' she added, presently, 'I do believe you had rather be as you are now than the girl you were then?'

'Oh, Aunt Mary, it is what Uncle Frank and you are— that—makes one feel—'

Ida could say no more. She once saw Michael's bright boyish face awed into pity, and had the kiss that sealed her earthly pardon, unconscious as he was of the evil she had attempted. There was the pledge of higher pardon, before her uncle and aunt left her to those nearer who could minister to her as she went down to the River ever flowing.

Before that time, however, Herbert had made known to Rose one of his great reasons for settling in Canada, namely, that he meant to take her back with him. He had told his uncle long ago, and Mrs. Alder was quite ready and eager to welcome her as a cousin. Even Mr. Rollstone could hardly have objected under these circumstances, and Rose only doubted about leaving her mother. It presently appeared, however, that Mrs. Morton wished to remain with Mrs. Rollstone. Westhaven was more to her than any other place, and her vanity had so entirely departed that she could best take comfort in her good old friend's congenial society. Constance offered to remain and obtain some daily governess or high school employment there; but it was to her relief that she found that the two old ladies did not wish it. There was a sense that her tastes and habits were so unlike theirs that they would always feel her to be like company and be on their best behaviour, and decidedly her mother would not 'stand in her light,' and would be best contented with visits from her and to Northmoor.

So, after the quietest of weddings in the beautiful St. James's Church, Herbert and Rose went out to be welcomed at Winnipeg, and Constance returned with her uncle to be a daughter to Aunt Mary—till such time as she was sought by the young Vicar of Northmoor.

Choose from Thousands of 1stWorldLibrary Classics By

A. M. Barnard	Booth Tarkington	Edward Everett Hale
Ada Leverson	Boyd Cable	Edward J. O'Biren
Adolphus William Ward	Bram Stoker	Edward S. Ellis
Aesop	C. Collodi	Edwin L. Arnold
Agatha Christie	C. E. Orr	Eleanor Atkins
Alexander Aaronsohn	C. M. Ingleby	Eleanor Hallowell Abbott
Alexander Kielland	Carolyn Wells	Eliot Gregory
Alexandre Dumas	Catherine Parr Traill	Elizabeth Gaskell
Alfred Gatty	Charles A. Eastman	Elizabeth McCracken
Alfred Ollivant	Charles Amory Beach	Elizabeth Von Arnim
Alice Duer Miller	Charles Dickens	Ellem Key
Alice Turner Curtis	Charles Dudley Warner	Emerson Hough
Alice Dunbar	Charles Farrar Browne	Emilie F. Carlen
Allen Chapman	Charles Ives	Emily Bronte
Alleyne Ireland	Charles Kingsley	Emily Dickinson
Ambrose Bierce	Charles Klein	Enid Bagnold
Amelia E. Barr	Charles Hanson Towne	Enilor Macartney Lane
Amory H. Bradford	Charles Lathrop Pack	Erasmus W. Jones
Andrew Lang	Charles Romyn Dake	Ernie Howard Pie
Andrew McFarland Davis	Charles Whibley	Ethel May Dell
Andy Adams	Charles Willing Beale	Ethel Turner
Angela Brazil	Charlotte M. Braeme	Ethel Watts Mumford
Anna Alice Chapin	Charlotte M. Yonge	Eugene Sue
Anna Sewell	Charlotte Perkins Stetson	Eugenie Foa
Annie Besant	Clair W. Hayes	Eugene Wood
Annie Hamilton Donnell	Clarence Day Jr.	Eustace Hale Ball
Annie Payson Call	Clarence E. Mulford	Evelyn Everett-green
Annie Roe Carr	Clemence Housman	Everard Cotes
Annonaymous	Confucius	F. H. Cheley
Anton Chekhov	Coningsby Dawson	F. J. Cross
Archibald Lee Fletcher	Cornelis DeWitt Wilcox	F. Marion Crawford
Arnold Bennett	Cyril Burleigh	Fannie E. Newberry
Arthur C. Benson	D. H. Lawrence	Federick Austin Ogg
Arthur Conan Doyle	Daniel Defoe	Ferdinand Ossendowski
Arthur M. Winfield	David Garnett	Fergus Hume
Arthur Ransome	Dinah Craik	Florence A. Kilpatrick
Arthur Schnitzler	Don Carlos Janes	Fremont B. Deering
Arthur Train	Donald Keyhoe	Francis Bacon
Atticus	Dorothy Kilner	Francis Darwin
B.H. Baden-Powell	Dougan Clark	Frances Hodgson Burnett
B. M. Bower	Douglas Fairbanks	Frances Parkinson Keyes
B. C. Chatterjee	E. Nesbit	Frank Gee Patchin
Baroness Emmuska Orczy	E. P. Roe	Frank Harris
Baroness Orczy	E. Phillips Oppenheim	Frank Jewett Mather
Basil King	E. S. Brooks	Frank L. Packard
Bayard Taylor	Earl Barnes	Frank V. Webster
Ben Macomber	Edgar Rice Burroughs	Frederic Stewart Isham
Bertha Muzzy Bower	Edith Van Dyne	Frederick Trevor Hill
Bjornstjerne Bjornson	Edith Wharton	Frederick Winslow Taylor

Friedrich Kerst	Hayden Carruth	James Branch Cabell
Friedrich Nietzsche	Helent Hunt Jackson	James DeMille
Fyodor Dostoyevsky	Helen Nicolay	James Joyce
G.A. Henty	Hendrik Conscience	James Lane Allen
G.K. Chesterton	Hendy David Thoreau	James Lane Allen
Gabrielle E. Jackson	Henri Barbusse	James Oliver Curwood
Garrett P. Serviss	Henrik Ibsen	James Oppenheim
Gaston Leroux	Henry Adams	James Otis
George A. Warren	Henry Ford	James R. Driscoll
George Ade	Henry Frost	Jane Abbott
Geroge Bernard Shaw	Henry James	Jane Austen
George Cary Eggleston	Henry Jones Ford	Jane L. Stewart
George Durston	Henry Seton Merriman	Janet Aldridge
George Ebers	Henry W Longfellow	Jens Peter Jacobsen
George Eliot	Herbert A. Giles	Jerome K. Jerome
George Gissing	Herbert Carter	Jessie Graham Flower
George MacDonald	Herbert N. Casson	John Buchan
George Meredith	Herman Hesse	John Burroughs
George Orwell	Hildegard G. Frey	John Cournos
George Sylvester Viereck	Homer	John F. Kennedy
George Tucker	Honore De Balzac	John Gay
George W. Cable	Horace B. Day	John Glasworthy
George Wharton James	Horace Walpole	John Habberton
Gertrude Atherton	Horatio Alger Jr.	John Joy Bell
Gordon Casserly	Howard Pyle	John Kendrick Bangs
Grace E. King	Howard R. Garis	John Milton
Grace Gallatin	Hugh Lofting	John Philip Sousa
Grace Greenwood	Hugh Walpole	John Taintor Foote
Grant Allen	Humphry Ward	Jonas Lauritz Idemil Lie
Guillermo A. Sherwell	Ian Maclaren	Jonathan Swift
Gulielma Zollinger	Inez Haynes Gillmore	Joseph A. Altsheler
Gustav Flaubert	Irving Bacheller	Joseph Carey
H. A. Cody	Isabel Cecilia Williams	Joseph Conrad
H. B. Irving	Isabel Hornibrook	Joseph E. Badger Jr
H.C. Bailey	Israel Abrahams	Joseph Hergesheimer
H. G. Wells	Ivan Turgenev	Joseph Jacobs
H. H. Munro	J.G.Austin	Jules Vernes
H. Irving Hancock	J. Henri Fabre	Julian Hawthrone
H. R. Naylor	J. M. Barrie	Julie A Lippmann
H. Rider Haggard	J. M. Walsh	Justin Huntly McCarthy
H. W. C. Davis	J. Macdonald Oxley	Kakuzo Okakura
Haldeman Julius	J. R. Miller	Karle Wilson Baker
Hall Caine	J. S. Fletcher	Kate Chopin
Hamilton Wright Mabie	J. S. Knowles	Kenneth Grahame
Hans Christian Andersen	J. Storer Clouston	Kenneth McGaffey
Harold Avery	J. W. Duffield	Kate Langley Bosher
Harold McGrath	Jack London	Kate Langley Bosher
Harriet Beecher Stowe	Jacob Abbott	Katherine Cecil Thurston
Harry Castlemon	James Allen	Katherine Stokes
Harry Coghill	James Andrews	L. A. Abbot
Harry Houidini	James Baldwin	L. T. Meade

L. Frank Baum
Latta Griswold
Laura Dent Crane
Laura Lee Hope
Laurence Housman
Lawrence Beasley
Leo Tolstoy
Leonid Andreyev
Lewis Carroll
Lewis Sperry Chafer
Lilian Bell
Lloyd Osbourne
Louis Hughes
Louis Joseph Vance
Louis Tracy
Louisa May Alcott
Lucy Fitch Perkins
Lucy Maud Montgomery
Luther Benson
Lydia Miller Middleton
Lyndon Orr
M. Corvus
M. H. Adams
Margaret E. Sangster
Margret Howth
Margaret Vandercook
Margaret W. Hungerford
Margret Penrose
Maria Edgeworth
Maria Thompson Daviess
Mariano Azuela
Marion Polk Angellotti
Mark Overton
Mark Twain
Mary Austin
Mary Catherine Crowley
Mary Cole
Mary Hastings Bradley
Mary Roberts Rinehart
Mary Rowlandson
M. Wollstonecraft Shelley
Maud Lindsay
Max Beerbohm
Myra Kelly
Nathaniel Hawthrone
Nicolo Machiavelli
O. F. Walton
Oscar Wilde

Owen Johnson
P.G. Wodehouse
Paul and Mabel Thorne
Paul G. Tomlinson
Paul Severing
Percy Brebner
Percy Keese Fitzhugh
Peter B. Kyne
Plato
Quincy Allen
R. Derby Holmes
R. L. Stevenson
R. S. Ball
Rabindranath Tagore
Rahul Alvares
Ralph Bonehill
Ralph Henry Barbour
Ralph Victor
Ralph Waldo Emmerson
Rene Descartes
Ray Cummings
Rex Beach
Rex E. Beach
Richard Harding Davis
Richard Jefferies
Richard Le Gallienne
Robert Barr
Robert Frost
Robert Gordon Anderson
Robert L. Drake
Robert Lansing
Robert Lynd
Robert Michael Ballantyne
Robert W. Chambers
Rosa Nouchette Carey
Rudyard Kipling
Saint Augustine
Samuel B. Allison
Samuel Hopkins Adams
Sarah Bernhardt
Sarah C. Hallowell
Selma Lagerlof
Sherwood Anderson
Sigmund Freud
Standish O'Grady
Stanley Weyman
Stella Benson
Stella M. Francis

Stephen Crane
Stewart Edward White
Stijn Streuvels
Swami Abhedananda
Swami Parmananda
T. S. Ackland
T. S. Arthur
The Princess Der Ling
Thomas A. Janvier
Thomas A Kempis
Thomas Anderton
Thomas Bailey Aldrich
Thomas Bulfinch
Thomas De Quincey
Thomas Dixon
Thomas H. Huxley
Thomas Hardy
Thomas More
Thornton W. Burgess
U. S. Grant
Upton Sinclair
Valentine Williams
Various Authors
Vaughan Kester
Victor Appleton
Victor G. Durham
Victoria Cross
Virginia Woolf
Wadsworth Camp
Walter Camp
Walter Scott
Washington Irving
Wilbur Lawton
Wilkie Collins
Willa Cather
Willard F. Baker
William Dean Howells
William le Queux
W. Makepeace Thackeray
William W. Walter
William Shakespeare
Winston Churchill
Yei Theodora Ozaki
Yogi Ramacharaka
Young E. Allison
Zane Grey

www.ingramcontent.com/pod-product-compliance
Lightning Source LLC
Chambersburg PA
CBHW021319250626
47155CB00002B/549